Baba's Gurukul
SHIRDI

Sterling titles on Shirdi Sai Baba

Baba's Gurukul

SHIRDI

Compiled by
Vinny Chitluri

STERLING PAPERBACKS
An imprint of
Sterling Publishers (P) Ltd.
A-59, Okhla Industrial Area, Phase-II,
New Delhi-110020.
Tel: 26387070, 26386209; Fax: 91-11-26383788
E-mail: mail@sterlingpublishers.com
www.sterlingpublishers.com

Baba's Gurukul – Shirdi
© 2009, Vinny Chitluri
ISBN 978 81 207 4770 8
Reprint 2011 , 2014

Printed in India

Printed and Published by Sterling Publishers Pvt. Ltd.,
New Delhi-110020.

Dedication and Acknowledgements

I would like to dedicate this book to Dr. Keshav B. Gavankar and Manjula S. Unfortunately I did not meet Dr. Gavankar, but I'm eternally grateful to him for writing all these 'reference' books. They are a wealth of information, wisdom, with a deep insight of Baba.

Manjula S, is a dear friend and my spiritual guru. She is well versed in the scriptures and Bhagvad Gita. She deciphered the meanings and significance of almost everything in Baba's Gurukul. When I repeatedly asked her to at least be a co-author, she smiled and refused.

I would like to thank Vishwanath (Baba) Iyer of Shirdi who is a walking encyclopedia on Shirdi. As he was born and bred in this village, he has seen it changing. He willingly filled in gaps of my memory and gave me much needed information.

I am grateful to Sada S. Ghode of Shirdi for patiently rereading the Marathi books innumerable times and explaining its meaning.

I owe a debt of gratitude to Sameer Phanse of Thana for happily doing the tedious task of editing the book.

My rinanubandhic ties with S K. Kapur (New Delhi) are deep. I wish to thank him for helping me in innumerable ways.

Finally my thanks to S K. Ghai of Sterling Publishers for undertaking the publication of the book for the benefit of Baba's devotees.

Preface

Baba spoke of the future of Shirdi to Mhalsapati and other devotees. He said, "There will be huge palatial buildings, big fairs will be held, high ranking officials will come here. My Brahmins will gather here". And so it came to pass. The small remote village called Shiladhi turned into what it is now. I have tried to show what Shirdi and the sacred sites were like in the 20's, the 80's and at present.

Each site has a spiritual significance and each devotee gets what he wants from it. A devotee goes to a sacred place with a purpose and that gets fulfilled and he returns with an answer. Those who come to learn from Baba's life and at each place they get an answer. What it is we do not know, but they are closer to the most important person in their lives?

Without a formal induction into a learning program each devotee finds an answer to his quest. He goes back a happier and contented person. Each devotee has a preference for a special site and gets an individual personal experience.

Devotees have many questions to ask about these sites and I have tried to explain their significance.

Vinny Chitluri

Contents

Introduction

At the time that Baba manifested in Shiladhi it was a small, remote village, in Kopergaon Taluka, in the district of Ahmednagar. This was a district of the composite Bombay Province up to 1960 (now called Maharashtra). Shiladhi was small about 3.3 sq miles, calculated on the basis of the census, of a medium-sized family. Now, it is spread far and wide.

In the 1884 *Bombay Gazetteer* (Vol. XVII) of Ahmednagar district, it is mentioned in a chart of 'Kopergaon villages of 1883'. It is grouped under 'Taraf Korhale thirty villages', where it is spelt as Shirdi. The Gazetteer says there is only one road in the Kopergaon Taluka to Malegaon. "This road enters the Kopergaon sub-division at the 45th mile from Ahmednagar near the village of Ashtagaon, and Shirdi is at its 53rd mile. The Godavari River is crossed by a wire-rope ferry."

In the 50's, as the bridge over the Godavari was low, it was often under water. Later the huge bridge was built. The Godavari flowed swiftly, and a boat used to ferry devotees to the other shore. Then the journey was by *tonga*; it was exciting to see the flag over the *Samadhi Mandir* far off from Neemgaon. Now there are so many buildings that it is not visible. Recently, a railway station has been built near Neemgaon.

Mamledar B V Dev first visited Shirdi in 1910. He recorded his impressions in the *Sai Leela Magazine*, in 1932. He states that Shirdi was originally known as '*Shiladhi*' or '*Shailadhi*'. At that time the village was tiny and had about 400 houses. A few were large while others were small mud huts. The village had two wells and two schools. One school was up to the 7th standard in the Marathi medium and the other was a Marathi mission school.

The village had two *panmalas* (betel leaf vineyards), two orchards, one flower garden, one sugar mill, one flour mill and a water mill. There was one *dharamshala* for pilgrims to stay in. Besides this, there were nine temples and two *masjids*.

The total population was about 2,586. The Muslims were the minority (about 10%) and the rest were Hindus. The Hindus were divided into the following castes – Brahmins, *Marwadis, Marathas, Dhangars* (shepherds), *Malis* (growers of fruits and vegetables), *Sonars* (goldsmiths), *Sutars* (carpenters), *Lohars* (Blacksmiths), *Kumbhars* (potters), *Parits* (washermen), *Mahars, Mangs Chamars* (tanners and leather workers), *Kolis, Bhils* (scheduled tribes), *Guravs* and *Vadars*. There was a wide cross section of castes. Shirdi though small and remote was quite prosperous. The population was of a working class and Shirdi seemed to be quite self-sufficient.

In the 20's and up to the 70's there were many '*Gow Shalas*' in and around Shirdi. Many of the neighbouring villages and villages as far away as Sinner and Nasik used to do '*Gow daan*' to Shirdi *kshetra*. They would bring a cow and release it in Shirdi; hence there were numerous *Gow Shalas*. It is interesting to note that Baba is given butter sweetened with sugar as prasad after *Kakad arati* .

There is an interesting legend in the *puranas*. The sage Gautama brought the river (originally the *Ganga*) from the matted locks of Lord Shiva. Lord Shiva once vigorously shook his locks and dashed them on the ground. At that site the Godavari or *Goda Mai* originated, atop the Bramhagiri mountain near Tryambakeshwar.

The word 'Godavari' is broken down as, *Go* which means *bhumi* (earth or land), *da* means *denara* (bestower) and *vari* means *shresth* (the best or excellent). So Godavari means the land that bestowed the best. The banks of the Godavari have nurtured many a saint. But at Shirdi, it nurtured the '*Parabramha*' who walked in the alleys and *gullies* and sanctified the soil. Shirdi is situated about eight miles south of the banks of the Godavari.

Shiladhi

Dr Keshav B Gavankar in his book titled *Shiladhi*, explains the meaning of Shiladhi very succinctly.

The word Shiladhi can be broken into two words. *Shila* means a mountain and *dhi* means '*budhi*.' The word '*budhi*' means intellect or wisdom. Thus, the meaning of Shiladhi is that '*gaon* or village whose intellect or wisdom is as calm or serene as a mountain'. Shiladhi is the village that brings calm and peace to the flitting mind.

Shiladhi *written by Dr Keshav B Gavankar*

Shiladhi the Seat of Spiritual Learning

The *Sadguru* (Baba) in his unique way drew devotees to Shirdi, who were well-versed in the scriptures. They were looking for a *Sadguru*, to help them reach their final goal which was *moksha*. Chandorkar, Dixit, Shama, Dabholkar and Das Ganu were some of them. They were steeped in Guru *bhakti* and were eager to progress on their spiritual path. Shiladhi was a seat of spiritual learning with Baba at the helm.

Thus, Shirdi became a *Gurukul*, with devotees in different stages of knowledge. For each devotee, according to his capability, the stage he had reached in spiritual development, there were different places akin to classrooms, so that he may learn and benefit from it. This procedure follows the natural course of learning.

1. For novices, the curriculum was '*Antah-bahya shuddhi*' that is cleanliness and purity of external body and *chitta*. The routine to be followed was '*snan sandhya*' or performing *sandhya* after bathing. They did *Naam smaran, bhajan, pujan, archan*, or practising the *nav vidha bhakti* with devotion. This is described in chapter 21 of the *Shri Sai Satcharita*. The classroom or place for them was the Gurusthan.

2.　The medium knowledgeable persons adopted were, '*Antah-bahya shuddhi*'

The practice of *varna ashram dharma* (the *dharma* according to the stage of life), *niyam* (to live life according to the laws prescribed in the *Vedas* and by *Manu*) and *Chandrayana vrat* (fasting according to the waxing and waning of the moon). For these devotees the classroom was the Gurusthan.

3.　The brightest and highly knowledgeable: They performed *chitta shuddhi,* followed by reading and meditating on the *Bhagvad Gita, Bramhasutra*, Upanishads, Vedanta and other religious texts. The classroom was the Chavadi.

4.　Those that were *pragya* or had reached the highest stage of knowledge: These devotees practised yoga like *dhauthi, neti, basthi, nauli* and *kapalbhathi*. They performed rigorous yoga and penance and were masters of *khanda* and *hatha* yoga. The classroom for them was the Lendi Baugh.

5.　The most brilliant and the best: They were always calm and peaceful. They had achieved *Atma Jnana* and were steeped in *vairagya* and in a state of *sat chit anand* and bliss. They were in *sahaja samadhi*, joy, peace, as they had boundless Guru *kripa* the classroom for them was Dwarka Mai.

There were teachers in this *Gurukul*, who helped devotees to reach the next stage of their spiritual development. Their role and *seva* is given below.

1. Nana Sahib Chandorkar

Without Baba asking him or ordering to deliver a message to a particular devotee, Nana had the foresight to do this. Nana on his own accord, with zeal told his friends and acquaintances about Baba's *leelas, updesh* and his own experiences. His *Sadguru* was in his thoughts day and night and invariably he turned the conversation to Baba.

Further more, he deciphered the meaning of the parables and prime words that Baba used. He related Baba's *leelas* to many scholars and was responsible for bringing the scholars to Baba's feet.

2. Madhavrao Deshpande (Shama)

Shama first introduced the devotee to Baba and told him of the purpose of his visit. Baba, asked about his welfare, then addressed his secret desire or query in cryptic language or in a parable. Shama then explained the meaning of Baba's words or parables to the devotee. The explanation given by Shama always satisfied devotees and filled them with peace. Shama had a deep understanding of Baba's gestures, cryptic words and parables. Thus he could explain the hidden meaning in them. Often Baba would look at a devotee and say something that seemed to have no relevance to the ongoing conversation; but Shama had the wisdom to explain what was said.

Baba often said, "Shamyia tell him something". Shama would tell him a *leela* that gave him the perfect answer. At other times Baba asked the devotee to go and chat with Shama. An apt example of this is given in *Shri Sai Satcharita*, chapter 18 when Baba sent Dabholkar to Shama, who told him the story of Radhabai Deshmukh. The *leela* calmed Dabholkar's restless mind and he realised how blessed he was.

The devotees always invited Baba to weddings or thread ceremonies of their children. Baba said, "Take my Shamyia with you." Shama went for the function and it would be trouble-free and a grand success. In fact, Baba sent Shama instead of going himself. Baba often asked him to stay a few days in the home and this brought peace and happiness to the family. As time went by, the devotees requested Shama to grace their homes and functions as Baba had taken *Mahasamadhi*.

Many devotees came to Shama and described their dream visions pertaining to Baba as they could not understand it. Shama deciphered it and explained it till the devotee was satisfied.

Another service that Shama happily did was to take the devotees to his home and according to Baba's instructions look after their needs and comfort. Then he would talk about Baba's *leelas*, Baba's *Brahma Jnana* and give instructions on '*Sagun bhakti*'.

3. Anna Sahib Dabholkar

In the 13th century, the Yadav dynasty of Devgiri flourished in Maharashtra. Their valiant king Ramaraja's minister was the famous

Hemadripanth. Hemadri was talented, virtuous, highly educated, a brilliant mathematician and accountant. He was the author of numerous books, some of which were used as theological reference books.

On Dabholkar's very first visit to Shirdi, Baba called him Hemadpanth (a corrupted version of Hemardripanth). Dabholkar was the first accountant-treasurer in Baba's *durbar* (the Shirdi Sai Baba Sansthan). Dabholkar was also the author of the *Shri Sai Satcharita*, which like Hemadri's book *Chaturvarg Chintamani* is replete with spiritual knowledge. It contains gems of *bhakti, Jnana, vairagya* and *yoga*.

Shri Sai Satcharita is studied by many devotees, who try to follow it to the letter; so that they can easily cross this *bhavsagar*. If there is one book that should be read and studied, it's *Shri Sai Satcharita*.

4. Das Ganu Maharaj

Das Ganu wrote *Bhakta Leelamrut* and *Sant Leelamrut* which describe the lives of the great saints of Maharashtra. He sought permission from Baba which he readily gave. These books were written in simple colloquial Marathi. Thus, the young and old could easily read and understand them. The readers could incorporate this knowledge into their daily lives. Those people who could read Marathi were thus greatly benefited.

Das Ganu also wrote the '*Ishavasya Bhavarthbodhini* '. When he was writing it he had many doubts. He came to Baba and laid his doubts before him. Baba asked him to go to Vile Parle and stay in Dixit's home. There his maid would clear his doubts. The *Ishavasya Upanishad* is a small book; but it has profound significance and meaning.   Shri Sai Satcharita *chapter 20*

Das Ganu wrote in simple Marathi. So people who couldn't understand Sanskrit could benefit from reading it.

He worked in the department of police; he was a poet and could compose poetry, extempore. He also had a passion for '*Lavani* and *Tamasha*'. He would dress like a woman and dance and sing. Baba knew his talent and potential to become a great poet. So he literally forced him to give up his job. Baba then channelled his talent towards *bhajans* and *kirtans*. Later, he was known as '*Sant kavi* Das Ganu Maharaj*'* and many a street is named after him.

At first, Das Ganu set out to perform *bhajans* and *kirtans* wearing an elaborate dress. He wore a beautiful *angarkha* and *uparna*. Baba saw his elaborate dress and asked him to take it off before him. Then Baba set him up in the style of Narada Muni. In this tradition, the *kirtankars* are not burdened with the outward trappings of dress. So Das Ganu performed *kirtans* with a bare chest, a flower garland around his neck and *chiplis* in his hand. Thus, Das Gunu besides spreading Baba's fame far and wide spoke on the reality of God, his power and *leelas* of great saints.

5. Kaka Sahib Dixit

Kaka was the perfect devotee and disciple. He followed Baba's words to the letter. He got up early in the morning and completed his rituals and *Pujas*, so that he had sufficient time to read, understand and explain the *pothi*. Every day he read and studied the *pothi*, as Baba had advised. Dixit explained the meaning of the *shlokas* in simple language. With the help of the *shloka* of the day he would explain Baba's words and give the meaning that Baba wanted to convey.

Baba often sent a devotee to him on the pretext of getting *dakshina*. At other times Baba said, "Go and sit in the *Wada*", or "Go and get *dakshina*." The amount that Baba asked for had a special meaning.

The only thought on Dixit's mind was his *Sadguru*. He talked about his experiences and *leelas* and those that he had witnessed from the time he came to Shirdi. He spoke about '*Tatva Jnana*' or the principles to live by like truth and honesty. He did not just talk about Baba's teachings, but also obeyed, followed and lived them. Thus, he taught by example.

Baba's word was a law for him and he obeyed it to the letter. An apt example is given in *Shri Sai Satcharita*, chapter 23 under the title 'Killing the Goat.' In Ovi 180-181 he says, "Before the Guru's word rules, regulations, prohibitions and taboos are not applicable. The attention of the disciple must be focused on the duty assigned to him by his Guru."

Ovi 181, "We are slaves to your command and will not question what is proper and what is not. We will give our life if need be, but will obey the Guru's word." These words show what a perfect disciple Dixit was.

Veda Jnana is *Brahma Jnana*. Baba asked many devotees to read and study the Upanishads, the *Gita*, or the *Jnaneshvari* on a daily basis. In the *Sabhamandap*, numerous devotees were asked to sit and read. In the evenings regular classes of Eknath's Bhagwat were held by Jog and Dixit in Sathe Wada and Dixit Wada.

Baba's Unique Gurukul

Unlike other schools and colleges Baba's *Gurukul* did not have any timetable; anyone who was thirsting for knowledge received it instantaneously. There were no entrance exams, no fees, breaks or vacations. Baba himself was always present to help the devotee go a step further in his spiritual development. Many students are refused entrance into schools, because of physical handicaps; but in Baba's *Gurukul* this was not a deterrent. Kaka Dixit walked with a limp; but he was the prime teacher of the *Gurukul*.

When a devotee sat before Baba, he looked at him intently. In a single glance he knew what his physical constitution was and any diseases that the devotee had. Baba knew the level of his spiritual development, his eagerness to progress and the reason for his question. Keeping all this in mind he answered the devotee. There was no age bar. Baba taught the young and the old, the robust and the weak and physically handicapped. In fact, any and everybody with a yearning for knowledge was welcome.

With the passage of time, numerous devotees flocked to Shirdi. Baba placed two acid tests of *'kanchan* and *kamini'* before them. One was in the form of *dakshina*. Sometimes Baba took all the money they had brought. Then he rewarded them with ten times the amount. The other test was to go to Radha Krishna Mai's residence. These two tests revealed their love for woman and wealth.

Baba in his conversations taught about the accumulation of wealth. He said, "Wealth should be made with honesty and integrity. Money ought not to be squandered, but used wisely, taking into account the time and place. Life should not be considered a burden; lead it joyously with your family and friends."

"Everyone should do *seva* of their Guru, parents, *gaon* and motherland. Thus, they can obtain *bhakti, jnana, vairagya* and *atman jnana*."

This seat of learning was very unique. In universities around the world education and knowledge are given when both the teacher and student are awake. Baba however imparted knowledge and guidance in dreams, or when the devotee was awake. Sometimes the devotee was in a *samadhi* state when Baba gave *sakshatkar* and cleared his doubts and answered his questions. Often it seemed that Baba was nodding off to sleep, but at that very time Baba was in a *samadhi* state or in bliss. Baba was and is always awake. Baba once told Mhalsapati that he slept with his eyes open.

Education is imparted through the medium of reading and writing. Baba however, made the devotee use the '*panch indriyias* and *karma indriyias*' for his welfare and business. Often Baba used humour to teach or get his view across. He had a very personal relationship with his devotees. He gave them apt nicknames that had profound hidden meanings. He answered their questions, cleared their dilemmas using various methods. He spoke to them sweetly and used his *leelas* and *chamatkars* that had a profound impact on their lives. He channelled them into the *bhakti marga*.

Sometimes, he shouted and used foul and abusive language. An apt example is given in *Shri Sai Satcharita*, chapter 41 of how Deo was made to read *Jnaneshvari*. At other times he hit them with his *satka* or with small pieces of bricks. He took hold of their head and banged it against the pillar or he lifted them above his head and whirled them around. All of them advanced a step or two further in their spiritual development after this treatment. Like the mother tortoise he watched them and looked after them eternally.

The main seat of learning was Shirdi and Shirdi Sai Baba Sansthan, with numerous smaller sister institutions around the world. But the devotees enrolled elsewhere did not feel blessed and satisfied until they made a pilgrimage to Shirdi and venerated all the seats of knowledge. However, there was one condition, they could not visit Shirdi until and unless Baba permitted them.

Because of the truthful nature of this village and all the qualities mentioned above, many a saint came and stayed here. As time passed by the name Shiladhi became Shirdi.

The saint named Devidas Maharaj was already residing at Shirdi when Baba returned with the marriage party of Chandbhai Patil. Then Jankidas Gosavi and Gangagir came.

Shri Sai Satcharita *chapter 5*

After Baba took up residence in Dwarka Mai, numerous saints and God men came to take his *darshan*.

The Vess of Shiladhi

If one goes out of the *Dakshina Mukhi Maruti Mandir* and walks towards Dwarka Mai, there is a brick that is placed horizontally. The brick is fixed above the level of the tiled flooring. This is the marker for the *vess* or entrance gate of Shiladhi. On auspicious occasions like a wedding the groom will break a coconut over this brick and then step into Shiladhi. On the festival of *Pola*, bulls are brought in harness till this *vess* and then let free to go home as they please. When a person dies in the village the bier is brought to this threshold and as a mark of respect, the bier is placed on the ground for a few minutes and then taken to the crematory.

The Four Shivs of Shiladhi

The *shiv* is the boundary or border of the village of Shirdi. The Northern *shiv* is near the Police Station, which is on the northern side of the Nagar-Manmad highway. On the opposite side is the Lakshmi Nagar cremation ground. The southern *shiv* is on the same highway in the opposite direction. It is called the Shirdi Sakori *shiv* and is at the Mhasoba temple. The western *shiv* is on the Pimpalvadi road near Lute Vasti. The eastern *shiv* is on Kankuri Road at the Mhasoba temple.

The Wells of Shiladhi

Water was drawn from numerous wells. There was a huge well in Saran Jane Baugh; this was in front of the Shani Mandir. There was another well in the *smashan bhoomi* (cremation ground). Dead bodies were cremated in the vacant area between what is now the museum (Dixit Wada hall) and the bathrooms and latrines. The bathrooms and latrines were located behind the present *Parayan Kaksh*. Since it was a cremation ground, there was a well there, as water is used extensively for the cremation rituals. Next to the hall in Dixit Wada there was a well and one well next to the present exit of *Samadhi Mandir*.

There was no electricity. Alternately kerosene oil lanterns and petromax were used as a source of illumination.

An old map of Shirdi (1875) is given in the photograph section. It gives a rough idea of how small Shiladhi was. This is a land survey map and the properties are called *ghat*. The number assigned to Shirdi is *gaon* 92. This map shows the shape of Shirdi. The village of Beragaon was officially joined to Shirdi on July 22 1947. Unfortunately, this map could not be scanned; so it is not in this book.

The map below gives the location of all the sacred places of worship in the Shirdi Sai Baba Sansthan.

MAP

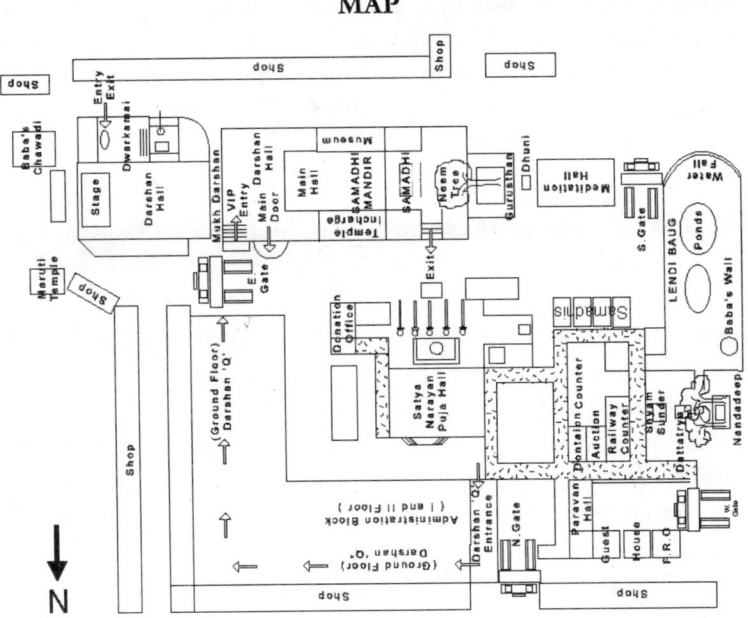

1

Gurupaduka Sthan (Gurusthan)

At the tender age of 16, Baba first manifested in Shirdi for the sake of his devotees. The young lad was seen sitting under the Neem tree in complete bliss, oblivious of his surroundings. Just glancing at him one could perceive that he was a *Brahmajnani*. *Maya* he had abandoned totally and *moksha* rolled at his feet. His handsome lustrous form revealed his divinity. The villagers were amazed to see the young lad lost in such hard penance. Hunger and thirst he knew not. He did not experience the heat of the day or the chill of the night.

Chopdar's mother would talk lovingly about the lad, "This lad fair and handsome, was first seen sitting calmly in deep mediation under the Neem tree," she said. The villagers on their way to work looked at the boy with awe. For in the day he did not seek anyone's company and at night he was not afraid of anything or anyone. They were puzzled as to where he came from.   Shri Sai Satcharita, chapter 4

This blessed Neem tree was already there, as if it was waiting for Baba to sit under its shade. In '*Sai Mahima Sthothra*' Upasani says, "This Neem tree surpasses the '*Kalpa Vriksha*' by showering ambrosia of Baba's grace." Many devotees are relieved of their ailments by eating its leaves. *Pradakshina* of the Gurusthan (**photo 1.1**) is done by many devotees, for destruction of their *Karmic* problems, spiritual enlightenment and fulfilment of their wishes.

Around April 2007, this neem tree was drying up. The Shirdi Sai Baba Sansthan got the horticulture department to treat it. Thus the Gurusthan had to be removed, so that the roots could get adequate supply of oxygen, nutrients and water. As Guru *Purnima* was fast approaching the present Gurusthan was constructed. To prevent repetition the word *Utthapan Vidhi* will be used hereafter.

The significance of the Neem tree is given under the 'Neem Trees' in Lendi Baugh. This again is done to avoid repetition.

Lord Shri Krishna himself had come to Shirdi in the '*sagun roopa*' (the living form) of Sai Baba. So it was but natural that there would be a charming, beautiful and peaceful *Vrindavan*.

Whenever Baba went to Rahata he brought saplings of marigold and different varieties of jasmine. These he planted by digging the dry and barren land around the neem tree. Everyday, a devotee named Vaman Tatya supplied him with two earthen pitchers. With these Baba watered the saplings and gave them life. For three years he drew water from the stone well and carried the pitchers on his shoulders to water the saplings. Thus grew a fragrant and luscious garden where the Samadhi Mandir now stands.

Gagangiri Maharaj does Naam Saptaha in Shirdi

Gangagiri Maharaj hailed from the village of Kaapus Vadgaon. He went from village to village performing *naam saptaha* (continuously reciting the lord's name for a week) and following the *Saptaha* he performed *annadaan*. Once, he came to Shirdi and performed *naam saptaha,* and *annadaan*. On that visit he saw Baba holding two pitchers of water in both his hands and then watering the plants. Nearby he saw Mhalsapati, standing and talking to some villagers. Gangagiri then went up to them and asked, "Who is this *Maharaj*?" Mhalsapati informed him that he was Sai Maharaj. Then full of admiration he said, "He is a diamond. If you think he is an ordinary stone lying in the rubble, you have not recognised his divinity"

Just then Baba went to Dwarka Mai and kept the pitchers. Gangagiri Maharaj followed him. Baba quickly kept the pitchers there and picked up a small stone in his hand, as if to throw it at Gangagiri Maharaj; but Gangagirie Maharaj just stood there smiling. "Go this way, and come through the *vess*," said Baba pointing the way. Gangagiri Maharaj did just as Baba had ordered. Then Baba welcomed him saying, "Come Ghangdev Maharaj " Later Baba, Mhalsapati and Gangiri Maharaj sat together and smoked a *chillim* in Dwarka Mai.

Shiladhi *written by Dr Keshav B Gavankar*

13

Anandnath Maharaj comes to Shirdi for Baba's Darshan

Anandnath Maharaj was a disciple of Swami Samarth of Akkalkot. His '*mutt*' (*ashram*) is near Yeola.

Nandram Marvadi, Dagdubhai Gayake, Shama and Tatya Kote Patil visited Yeola once to take his *darshan*. After taking his *darshan* they sat in their bullock cart to return to Shirdi. All of a sudden Anandnath Maharaj came to their bullock cart and sat in it. Then all of them came to Shirdi. Upon seeing Baba he said, "This *Maharaj* is a diamond, a rare diamond. You people must have a good perception of his spirituality and divinity." After taking Baba's *darshan*, he returned to his *ashram*.

Devi Das was already in Shirdi when Baba arrived there with the marriage party of Chand Bhai. Devi Das was a *Gosavi* and was bare bodied except for a *langot*. Though he was just about 10 years old, he was highly spiritual and enlightened. Many of the residents of Shirdi like Tatya and Kashiram became his disciples.

He stayed in Maruti Mandir and Baba often spent time talking to him. It was this child *yogi* that vanquished Javar Ali in the religious debate and drove him out of Shirdi. Shri Sai Satcharita, *chapter 5*

Janki Das was a saint from the *Gosavi Mahaunbhavi* sect. Baba often went and chatted with him. At other times Janki Das came to Baba and chatted with him.

Baba was silent most of the time and did not waste time in idle chatter.

The Cellar Near the Neem Tree

The villagers could not control their curiosity regarding the young lad. One day a group of villagers went up to him and politely asked, "*Maharaj* who are you? And where have you come from?" But Baba remained silent. Then the group went to Khandoba Mandir and earnestly prayed for an answer.

Then a strange incident happened. A few people were possessed by the sprit of Lord Khandoba. The rest of the group asked the spirit about the lad. Lord Khandoba asked them to bring a hoe and dig in a particular spot. They did as instructed and found the cellar. Then the spirit spoke thus, "For twelve years this lad did penance here."
Shri Sai Satcharita *chapter 4*

Dr Keshav B Gavankar in his book titled *Shiladhi* gives a slightly different and a more detailed account. It is as follows: Baba at that time stayed for a few days under the Neem tree and for a few days in the *Masjid*. The villagers were curious about him. One day the villagers asked him politely who he was and why he sat there under the Neem tree. But Baba did not respond to their queries. In the end they sought Lord Khandoba's help. And they went in a group to the temple. There they got a revelation that there was a cellar (**photo 1.2**) about 12' deep. The cellar was directly below the area where Baba sat.

At that time Sathe Wada was existent. It had an entrance facing east and an exit facing west. There were steps leading to the entrance. They dug up the area adjacent to the steps and found a cellar. It was 10' in length and 10' in breadth and 12' high. Inside it they found a *paat* (low stool), next to which were lamps that were lit. On the *paat* there was a *jaap mala* (rosary) and a *Gomukhi* (a glove shaped like a cows mouth, in which the hand holding the rosary is placed when doing *naam jaap*). The villagers were amazed to see this.

They came to Baba and besought him to tell them something about the cellar. Baba answered, "This is the place of my *Sadguru Maharaj*." To prove this he placed his right hand on a branch of the Neem tree. That was the branch facing the east and said, "This is the truth and from today the bitterness of this side of the Neem will disappear." Thus it came to pass that the leaves on the right side are not bitter. The villagers then covered the portion that was dug. They placed the mud over as it was before. Then Baba said, "Anyone who applies slurry of cow dung on this area, on Thursday and Friday and offers incense sticks, will be benefited greatly." Devotees offer incense sticks and fragrant myrrh there even today.

The Gurusthan or Guru Padukasthan

In the 1920's Gurusthan (**photo 1.3**) was a small temple facing west adjacent to the Neem tree. In *Ashvin Shudh 10, Shake 1863* (30-09-1941) a beautiful temple was reconstructed. This west facing temple was on a small platform, about 1' high. It had bass relief peacocks and flowers painted with delightfully bright colours. There was a small *kalasha* on top.

In 1974, this small shrine was enclosed in a bigger temple. Baba's idol was placed to the right of the small shrine, while the Neem tree was to the left of it. The marble *padukas* were in front of the Neem tree on a pedestal.

Baba's Idol

This marble idol (**photo 1.4**) is about 3' in height and is of "Baba sitting on the stone" posture. On *Guru Purnima* of 1974 *prathistha* of this idol took place with all rituals. Yasvanthrao D Dave a devotee from Mumbai donated the idol. It was sculpted by Harish Balaji Talim (son of the late Balaji Vasanth Talim, who had sculpted the idol of Baba for the *Samadhi Mandir*).

In the year 2007, this idol was covered from head to toe and placed in the Museum. The idol will be kept like this till it is placed back in Gurusthan. This is '*Utthapan vidhi*'. When *pran prathistha puja* is performed the *pujari* blows life into the idol. If for some reason the idol has to be moved and ritualistic *puja* and *bhog* cannot be offered for that period of time this *vidhi* is done. The *atman* or life force of the idol is requested to be seated in a copper *kalasha*. The *kalasha* is filled with water; the mouth is covered with a cloth and kept aside. When it is time for the idol to be moved back again, elaborate rituals are performed. The *pran* or life force from the *kalasha* is requested to enter the idol. This completes the '*Utthapan vidhi*'.

16

In the case of Baba's idol, the Neem tree was dying; so the old Gurusthan was broken and a smaller version was made.

Baba's Original Photograph

During Baba's sojourn in Shirdi, an original photograph (**photo 1.5**) was installed in the small shrine. *Arati* was performed twice a day by Bapu Sahib Jog. Later it was discontinued on Baba's advice. This photograph was noteworthy for giving *saksatkar* and *darshan* of the *ishta devta* of many a devotee.

On 30-9-1952, which was the 3rd day of the festival of Baba's 34th *mahasamadhi*, this photograph was changed. The Sansthan felt that the photograph was old, so it was replaced by a photograph donated by Shri Naryanrao Devhare. At 11 a.m. with due rituals, *sthapana* of the photograph was done by Shri Vasantrao Naryan Gowrakshakar.

Sai Leela Magazine. Ank 4. Year 29 October, November December 1952

Alankar is done daily in the morning by the *pujari* in charge of the Gurusthan. *Bhog* is offered at 11.30 a.m. and after *dhup* (evening) *arati*.

The Possible Meaning of "Baba Sitting on the Stone" Pose

Baba has placed his left leg firmly on the ground. The right leg is across the left leg at exactly 50 %, i.e. on the knee. His left hand is on the right leg (As is also seen in sitting in front of *Dhuni Mai* pose). His right hand is not visible as it is behind the right leg. This pose could be an instruction as to how one should live one's life.

Through this pose, Baba is instructing us to control or rule over *maya*. The stone represents *maya*. One should sit on it. Move karma *indriyias* very firmly without allowing them to wander about according to their wish. This is represented by the firmly placed left leg. Do the inward journey to find the real 'I', this is achieved through *antahkarna chatusaya* with *adhimanas*. This is represented by the right hand which is hidden behind the right leg. With the insight and support of the inward journey allow the *Jnana indriyas* to exert apt and legitimate pressure on the karma *indriyias*. This is represented by the right leg. At the same time get detached from *kamini, kanchan* and *Kashyap*, represented by middle, ring and little fingers respectively of the left hand. Make every effort to merge *aham* represented by the index finger of the left hand with *parabrahma* represented by the thumb of the left hand.

The rest of the fingers are not visible. The *trigunas*, three *shariras* should act on the *arishadvargas*. The *panch bhoothas, panch pranas*, should be focused on His lotus feet. The inward journey is possible only by sitting on the seat of *maya*, which is attractive and has lucrative frills. (This stone has 9 scallops below, that look like frills). The stone represents *maya*, so one should not carry it on the head, rather be firmly seated on it.

Shiva Linga

In front of Baba's photograph is this *Shiva Linga* (**photo 1.6**). The *shalunka* faces north, while the *nandi* faces east and is in front of Baba's photograph. The wonderful story of this *Shiva Linga* is given in chapter 28 of *Shri Sai Satcharita*. Baba blessed Megha by giving him *saksatkar* and then gave him this *Shiva Linga*.

Shiva means auspiciousness and *Linga* means a symbol. So *Shiva Linga* is the symbol of the great God of the universe, who is all auspiciousness. *Shiva* also means 'one in whom the whole creation sleeps after dissolution'. *Linga* also means the same, a place where created objects get dissolved during dissolution of this universe.

The Shiva Linga can be '*Cala*' or movable and '*Acala*' or immovable. The *Acala Lingas* are those installed in temples. Hence the '*Utthapan vidhi*' was performed. This *Shiva Linga* is a *Bane Linga*, so it does not have the traditional platforms. *Bane Lingas* are found in the Narmada River.

Every day, this *Shiva Linga* is bathed and adorned. On *Maha Shivaratri*, *Rudrabhishek* and elaborate rituals are done at the time of *Lingodbhav*. This *Shiva Linga* was installed in 1912 after Megha passed away.

Baba's Padukas

In chapter 5 of *Shri Sai Satcharita* the story of the *padukas* (photo 1.7) is given. Dr Keshav B Gavankar in his book titled *Shiladhi* gives a more detailed and slightly different account. The devotee should read both the versions together.

Dr Ramrao Kothari lived in Mumbai; he made a pilgrimage to Shirdi in *Shake* 1834 (in 1912). Dr Kothari's medical assistant and his friend Bhai Krishnaji Alibagkar were also devoted to Baba. Unfortunately, the name of the medical assistant is not known. Alibagkar and the medical assistant had visited Shirdi several times earlier. They visited Shirdi again in 1912.

One evening Sagunmeru Naik, Kamlakar Dixit, Alibagkar and the medical assistant were chatting together. The conversation turned to Baba's advent in Shirdi. They decided that the area adjacent to Sathe Wada, under the Neem tree should be revered. As Baba sat there, this site should be marked with the installation of his *padukas*. Alibagkar immediately went and got *padukas* made of a rough ordinary stone and brought them. Seeing the *padukas* the medical assistant said, "Do you truly want to install these ordinary *padukas*? If my employer was aware of our plan, he would gladly have got marble *padukas* made."

They informed Dr Kothari of their plan. He got a drawing of a pair of marble *padukas* and brought them to Shirdi. The doctor being friendly with Upasani showed him the drawing and told him about the plan. Upasani said, "Your plan is great. Instead of installing bare *padukas*, if there are motifs of *shankha, chakra, Gada* and *padma* it will look beautiful. The *padukas* should not lie on the floor. They ought to be on a marble pedestal. The pedestal should have marble on all four sides. On the front panel the sacredness of the Neem tree and the greatness of having *darshan* of the *Sadguru* Shri Sai Baba may be inscribed." Dr Kothari gladly agreed with the suggestion.

The motifs mentioned above are in the four hands of Lord Vishnu. The sound that emits from the *shankha* (conch) is the sound of *'pranav'* or *aum*. It symbolises *Naad Brahma* or God in the form of sound. The *chakra* or wheel, symbolizes the one who turns the wheel of *samsara* (life). *Gada* or mace known as *Kaumodki* stands for a category of *'budh'*. *Padma* or lotus is the symbol of purity and eternal peace.

On the front panel was inscribed the 4th verse of *Shri Sainath Mahima Stotra*, written by Upasani (**photo 1.8**). The verse means, "I bow to Lord *Sadguru* Sainath, whose constant abode was at the foot of this Neem tree. Thereby has turned into nectar its bitter and distasteful taste. Because he has exalted this tree above the legendary *Kalpvirksha* (wish fulfilling tree)."

Sthapana of the Padukas

Dr Kothari got beautiful marble *padukas* prepared and sent them to Shirdi. They were kept in Khandoba Mandir for two days. Baba said, "On *Shravan sudh Purnima* perform the *sthapana* of the *padukas* under the Neem tree." On that day at 11 a.m., Govind Kamlakar Dixit carried the *padukas* on his head, in procession to Dwarka Mai and placed them at Baba's feet. Baba touched them saying, "These are the feet of the Lord. Keep them below the Neem tree."

A Parsee devotee from Mumbai, named Pastha Seth, sent a money order of 25 rupees as *dakshina* to Baba. It arrived a day before the installation, addressed to Alibagkar, who handed over it to Baba. Baba said, "Keep it as we will need the money tomorrow for the installation of the *padukas*." Dr Kothari however did not send any money.

On the day of the installation Upasani, Jog, Bhate and Dada Kelkar along with a host of devotees participated in the ceremony. They spent 100 rupees on the installation and the feast that followed. Baba gave 25 rupees and 75 rupees were contributed by Alibagkar,

Vasudev Appaji, Sathe and Kamlakar. Four Brahmins representing the four Vedas came from Kopergaon and performed the ceremony. The villagers joyously participated in the function.

Akkalkot Maharaj was Alibagkar's chosen deity and he wished to go there. Baba said, "*Arre* what is there in Akkalkot? Why are you going there? Swami Samarth is here in Shirdi itself." So Bhai did not go to Akkalkot and thereafter visited Shirdi frequently.

Shiladhi by Dr K B Gavankar

Kamlakar, then L K Jakadi did *mangal snan* and *puja* of the *padukas* daily. Now the *pujari* from the Sansthan does it. At present they have silver padukas. In 2007 they were installed on a small platform about 5" in height following the *Utthapan vidhi*.

The Ever Burning Lamps

Two ever burning lamps (**photo 1.9**) were placed on the wall on either side of the Neem tree. They were enclosed in a silver casing with a glass door. They were placed at a height of about 5′, so that the *pujari* could attend to them easily. Daily the wicks were trimmed, replenished with oil and new wicks used whenever necessary. This was done without allowing the *jyoth* (lit end) to be extinguished; as the *jyoth* is burning since Baba's time.

Following the installation of the *padukas*, Dr Kothari sent two rupees every month for lighting the lamps. Then Sagunmeru Naik did this service. Now the Sansthan does it. Since *Guru Purnima* of 2007, there is only one small 'ever burning' lamp. This lamp is kept in the right hand corner and towards the front of Baba's photograph. (**photo 1.10**). This photograph gives a view of the interior of the Gurusthan in days gone by. The devotees can see for themselves what it looks like now.

The Sacred Neem Tree

The *Audumbar* and *Ashwatha* are considered sacred. Baba made this tree (**photo 1.11**) sacred by sitting under her shade. It is believed that the Neem tree is the abode of Goddesses and it is also referred to as *Neenari*. In *Chaitra Maas* after *amavyasia* Durga and Maha Kali reside on the tree. So devotees worship the tree and eat its leaves mixed with pepper and sugar, as it has curative properties. Elleyamma sometimes assumes the form of a young neem tree. The goddess of small pox, Sitla Devi is believed to reside on this tree. Hence, this tree is worshipped at the onset of the disease and a paste made of the leaves is applied to the skin. A detailed account and significance of the neem tree is given under the heading, 'The Neem Trees' in the section on Lendi Baugh.

2

The Mashid or Dwarka Mai

In chapter 22 of *Shri Sai Satcharita* Baba says, "*Mashidmayee* is her name, will she ever go back on her promise?"
A mother is always full of love and tenderly merciful towards her child." *Mashid* or ma+shi+da means refuge at the feet of Lord Shiva. In Shirdi the *Parabramha* gave refuge and is still giving refuge to multitudes of devotees that flock there.

He called it *Dwaravati* and *Dwarka Maatha* (**photo 2.1**), and said that those who sit in her lap should be fearless as no harm will befall them. She was *mothi krupalu*, full of compassion and would take you across the ocean of worldly existence. This gives a glimpse of the love he had for her.

The word Dwarka can be broken into Dwar+ka. *Dwar* means the door and *ka* means Brahman. Thus, it is the door or gateway to get to or reach *Brahman*. Dwarka is that place where one can get freedom from the bondage of *karmic* actions. Dwarka is also known as *Mukthidham* and *Mokshpuri*.

Narad Muni extols Dwarka saying that it is a sacred *yagna bhumi* that bestows *moksha* on the pilgrims. By having its *darshan*, one becomes like Lord Narayana. The pilgrim who visits it, hears its story and does charity however miniscule, becomes immortal. Our Dwarka Mai grants all this and more.

It was here that Baba spent 60 years in bliss. Here Baba granted his devotees wishes and nurtured them like the mother tortoise. Finally, he took *Maha Samadhi* in his beloved *Mashidmayee*.

What did this Masjid *look like?*

This *masjid* that Baba extolled was old and dilapidated. There were deep pits and huge holes in the floor. Each and every nook and corner had garbage dumped in it. It was in this ambience that he stayed blissfully smoking his *chillim*, by day and night. To appease his hunger he took *bhiksha* (alms) from five houses. Whether the food was stale or delicious he knew not.

On his body were torn and tattered clothes and then was it possible for the people to recognise his divinity. Often he roamed in the forest nearby. There he would sit under the *Babul* tree (a small tree full of thorns), often talking to some unknown entity and waving his hands about in a threatening manner. The villagers saw his lifestyle and took little notice of him.

The only time they interacted with him was when someone in the family was sick and they needed some medicines. Baba dispensed his medicines readily. If the patient did not recover quickly, he himself went and nursed him back to health.

Baba's divinity dawned on the villagers only after Nana Sahib Chandorkar's visits to Shirdi. He was convinced of Baba's superhuman powers and divinity. Although, Gangagiri Maharaj had told the villagers this, "He is a valuable diamond lying in a heap of rubbish. It is your good fortune that he has come to stay amongst you."

The *Sadguru* manifests to uplift his devotees. His only concern is their welfare in every aspect of life. He is eager that they progress spiritually and that they are filled with love and bliss. The devotees are also eager to do *Guru seva*, charitable deeds and fulfil his wishes.

Repair of the Masjid
Nana Sahib's heart was bursting with love and devotion. He was eager to renovate and repair the old and dilapidated *masjid*. His only thought was, "How will I get permission to make the *masjid* more habitable?" Baba however was quite content and did not grant him permission. Nonetheless with this thought in his mind he went to Shirdi.

The next morning Nana was standing outside the *masjid* and waiting for Mhalsapati, who had gone to get his *bhiksha*. Having received it, he was about to enter the *masjid*, when Nana accosted him. Nana was eager to tell him of his plan. At that very moment Baba called out to Mhalsapati.

24

Mhalsapati immediately went to Baba, who said, "*Arre* Bhagat, who is standing outside?" Mhalsapati told him that it was Chandorkar. Innocently Baba said, "Is that so? Bhagat I wanted to have your opinion on this matter. That Nana says, 'Baba, I would like to build a new *masjid*.' Now don't you think our old *masjid* is good enough for us?" To this Mhalsapati replied, "Baba let him build a new *masjid*. It will be very useful for both of us, as we will have a place to sit and to sleep when the time comes." Then Baba agreed and gave his consent.

As soon as Baba gave his consent, Mhalsapati called out to Nana and asked him to start the work. Nana immediately brought a coconut and broke it. Thus, on Mhalsapati's advice Nana was allowed to renovate the *masjid*. And Kaka Dixit was allowed to do the flooring.

Shiladhi *by Dr Keshav B Gavankar*

Gopal Gund who started the *urs* had wished to renovate the *masjid*; but this task was for Chandorkar and Dixit.

Shri Sai Satcharita, *chapter 6*

The three carpenter brothers Kondaji, Gabaji and Tukaram Sutar provided the greatest help. All the woodwork was done by them. After the renovation the management of the *masjid* continued with them for many years. Till Baba's *Mahasamadhi* Tukaram undertook the sweeping of the *masjid*. He took care of Baba's needs like heating water and giving it to Baba to wash his face and mouth. Baba would not allow any other person to do this.

Shri Sai Baba of Shirdi *by the Late Rao Bahadur M W Pradhan*

Dwarka Mai in the 1920s

Each and every article in Dwarka Mai (**photo 2.2**) fills devotee's heart with love, joy and peace. Baba spent 60 years here; his touch has filled every stone, brick and woodwork with life. This is the place where he fondly asked about each devotee's welfare. and told *goshties* (stories). Like a fond mother he fed devotees sweets.

Sometimes he cut fruits into small pieces and put small morsels into their mouth.

In the place that he sat there was a huge portrait painted by Shamrao R Jaykar that faces the south. Now a copy of that portrait is there and the original portrait is kept on the first floor of the Museum. This masterpiece is so famous that it is often referred to as the Dwarka Mai pose. Below this portrait was a *chappi* (a wet cloth that is wound around the end of the *chillim*) and a *chillim*. A set of marble *padukas* were installed directly in front of the portrait for the devotees to do *namaskar*. The *Nimbara* was garlanded daily and draped with a beautiful shawl. Next to it were three ever burning lamps. The lamps are still there. There were two querns next to the lamps. Baba used the bigger quern when he ground wheat to drive away the cholera epidemic. He used the smaller one to grind pulses and spices when he wanted to do *annadaan*. Beside the lamps was, and still is, a sack filled with wheat.

To the left, in the alcove was the clay *maath* (water pot). In the corner near the *maath* were a stack of *chillims*, that are now in the museum. Next to these were Baba's *bhiksha* utensils, like the *tumrel* and *kolamba*. The *tumrels* are now kept in the museum. In front was the open *Dhuni Mai*. Then a small wall was erected around it and the *Dhuni Mai* was enclosed. In a cupboard next to the *Dhuni Mai* heaps of Baba's *kafnis* were neatly folded and stored. Now Baba's *kafni* is hung in the museum. *Shiladhi by Dr Keshav B Gavankar*

At present the cupboard is used to store Baba's *alankar* items like *chandan, ashtagandh* and *kumkum*. In the cupboard on the left, the articles that he needs for the night are stored. These articles are the mosquito net, the copper *kalasha* for water and a *phool patra* (this is a flat bottomed, copper tumbler that is kept over the mouth of the *kalasha*) and the kerosene oil lantern.

In 1959 Shirdi Sai Baba Sansthan made some more renovations. In 1998 the Sansthan redid the *Dhuni Mai* and laid heat resistant bricks at the base. They also made a chimney. While this work was going on for a few days the *Jyot* (fire) was maintained in a small, temporary *Dhuni Mai*.

The Sabhamandap (1911)

The area in front of Dwarka Mai was a vacant plot. Devotees stood there and attended *aratis*, often in scorching heat and rain. Dixit thought that if a *Sabhamandap* (**photo 2.3**) or portico was built, it would provide shelter for devotees from the elements. He was determined to build it, no matter what it may cost.

He bought tall iron pillars and angled brackets. On the day that Baba slept in Chavadi, he and the other devotees worked all night. The next morning, when Baba came to Dwarka Mai, he swiftly pulled out the pillars.

In *Shri Sai Satcharita,* chapter 6 *Ovi 127-147,* a detailed account is given under, "the renovation of the *masjid* and construction of the *Sabhamandap.*"

Thanks to Dixit's dedication and determination, we devotees can enjoy its comfort. In this *mandap* many *palkis* stop awhile. Devotees use it for exchanging garlands on their weddings, for christening ceremonies and *Anna Prash* (the ceremony of solid food being given to the child). But most importantly, devotees recite the *Vishnu Sahasranama,* do Baba's *Naam Jaap* and read *Shri Sai Satcharita.*

Thus, Dwarka Mai had two parts, the *sanctum sanctorum* which is the *Masjid* or Dwarka Mai and the *Sabhamandap.*

The *sanctum sanctorum* faces east. Three steps lead inside (**photo 2.4**); it is 17′ in length and 15′ in breadth.

The entrance to the *Sabhamandap* faces south. The roof has CI corrugated tin sheets. These sheets were donated by Baba's ardent devotee Capt. Darruwala as a gesture of gratitude. Through his mysterious ways Baba saved him, his crew and some ships from the enemy during the Russo-Japanese war of 1905. The roof is supported by 12 iron pillars, 15′ long.

There are small niches in the eastern wall, seven on the right and ten on the left, of the shrine that houses Baba's photograph. In the past devotees used to place lighted *Divas* (earthen lamps) as Baba loved to light *Divas.* The length of the *Sabhamandap* is about 48′ from the *otta* (platform) to the shrine and the breadth is 38′.

There is a room that shares the eastern wall of the *Sabhamandap*. Its door faces east. The signboard above it reads, "Shyam Sunder Hall."

The Bell

This huge brass bell (**photo 2.5**) is tied above and to the left of the entrance of the *Sabhamandap*. It is not the original bell and has been changed many times. It is rung three times a day, at 4. a.m, 11.30 a.m. and at 8.30 p.m. It is rung by the priest, calling the devotees for the *arati*. If it is rung at any other time it, signals that an untoward incident has occurred somewhere in the village. The villagers assemble in the pavilion and go to the place of the calamity and set it right. This practice continues to date; hence the gong is tied to the grill.

Mention is made of it in *Shri Sai Satcharita*, chapter 19. When Baba sent Dabholkar to Shama's house to get *dakshina* and chat awhile Shama narrated the story of Radhabai Deshmukh. Just as he finished narrating this story the bell rang and both of them hurried to the *masjid* for the noon *arati*.

Flags (*nishans*) of Dwarka Mai

Gopal Gund was devoted to Baba. He did not have any children but with Baba's blessings a son was born to him. He felt that an annual *yatra* (fair) should be held in Shirdi. He told the prominent devotees of Shirdi, like Tatya Kote, Dada Patil and Shama about it. They all liked the idea very much and everyone started making preparations for it. However *Kulkarni* (the Revenue Officer) opposed it. Hence the District Collector did not grant them permission to hold the fair. But they single mindedly pursued it and finally got permission to hold the fair.

They chose the festival of Rama Navami to hold the fair. Tatya Kote supervised all the arrangements. Gopal Gund asked his friend Dammuanna Rasne to supply a flag for the occasion. Nana Sahib Nimonkar supplied another flag. Both these flags (**photo 2.6, 2.7**) were taken in procession through the village to the accompaniment of musical instruments. Then these flags were fixed atop the Dwarka Mai.

Even today this ritual is performed. The great grandson of Dammuanna, Pradeep Rasne brings an ochre coloured flag. He along with his family comes from Ahmednagar. While the great grandson of Nana Sahib Nimonkar, Chandrakant Deshpande Nimonkar brings a green coloured flag from Pune.

The Significance of the Nishan

It is a banner called *dhvaja* and is a common feature in Hindu temples. The *dhvajas* are made of cloth and are hoisted atop temples, taken by *padyatris* to holy places like Pandharpur and Shirdi. The temple or place of worship is considered as the palace of the deity. He is the emperor of emperors and to honour him the flags are hoisted. Flags denote the area of territory of a particular ruler or a country. Similarly the flags of Dwarka Mai indicate the palace of the *Parabramha* Shri Sadguru Sai Baba.

The Small Red Pillar

This small red pillar (**photo 2.8**) stands in front of the *choolh*. Baba often sat near the *choolh* and rested his back against the pillar. Whenever Baba went out of the sanctum sanctorum, he did *pradakshina* (circumambulation) of this pillar, and also when he returned. *Pradakshina* is done of a temple or a sacred book or a holy tree. One can do the same and utilise the favour of this pillar.

The unique feature of this pillar is that if anyone with a painful back or joints leans against it, the pain abates. Many a devotee can be seen leaning against it. Some devotees read *Shri Sai Satcharita*, others sing the *arati* leaning against it. Others meditate close to it.

Nana Sahib Dengle was an ardent devotee. He wished to perform ritualistic worship of Baba. So he came with all the *puja* materials and sought Baba's permission. He was denied permission, however Baba asked him to perform the ritual to this pillar. Every morning the *pujari* of Dwarka Mai applies *ashtagandh* (a mixture of sandal wood powder and saffron powder) to this pillar. Now a grill enclosure has been built around it for its preservation.

Three Steps in Front of the Pillar

These three steps (**photo 2.9**) are on the southern side of Dwarka Mai. Baba used these steps when he went in and out of the sanctum sanctorum.

Significance of the three steps of Dwarka Mai:

The three steps represent the three *gunas*. These *trigunas* refer to three fundamental components of *prakriti* or *maya*. This is the basic matrix of which this universe is created. These *trigunas* are *Sattva*, *Rajas* and *Tamas*. These *gunas* are not qualities or attributes, but they are fundamental subtle elements which constitute *prakriti*, like the cords of a rope. They bind the *jeevatma* to body.

Sattva increases when the other two decrease. It is characterised by right knowledge, purity, happiness and righteous actions, etc. Thus after death, they take us to higher worlds.

Rajas, when it increases the other two are low. It provides a thirst for selfish actions, anger, greed, lust, involvement, suffering and egoism. After death it brings the *jeeva* back to earth.

Tamas increases when the other two are low. It is characterised by ignorance, dullness, sloth and sin. After death the *jeeva* goes to lower worlds.

To reach the *Parabramha* one has to be *gunatita*. This is possible by doing *sadhana*, under the tutelage of a *Sadguru*. But for his grace this is next to impossible. Therefore, one has to rise above the *trigunas* to establish the pure *Sattva* or 'Self'. This can be accomplished by treating the pair of opposites with equanimity, by remaining unconcerned about losses or gains, etc. by remaining calmly aloof and above all being totally surrendered to Him.

Thereby, by climbing the three steps of the Dwarka Mai one will reach the state of attributeless *Parabramha*.

Padukas in Front of the Chariot Room

Every morning Baba stood here leaning against the wall. He stood there for a while and looked at the sun. There are two pairs of *padukas*, to mark the spot. A small set of *padukas* is on top of the southern wall. This is where Baba placed his right palm while leaning against the wall. Just below the small *padukas* is a small shrine enclosing a bigger set of *padukas* (**photo 2.10**). This is the site of Baba's holy *charan* (sacred feet).

Daily worship is done by the *pujari* of Dwarka Mai, with *ashtagandh*.

The Choolh

In chapter 38 of *Shri Sai Satcharita* under the heading, "The description of the *Handi*," a detailed account of Baba's *annadaan* is given. The *choolha* (**photo 2.11**) is a semicircular earthen hearth or oven. Small faggots of wood are placed in its cavity and lit, while the *handi* or utensil is placed on top of the rim. This *choolha* is directly in front of the red pillar, in the *Sabhamandap*.

The *Shastras* (scriptures) prescribe charity for removal of all the woes of *Kali Yuga* (this era). Of all forms of charity *annadaan* is the highest, as every one feels the pangs of hunger. As Baba took a *sagun roopa*, he also did *annadaan*. Whenever Baba did *annadaan* he used this *choolha*.

Baba used either of the two copper *handis*. The smaller one could feed 50 people, while the bigger one could feed 100 people to satiation with some food remaining. Baba was very meticulous about the salt, condiments, garnishing and other ingredients. He went to the grocer and the bazaar to buy exactly what was required and paid for it in cash. He himself ground the wheat, *jowari* and pulses on the quern and then prepared the food. These *handis* and quern are now kept in the museum.

He often prepared *meetha chawal* (sweet rice), *mutton pulav* (spicy rice with bits of mutton in it), *varan* (soup like lentil or *dal*) with wheat dumplings in it. Sometimes he made tasty *mung dal* dumplings and put them in the *varan*. Often instead of using the ladle, he pulled up the sleeve of his *kafni* and churned the sizzling hot food with his bare hands. Yet there was not a trace of burns or scalding on his hands.

After the food was cooked to his satisfaction he carried it to the sanctum sanctorum. There a *Maulavi* offered *'fatiah'* or prayers. Then Baba sent the food to the homes of Mhalsapati and Tatya. The remaining food, Baba served to all the devotees assembled there to their utmost satisfaction. "Have some more, take some more," coaxed Baba.

The Possible Meaning of the Choolha

One has to travel inward to know the meaning of *choolha*. Food is the cause of birth of any being. The cycle of the evaporation of water that falls as rain on the seeds that result in a harvest of grain. The grain is eaten by a human being that gets converted into a sperm or egg. Union of the two results in birth of a living being. The human being is then baked or cooked in the fire of *'prarabdha'*. One does not know how long one has to go through this process to be completely *pukka* or ready. Only a *Sadguru* by his grace i.e., by putting his hand in the scalding food and churning it around can reduce the duration of this process. So the *choolha* represents the fire that takes away two-thirds of the suffering from one's *prarabdha*.

Another explanation can be as follows. The *choolha* contains the fire of *maya*, on which vessel or body is placed. Thus, we are boiling in the water known as karma. These *karmas* are *sanchita, prarabdha* and *aagami*, which result in suffering and happiness. This leads to the never ending vicious cycle of birth and death.

32

We however, by concentration and total surrender to the *sadguru*, should make ourselves ready to be boiled in the water of the *sadhana* path. With this effort on our part he will definitely put his hand in the vessel and lift us to eternity.

The *quern* and the *handis* used by Baba were at first kept in the show room of *Samadhi Mandir*. Now they are in the museum.

The Chariot (Rath) Room

This room is on the left side of the main entrance to Dwarka Mai. The old chariot (**photo 2.12**) used to be kept in it. This chariot was presented to Baba by Avasthi and Rege. The chariot was first taken in procession on *Guru Purnima* of 1918. The devotees entreated Baba for permission and reluctantly he agreed. Baba never sat in this chariot. On festivals this *rath* is taken in procession throughout the village.

Previously, this room was used to store containers of hot *udi* before it was sieved. The chariot was then taken and kept in the extension of the *Samadhi Mandir*. Now, the right wall has small trap doors; so the *udi* is shoveled directly into trays from *Dhuni Mai*. The rest of the room is used to store sacks of *gowri* (cow dung cakes) and logs of wood to feed *Dhuni Mai*. The chariot was kept for sometime in the extension of *Samadhi Mandir* (**photo 2.13**). After the Museum was built, it is housed there in the hall on the ground floor.

The Dhuni Mai

This everlasting *dhuni* (**photo 2.14, 2.14a**) was lit by Baba himself, more than 150 years ago and is still burning. The word *dhuni* possibly comes from the root word *dhun*, which means to kindle or waft. Even during the cholera epidemic, when the *panchayat* ordained that no fuel cart be allowed to come into the village, Baba went to the fuel cart and bought wood for his *dhuni*. Baba went at regular intervals to the forest nearby and carried huge logs of wood for his *dhuni*. The smoke and soot that emitted from Dhuni Mai touched or covered the devotees seated there was akin to *bhasma snan*.

The *dhuni* is 7' long and 5'2'' wide. Devotees offer wood, *gowri*, *ghee*, *nav dhanya* and five types of wood to this sacred *dhuni*. Now this cannot be done by individual devotees as the *dhuni* is boarded with a mesh. This is a precaution taken by the Sansthan in order to preserve *Dhuni Mai's* sanctity, as devotees used to put the *loban* along with the plastic wrapper and other undesirable articles. A huge drum is placed near the *dhuni*, so devotees can place their offerings in it and it is later offered by the priest.

Everyday at about 11 a.m, *dhuni puja* is done by the Sansthan. Eleven coconuts, wood and *gowri* are offered to *Dhuni Mai* at this time. The priest from the *Samadhi Mandir* does *Vaishva Dev (Agni) puja* with *anna ahuti* (cooked rice mixed with *ghee*). Sagunmeru Naik did this *puja* daily upon Baba's instructions. A detailed account of his life and how Baba instructed him to do this *puja* is given in the book titled *Baba's Vani*.

In our daily lives we kill a lot of insects, flies and mosquitoes. Thus accumulating a lot of sins. To get absolved from these sins we should feed the *agni*, the ants (*pipilika*) with sugar, feed the dog (*shwaan*), the crow (*kow*) and the cow (*gow*). It is often impossible to do this; so Baba in his mercy did this for us. Now the Sansthan is doing it for us every day by performing the *Vaishva Dev puja*.

Every action that Baba did is pregnant with wisdom. All systems of philosophy, all the *yogas* and 'isms' can be found in his life. His life itself is a teaching depending on how one can learn from it.

Baba by lighting and worshipping *Dhuni Mai,* has taught us the *marga* or path of realising the 'Supreme Self'. How?

Baba teaches to do our duty, without attachment. One should first fight with one's own (six) internal enemies. Conquer the lower nature, which is the cause of the pair of opposites like joy and sorrow, love and hate, hope and despair, so on and so forth. These passions are the eternal enemy of the 'seeker of truth'.

This is the fire of desire that keeps burning all the time. It consumes everything, but still remains unsatisfied. We in our ignorance keep feeding it and ultimately we are consumed by it. This is the fire of the materialistic life.

Baba directs us not to feed the fire of desire, but the fire of knowledge, the *Dhuni Mai.* So we have to keep on feeding her our six internal enemies. The final offering is the offering of ourselves or *aham* or the false ego. Thereby, we become the purest, which we are, the supreme 'Self'.

The *Dhuni Mai* reminds us of the power of fire, not only to grant the knowledge of 'Self', it is also the seat of *Parabrahma.* This is given in the *Bhagvad Gita* chapter 4 *shloka* 14 and 15: "Living beings evolve from food, food grows from the rain, rain falls from sacrifice (*yajna* – fire). Sacrifice springs from action. Action issues forth from the creator and the later issues forth from the indestructible. There the all pervading *Brahma* which is ever present in fire (sacrifice)."

Baba in his mercy is doing *Dhuni Puja* for us.

The Small Silver Padukas in Front of Dhuni Mai

These small silver *padukas* (**photo 2.15**) are in the north-west corner and in front of Dhuni Mai. This is the sacred place where Baba sat every morning. He could be seen sitting there before 5 a.m. This time he spent in solitude. At that time the devotees were not allowed to approach him. The *sevakaris* however entered the sanctum sanctorum and swept and cleaned it. Bhagoji Shinde was the first devotee to go to Baba and massage his burnt hand.

Baba sat near the pillar, which is adjacent to the *padukas*. Baba was very fond of the pillar and asked many a devotee to perform *Puja* to it. The details are given under the heading *Guru Puja*. There is an original photograph of Baba sitting in front of *Dhuni Mai*.

The Possible Meaning of 'Baba Sitting in Front of Dhuni Mai' Posture

This pose (**photo 2.16**) possibly represents the 'inward journey' that we have to take to reach 'Him' and be one with him. This journey is started with the first step of withdrawing our Karma *indriyias* totally from this mundane life. This is represented by the left leg which is not seen.

Control the *Jnana indriyias*, which are to act over Karma *indriyias*, which is represented by the right leg over the left leg.

This is achieved by following the messages heard or insight derived from this inward journey. This is represented by the closed fist of the right hand, which is kept next to the ear. An invisible *antarkarna chatustaya* with *adhimanas* as support is represented by the right hand kept next to the right ear.

The left hand over the right leg represents surrendering to him in totality. We have to surrender all of the following: the three *shairiras*, the *trigunas*, the *arishadvargas*, the 5 *pranas* and the 5 *koshas*. This is achieved by following the *Jnana marga*, *Bhakti marga*, Karma *marga* or the blend of these three.

The Kolamba

This *kolamba* (**photo 2.17**) is an earthen container which was used by Baba to mix the food received by *bhiksha*. This mixture known as *kala* would then be distributed to numerous devotees, birds, cats and dogs. Baba himself ate very little of the remaining food.

The significance of the *kolamba* lies in the fact that it is made of clay and thus may break at any time. Just as the human body is transient and death may strike at any moment, the body also acts as a container to mix the various acts of life. These actions and their consequences are akin to the food got by begging from our own doings. The taste of the food may be sweet (happiness) or sour (sorrow). Baba by mixing the food is teaching us to receive the happenings in our lives with equanimity.

The food will taste sweet, sour or bitter as long as it is in contact with the tongue. Once it crosses the tongue no taste is experienced, as there are no separate compartments in the digestive system. For the digestive system different types of food are the same for it to conduct its function.

This six centimetre long organ, the tongue is the most important organ of our body. We do all kinds of deeds just to fulfil its needs, not only for ourselves, but even for our 'nth' generation. We are trying to amass and hoard wealth, but we are not sure of our very own existence, thus becoming a slave to passions, thereby hiding the real 'Self'.

Baba is teaching us not to become a slave of the tongue, which is the origin of passions. Having the tongue under our control, we can march towards the supreme. By the grace of *Sadguru* (Baba), we can follow his sacred footsteps.

The Maath or Water Pot

The *maath* is an earthen pot in which he stored water. Baba's *maath* (**photo 2.18**) was placed on a stand made of coiled cloth next to the *Kolamba*. The *maath* kept in Dwarka Mai has been changed numerous times. However, the stand (coiled cloth) is in the museum.

Rain falls on the earth; seeds sprout and become trees. Then they produce fruit and these are eaten by human beings. When there is union of the sperm and ova, the beginning of a new life occurs. From there a child grows. It is in the womb for nine months and is then born.

The potter mixes the clay to proper consistency, gives it a shape and then incubates it in a kiln. Only when it is perfectly baked does he take it out. The *kumbhar* is symbolic of God. The *maath* symbolises the human body that can break (die) at any time and to mud it finally returns. Thus, the *maath* emphasises the transient or temporary nature of human life.

Water represents *atman* (soul). It is the life-giving element to the body. Water is odourless, shapeless and colourless; so also the soul. It is *Nirlingi* (genderless), *Nirliptha* (not affected by anything) and *Nirvikari* (formless). So it will take the identity of any living being, just as water takes the shape of any container. The lesson here is that all *Atmans* are the same and that Baba is in all of them. Mrs Tarkhad feeds a hungry dog and Baba is satiated (Shri Sai Satcharita, *chapter 9*).

The second explanation is in the philosophical treatises. The word *ghata* is used to indicate the body, since it is as fragile as the mud pot. A mud pot decorated with Mango leaves and a coconut, becomes a *kalasa* fit to invoke any deity ceremonially into it. It is one of the four receptacles, the other three being *agni*, *vighraha* and *sthandila* (consecrated platform).

In *Hatha yoga*, *ghata* or *ghatavastha* indicates the state of *pranayam*, wherein the *prana* and the *apana* are in a balanced state, leading to the union of the *jiva* (individual soul) with '*paramaathma*' (the supreme). With these facts let us try to decipher the meaning.

38

Baba wants us to understand the transient nature of the body, not to pamper it and give undue prominence to the false 'I' or the *aham* in us. As the body will certainly die at any time just as the mud pot will break. He wants us to understand that the mud pot filled with water represents the body filled with the *atman* (an *amsha* of *paramaathama*) is so sacred that it can invoke divinity and that which is to fuse with the supreme or *Parabramha*. Therefore we should not misuse this sacred body. Though the body is transient in nature, it can be used to reach Him.

If we cannot practice *Hatha yoga* what can we do?
Then we can sincerely and completely devote ourselves to our duty. In simple terms, we should not be depressed with failure and elated with success. Baba wants us to do selfless work which is not lifeless and listless work, rather it is livelier than selfish work. By inculcating this mode we are not resorting to fate, i.e., not fatalism. Fatalism is the result of *tamoguna* or inertia, sloth and infidelity. Fatalism means aversion towards duty or work as a result of a lack of understanding. Where as in *Karmayoga* there is neither aversion to work nor is there attachment to the fruits of action. This is precisely what Shri Krishna says in the *Bhagvad Gita*, chapter 3 *shloka* 47 and 48, "You have a right to perform your prescribed duty, but you are not entitled to the fruits of action. Neither consider yourself the cause of the results, nor be attached to not doing your duty." In *shloka* 48 Shri Krishna says, "Perform your duty equipoised, Arjuna, abandoning all attachment to success or failure. Such equanimity is called *yoga*." Baba is instructing us with the same concept in his laboratory, the Dwarka Mai, by using the apparatus like the *kolamba* and *maath*.

How is Baba Converting *Hatha Yoga* into Karma Yoga?
Baba wants us to be the water in the pot, which by itself is pure. However it can derive any odour, taste, shape and colour depending on the nature of the element that is added to it, otherwise it is unaffected. Likewise, Baba wants us to be unaffected, i.e., to retain the nature of the soul which is like the water in the pot. On the other hand, being unaffected and unattached one can unite with the *Parabramha*.

The Magical Chillim (clay pipe)

The magical *chillim* (**photo 2.19**) like Baba's *satka* was his constant companion during his sojourn on earth. Blessed was the potter who made them and blessed was the clay that touched Baba's hands and lips.

On the right side of the *maath* in the corner was a stack of *chillims'* that Baba had smoked. And next to them in another heap were new and unused *chillims*. This was the arrangement during Baba's lifetime. Till about 1930, these *chillims* were kept this way. Now the unused new *chillims* are in the museum in Dixit Wada.

Chandbhai Patil was a truly blessed soul, who got the first taste of Baba's *chillim*. The *rinanubandhic* ties between them were great. Baba after smoking and sharing his *chillim* actually went and stayed with Chandbhai. He was the '*nimithi*' (instrumental) in bringing Baba back to Shirdi, along with his marriage party.

Baba bestowed his grace on many a devotee by allowing them to smoke his *chillim*. The most amazing story is of Balaram Dhurandar (Shri Sai Satcharita, *chapter 51*). He was troubled by bouts of cough and had asthma for six years. On his visit to Shirdi he went to Dwarka Mai one afternoon and with great humility started pressing Baba's feet. Baba handed him his *chillim* to smoke. Balaram accepted it as *prasad* and took a puff. The very thought of smoking was painful and alien to him. He had utmost faith in Baba, so he smoked a while and humbly returned the *chillim* to Baba.

Lo! His asthma had vanished and he was relieved of the tightness in his chest. He wasn't tormented by breathlessness or coughing bouts thereafter. However, on the day that Baba took *Mahasamadhi* his asthma was triggered and he coughed all day. That day and only that day did he cough and wasn't bothered by it again. How could he ever forget the miracle of the clay pipe?

Ganesh S Khaparde was a renowned, wealthy lawyer from Amravati. He was a loyal aide of Lokmanya Tilak, who was serving a six-year sentence in Burma. Baba kept Khaparde in Shirdi and rescued him from the clutches of the British, who were waiting for a chance to prosecute him for treason and sedition.

Khaparde was a spiritual man, well versed in Sanskrit, the *Shastras* and the *Puranas*. Time and again during the *arati* Baba made mystic signs and offered his *chillim*, when he could unravel the answers. At times the *chillim* calmed his restless mind and gave him reassurance. On 22nd January, 1912 Khaparde writes. "During the course of worship he (Baba) put two flowers in his nostrils and two others between his ears and head. I thought this was his instruction and when I interpreted it in my mind, he offered his *chillim* to me and thus confirmed it."

Krishnaji J Bhishma, the author of *Sai Sagunopasna* (*Arati* book), was disgusted by the thought of devotees drinking *paad tirth* of a Muslim Sai Baba. He was horrified to see Brahmin devotees puff the *chillim* after Baba had smoked it and mentally he resolved not to do both. One day Baba narrated a story to him. It was the same dream vision that he had had earlier. While narrating the story Baba casually passed his *chillim* to Bhishma. He took a puff and was thrown into bliss and ecstasy, which changed for life. At that very moment he became an ardent devotee.

Bhagoji Shinde and Mhalsapati smoked the *chillim* with Baba every morning. Now the *chillim* is offered to Baba's photograph in the Chavadi during Adkar's *Arati Sai Baba soukhyadatara jeeva*.

The Hooks on the Ceiling

These hooks (**photo 2.20**) are on the ceiling in front of the *Nimbar*. Nana Sahib Dengle brought a plank about 8″ wide and 5′ in length and gave it to Baba. He thought that Baba could sleep on it instead of sleeping on the floor. Baba however tied the plank with old rags to the hooks on the ceiling. After lighting four earthen lamps he placed them in each corner of the plank. Baba then slept on the plank. One could see him either sitting there with his head bent or sleeping on the plank. Many people wondered how he got up and down from this plank. They tried to watch this *leela*, but were not successful. Then one day Baba broke the plank. This *leela* is described in great detail in the *Shri Sai Satcharita*, chapter 10.

Das Ganu states, "The plank hung so close to the ceiling that no one could sit upright. One could only sit by bending one's body like an arch. Yet this great *yogi* slept on it." *Bhakta Leela Amrit chapter 31*

Baba is *Parabramha*. One who is without birth, body, age and death. So how could they see him in the *Anima* or the formless state.

The Nimbar or Allah Mia Che Jagha

Upon ascending the central steps of the sanctum sanctorum the *nimbar* is directly in front. The *nimbar* or *allah mia che jagha* (the place of Allah Mia) (**photo 2.21**) is the arched structure in the wall. It is in the western wall of Dwarka Mai. It is garlanded daily and often is venerated with a shawl.

In a *masjid the nimbar* is said to represent the *darga* of Mecca. The devout Muslims do *Namaz* in front of it. Mention is made of the *nimbar* in several places in the *Shri Sai Satcharita*. The *urs* started in 1897. During that *yatra* (fair) the 'Sandal Procession' also took place. This procession is held in honour of great Muslim saints. A detailed account of it is given under the heading 'The *urs* and sandal procession'. This sandal procession was started by Amir Shakkar Dalal of Kohrala. Now the descendants of Abdul Baba carry on this tradition. *Shri Sai Satcharita, chapter 6*

After the noon *arati*, the devotees went home. Baba then went inside and sat behind a curtain, with his back to the *nimbar* for his meal. There were two rows of devotees, one on each side. After all the *naivedya* was mixed together, (*kaala*) Baba offered it to God. Then Shama and Nimonkar served it and everyone ate to their hearts' content. *Shri Sai Satcharita, chapter 38*

The Ever Burning Lamps

Baba was very fond of lighted *Divas* (earthen lamps) (**photo 2.21a**). From the beginning of his stay in Dwarka Mai, Baba lit *Divas* daily. And they burnt perpetually. Baba celebrated Diwali with numerous lamps. He tore thin strips of cloth and twisted them to use them as wicks. Often he tore his old *kafni* into thin strips and used them as wicks.

In *Shri Sai Satcharita*, chapter 5, the *leela* of his lighting lamps with water is given. One day the grocers refused to give him oil. He took an empty tumbler that had a smidgen of oil in it. He filled it with water and drank it. Thus offering it to God and then lit the lamps. Lo! They burnt throughout the night.

The *jyoth* has been burning perpetually since then. When the brass lamps are cleaned the wicks are temporarily placed in another lamp. The oil dripping from these lamps has healing properties. Numerous devotees have used it for arthritis, migraine and other ailments with wonderful results.

The Jaath or Quern

In *Shri Sai Satcharita*, *chapter 1* the wonderful *leela* of Baba grinding wheat is described. Early one morning Baba sat down at the quern to grind wheat. Four village women saw this. They took the peg of the quern (**photo 2.22**) from his hand and started grinding the wheat. While doing this they thought, 'Baba has no kith or kin and subsists on *bhiksha*. So he will give us the flour'. After all the wheat was ground they divided it into four portions for themselves. Baba then used very foul and abusive language. He said, *Phukat khau randa* (free looting prostitute) and told them to take the flour and throw it on the village boundary. At that time, cholera was raging through the village. Seven people had already succumbed to it. This was Baba's remedy to stop the epidemic. Since then, cholera has not occurred in Shirdi, although the neighbouring villages are often afflicted. What was the relationship between cholera and wheat flour?

Cholera is called *Mahamaari* or the great killer. *Mahamaari* means sure death every time it strikes. There is no greater fear than the fear of death. Birth is followed by death at sometime for sure. One who has conquered the fear of death is immortal. So if one wants to conquer the cycle of birth and death, one has to be liberated and free.

If the ultimate goal is liberation then why is one bound? The fact is that human beings are bound by *karma* (actions) and *maya*. In fact *karma* and *maya* are inseparably interlinked. They are the two facets of life.

The Katho Upanishad says that some people want to take rebirth, so they enter the womb of a human being. Others enter the embryo of the seed of a tree and subsequently become a tree. But most importantly the type of *Karma* performed and the knowledge attained from it is the primary deciding factor for the next birth.

1. The sack of wheat is filled with *Sanchita* (accumulated) *karmas*. Those actions done during innumerable lifetimes in the past is *Sanchita karma*.

2. Wheat that is measured out on the winnowing fan, is taken from the sack of *Sanchita karma* to be used in this lifetime. It is *Prarabdha karma*. Or simply, put it is what we are enjoying or suffering right from birth in this life.

3. *Kriyaman* is that *karma* that we perform in this life and the *Sanchita karma* that is not exhausted.

The Sack of Wheat

During Baba's sojourn in Shirdi, this sack of wheat (**photo 2.23**) was kept resting against the wall of Dwarka Mai. Now the sack of wheat is kept in a small cupboard, with a glass door. The cupboard is next to the quern. Balaji Patil Nevaskar did selfless *seva* and swept all the streets that Baba trod on.

Every year when there was a harvest, he brought the entire yield of grain and gave it to Baba. He and his family lived on that quantity of grain that Baba gave him. Whether the amount was large or small did not matter to him, as he believed that it belonged to Baba. This practice he continued till he died. Then his son continued the tradition. Baba used to eat *chapattis* made out of this wheat.

In *Shri Sai Satcharita, chapter 35* the *leela* of annual *shradha* ceremony is given, when thrice the number of guests invited had arrived. The mother-in-law said, "Food belongs to Baba and not a grain of it is ours. He alone will come to our rescue. Any shortcomings will be his, not ours." Then she took some *udi* and put a little in every vessel and covered it with a cloth and served it. Every guest ate to his heart's content. After the guests left she uncovered the vessels. Lo! The same amount of food that they had started with remained in every vessel.

The significance of Quern or Hand Mill.
Baba lived in Shirdi for 60 years and he ground mental, physical afflictions and miseries of innumerable devotees. The two grinding stones signify *karma*, which is the lower stone and *Bhakti*, the upper stone. The handle is *Jnana. Jnana* (knowledge) or self-realisation is not possible unless there is the prior act of grinding of all our impulses, desires, sins, *trigunas* and ego. Ego is so subtle that it is very hard to get rid of.

Once Kabir saw a woman grinding corn and said, "I am weeping, because I feel the agony of being crushed in this wheel of worldly existence, like the corn." His Guru reassured him saying, "Do not be afraid, but hold tightly the handle of knowledge of the hand mill and do not wander far away. Turn inward to the centre and you are sure to be saved." Shri Sai Satcharita, *chapter 1 written by Nagesh V Gunaji*

Another explanation is as follows. If one is born one has to perform *karma*, which leads to the cycle of rebirth. One should perform *Nishkama* (selfless) *karma* or *karma* without looking for the fruits of action. Only then can one destroy the *karma beej* or the seed that yields the harvest, or rebirth.

In *Jnaneshvari, chapter 18 verse 205*, the remedy is given succinctly. "When action is performed there are two binding factors namely the pride of being the doer and hope and expectation of enjoying the fruit or outcome. This creates bondage." says Lord Krishna.

How can One Become Free from the Shackles of Bondage?

The *bhakti marga* is the easiest and best path to follow. This can be achieved by visualising the quern. A quern has two grinding stones. The lower stone is stable and is symbolic of *saburi* and the upper one is *nista*. *Saburi* is joyous, courageous, forbearance or patience. Baba says, "*Saburi* overcomes sin, suffering and adversity; averts disaster ingenuously and drives away all fear."

Nista is unwavering faith. Oblivious of hunger and thirst, day and night is spent in loving devotion. Thus, the upper grinding stone is rotated with determination and concentration and the goal is achieved. Thus, wheat flour is obtained i.e., *karma beej* is destroyed.

The quern will not rotate without the handle or the wooden peg. This peg has to be knocked firmly into the socket or hole of the upper grinding stone; so that it does not become loose while grinding. In one quern at one time there is only one peg, which is fitted into the upper stone (*nista*). This peg guides the rotation of the stone. This wooden peg represents the *Sadguru*. You should have one *Sadguru* (Sai Baba) who will show and guide you along the path. Then you will be able to pull up your sleeves and rotate the quern of *nista* and *saburi* in that direction. Then the wheat of *prarabdha* will be ground easily and the flour will be readily viable. The *karma beej* is destroyed, the cycle of birth and death is halted, *Mahamaari* is stopped and *moksha* is obtained.

Baba said, "*Aalya randa phukat khao*". The word *randa* means a prostitute. The prostitute comes running to loot you of *vivek, budhi*, respect, heath, wealth, peace of mind and finally happiness of the family. This prostitute is *maya*.

Jeev atman yearns for *moksha*, but right from birth he is surrounded by *maya*. With the passage of time this *maya* lures him, entangles him, till he is totally submerged. It is up to that person to set himself free from her clutches.

There are three types of people in this world. They are *Jnani,* *Ajnani* and *Mumukshu* (seekers). *Jnani* is calm, peaceful, and *stheer* (unwavering). Since they are *jeevan mukth,* they are carefree, although they live in this *maya* engulfed world, it has no effect on them.

The second type is *Ajnani,* who are ignorant and submerged in *Maya.* If *tatva jnana* is explained to them, it would be akin to singing the *Gita* before a donkey.

The third group is the *mumukshus.* They choose one path like *Bhakti, Jnana, Yoga* or *Karma,* and progress steadily. Their determination is steadfast and God himself helps them along the way. The prostitute *maya* deviously tries to lure them away; but they are neither tempted, nor affected by her. They see their goal clearly and are determined to achieve it. They with their effort become *yogis.* But around the corner the next temptress is waiting and she is *siddhi.* If the *yogi* is entangled with *siddhis* he is inviting his own downfall.

Four women came running and hastily climbed the steps of the *Masjid.* These four women are symbolic of the first four *deh siddhis.* These are *anima, mahima, garima* and *laghima.* They may represent the *asta maha siddhis* and *upsiddhis.* He has to fight, use abusive language and drive them away (like Baba did), only then will he get *mukti* and *atman darshan.*

Once he realises who the free looting prostitutes are and what their goal is, he can claim the wheat as his own property. That he has not borrowed it from the prostitute's father. The father is symbolic of ignorance, *tamas, deh ankhar.* Only then can he laugh and grind his own wheat and go and throw it on the *shiv* or boundary, without giving it away. This culminates in his attaining *moksha.*

This is the meaning of the *leela* of Baba grinding wheat.

Portrait of Baba in Front of Dhuni Mai (Dwarka Mai Pose)

This portrait (**photo 2.24**) is an oil painting by the famous artist Shyamrao Ramchandra Jaikar. Moreshwar Pradhan brought Jaikar to Shirdi and requested him to make two portraits of Baba. After Jaikar met Baba, he on his own accord made more than two paintings.

This portrait was presented to the Sansthan after Baba's *Mahasamadhi*. It was installed the very place that Baba sat. As the portrait was made with Baba's consent, it has such incredible feature that when a devotee looks at it with love and devotion, he gets the 'living experience' of Baba in it.

Devotees could not leave Shirdi without Baba's permission. When they wanted to leave they came to Baba in Dwarka Mai and sought his permission. Baba gave them *udi* and his blessings and they had a safe journey. Even today devotees go to this portrait, prostrate and ask for permission. Then they take *udi* and have a safe journey home. At present, Jaikar's original portrait of Baba is kept in the museum. The one in Dwarka Mai is a copy.

This famous and beautiful portrait is a masterpiece and is widely known as 'the Dwarka Mai Pose' .

The Possible Meaning of the Dwarka Mai Pose

Baba is sitting next to the railing and his silhouette is in the form of a triangle with the apex at his head with the *Bilva* leaf on it. It signifies *Mount Meru* the abode of mother *Parvati*. So he is the mother calling his children (us) to come and take refuge in him. The *Kakad arati* says, "*Tu shanti kshmecha meru ho. Tu bhavarnavice taru guruvara* (You are the mountain *Meru* of peace and forgiveness. You are the bark that ferries us across this mundane existence)."

By this posture (**photo 2.24a**) Baba is instructing us to totally surrender at his lotus feet. This is done by offering the *panch pranas, arishadvargas, trigunas, karma indriyias* and *jnana indriyas* represented by the five fingers of the left hand. *Manas, budhi* and *chitta* are represented by three fingers of the right hand that are not visible. The index finger is pointing down representing *aham* pride and ego. The thumb represents *Sadguru* or *Parabramha* which is turned in pointing to himself. It is the *Sadguru* or *Parabramha* who can cleanse the *jeev atman* of all impurities and undesirable traits.

This is total surrender to his lotus feet. He is assuring us, nay promising us (represented by his firmly placed right foot) that he will take us on his lap, represented by his left foot. Thus, this pose is an assurance that he is prepared to take us on his lap like a mother, provided we surrender in toto. This is a copy of the original painting. The original is housed on the top floor of the museum.

Every night the priest places a *kalasha* filled with water and a kerosene oil lantern that is lit. The portrait is covered with a mosquito net. It is believed that when a human being sleeps the *atman* leaves the body and travels about here and there. Finally, it comes back to the body; water is a binding force that helps it to identify the proper body. The light from the lantern does the same.

The Padukas in Front of Baba's Portrait

These were silver covered *padukas* (**photo 2.25**) in front of the portrait painted by Jaikar. They were mounted on a granite platform about 3″ above the floor. After Baba's *Mahasamadhi* Shama stayed on in Dixit Wada. When the Sansthan was formed, Shama was asked to pay rent. Shama left Dixit Wada, but took Baba's *padukas* and the photograph with him to his house. The Sansthan requested Shama to return them, but he refused at first. Then Dhumal went to his home with a big procession, Shama handed over all articles.

These *padukas* are worshipped daily in the morning by the *pujari* of Dwarka Mai and decorated with *ashtagandh*. The *pujari* of the *Samadhi Mandir* comes to Dwarka Mai between 11.30. and 12 noon to perform *Vaishva Dev puja*. He cleans Baba's photograph and the *padukas* and applies fresh *ashtagandh*. Now these *padukas* are installed on a pedestal about 3′ high and are covered with gold foil.

The Kathada (railing) on which Baba Rested his Hand

This is the railing (**photo 2.26**) on which Baba rested his left hand. Baba sat near the wall, but he did not lean against it. He always sat upright.

In the north-east corner Baba sat in the direction of *Ishaanya*. His legs outstretched, showering His blessings on the devotees. There are eight directions or quarters in this world, each protected by a deity or *dikpal*. Baba sat in the north-east corner which is protected by *Ishaanya*, whose vehicle is an ox. This symbolises that each individual goes a certain direction or follows a certain path that makes or mars his life, according to his *vasanas*. It is Lord *Ishaanya* who guides the world. He comes riding on the *Vrishabha* to exhaust the accumulated *vasanas* of the *jeevas*. Thus, Baba sitting in the north-east guides the individual in the right direction. Therefore, any *puja* starts with *ashta dik bandhan* (the eight direction bondage) is done. Then the mind of the individual is arrested from taking any particular direction. He discovers his own true nature.

Baba sat facing the south; he is *Dakshinamoorty*. The ever smiling Guru, this south faced Guru symbolises the fact that a man of realisation has transcended time. That the Guru's grace is being showered on the devotees who are caught in the net of *Yama*, the Lord of death. The Guru leads the disciple to immortality. South is the special domain of *Yama*. *Yama* means control; it can be self-control, as well as a limitation over ones' capacity.

50

This railing had been painted many times. If one lovingly rests one's forehead on the railing, one can feel a gentle depression where Baba probably rested his hand. Recently, they have placed a plastic cover over the whole railing.

Baba's Asana

Baba's *asana* [seat] was a sack. In the sack the direction of the weave is very visible. There is a horizontal weave which symbolises the hopes, aspirations, goals and greed of man for materialistic things. This weave represents all the *karmas* that he performs to attain these goals. The vertical weave is the *Sadguru's* will or intervention. These intersections are milestones in his life when he has achieved or has not achieved his goal. The sack symbolises the essence of life. We wish for thousands of things, but the result depends on *Sadguru's* wish. So we should happily receive and accept what he gives us.

Dixit was very concerned about Baba sitting on the cold floor. It got so cold in winter that it was impossible to stand on the tiles that he had laid. Baba sat on that floor for hours together. As Baba would not accept a cotton mattress, immediately he set out and made a mattress of sack cloth. Baba did not object to this. That evening after his rounds, Baba asked them to remove the mattress. So every evening Dixit would take the mattress to his *Wada* and return with it early next morning. So the sack mattress became Baba's *asana*. A detailed account of Baba's *asana* is given in the book titled *Baba's Rinanubandh*.
Sai Leela Margashrish Shake 1857 year 12 (1936)

The Udi Stand

The *kathada* is attached to a pillar, and to this pillar the *udi* stand (**photo 2.27**) or container was fixed. *Udi*, the sacred ash that came from Baba's *Dhuni Mai,* was plentiful and Baba gave a palm full of *udi* to his devotees. This *udi* is called 'angara, rakh, bhasma and vibhuti'. It is the gift of *Dhuni Mai*. That wonderful *Dhuni Mai* that Baba lit when he came to stay in Dwarka Mai.

When Baba was in a cheerful mood he sang, in a melodious voice, "Shri Rama has come. He has come during his wanderings. And he has brought bags full of *udi*." The *Akhand Dhuni Mai* yields abundant *udi* even now and will continue to do so till the end of time.

Shri Sai Satcharita, *chapter 33*

During the day, Baba wandered about here and there, but he always returned to Dwarka Mai at night. In the early days of his stay in Shirdi, Baba gave medicines to the sick and infirm. If the patient did not improve as expected, Baba went and nursed the patient. This he did without accepting any payment. After a few years, he stopped dispensing medicines and started giving *udi*. He told Dixit, "Earlier I used to give medicines to sick people. Then I stopped doing this and I started saying Hari, Hari and I found Hari."

In *Shri Sai Satcharita*, chapter 33 and 44, the *leelas* and greatness of the *udi* are given beautifully. The *leela* of Moti Ram Jani is given here as it has some more details: there lived in Nasik a Brahmin named Jani. Before Baba took *Mahasamadhi* he had the good fortune of visiting Shirdi twice. After Baba's *Mahasamadhi*, he was unable to have *darshan* of Baba's *Samadhi* for three years. This upset him a great deal; but because of ill health, he was unable to visit Shirdi.

Once he was extremely sick, for a considerable period of time. One night he had a dream vision and he saw Baba coming out of a long tunnel. Then Baba came close to his bed and said, "Do not worry. From tomorrow you will start improving and in eight days you will be healthy again. Here take this *udi* and keep it with you. This *udi* means that I am with you all the time. Then why are you frightened?" After having said this Baba disappeared. True to Baba's words Jani felt better the very next day and within a week he was hale and hearty.

Sai Baba Hach Chamatkar by Dr Keshav B Gavankar

Baba went into the forests around Shirdi and brought wood for *Dhuni Mai*. Sometimes he went to forests far away and brought huge logs of wood. This he did himself; there was always a stack of logs near the Dwarka Mai. These logs he fed to his *Dhuni* and the ash or *udi* he applied to devotee's forehead. Baba had a unique way of applying *udi*. He applied the *udi* exactly in the centre between the eyebrows.

This spot is the *brukuti*; it is the house of *Brahman*. *Brahman* enables you to get self-realisation or realise the true Self. This spot is also where the *Ajna chakra* is seated, when the *Kundalini* is awakened. This *Ajna chakra* resembles a lotus. It is white in colour and is one of the *satchakras*. It is the centre of the principle of the mind. Baba referred to this spot as the 17th *kala*. The meaning of the 17th *kala* is given later.

The word *bhasma* means sacred ash, representing the transient nature of the universe. One day, all existing things will burn to ashes. The wise do not develop any attachment to them. The use of *bhasma* on the body ought to remind us of the transient nature of the world, so we should contemplate on the permanent or the *Parabramha*.

Vibhuti means 'all pervading' or omnipresent. Baba had a unique way of applying *udi*. Often he took the *udi* between his thumb and forefinger and applied it on the *Anja chakra*. He pressed his thumb laden with *udi* on this *chakra* and then drew his thumb in an upward direction.

What did it indicate? Why is this spot called the 17th *kala*?

In the *Prasna Upanishad (Atharvaveda)* in the sixth chapter Sukesha asks Pipalada, "Do you know the '*sodas kala*' *purusha*? Or the person with 16 attributes?

Pipalada replies that this is one's own body. He is the *atman*. He is the creator. He first created the 1. *prana*, the totality of the subtle creation. From this *prana* the others evolved. They are as follows 2.*Shraddha* or faith, 3. *Akasha* (sky), 4.*Vayu* or the wind and air, 5. *Jyothi* or fire, 6. *Apas* or water, 7. *Prithvi* (earth), 8. *Indriyas* (sense organs), 9. *Manas* (mind), 10. *Anna* (food), 11. *Virya* (strength), 12. *Tapas* (austerity), 13. *Mantras* (Vedas), 14. *Karmas* (Vedic rituals), 15. *Lokas* (the various worlds) and 16. *Nama* (names of objects in creation).

Though a *purusha* is made up of 16 attributes, he is perpetually searching for the truth and wants to realise the *atman*. He cannot achieve it, as he is submerged in *maya*. Only the *Sadguru* with his grace can show him the right path.

Baba by applying *Bhasma* on the *Ajna chakra*, the centre of the principle of the mind, makes the *purusha* understand that he is drowned in *maya*. And that this transient world will one day be reduced to ashes. Thus Baba is instructing us to treat *bhasma* as a path leading to *vibhuti* or the all pervading (*Parabramha*). This can be accomplished through *dharana*, i.e., fixing the mind on him; *dhyana* (meditating on him) which results in *samadhi* (super conscious experience).

This is what Krishna instructs Arjuna in *Vibhuti Yoga* of the *Bhagvad Gita*, "What is the use of knowing all these details? It can only confuse the mind. It is enough if you know that I pervade this entire universe through a small fraction of my *yogic* powers. If you know this and remember me at all times that will release you from this bondage."

In order to get released from the bondage of *maya*, develop *samyama* or control of the mind by applying *udi*.

The meaning of *udi* is detachment based on discriminating knowledge. The literal meaning of *udi* is 'to go'. Baba gave *udi* to his devotees with his blessings, so that they could go to a higher plane in their spiritual endeavour.

What Does *Udi* Teach us?
The body that we pamper with pride will die and turn into ash. So be alert, as we are surrounded by *maya*, *maha maya* and *adi maya* (forms of illusion) on all four sides. *Udi* teaches us that *Brahman* is truth and the *Brahmand* or the universe (this world) is untrue or false.

In this world of *maya* no one, be it brother or sister, relative or friend is really your's. Money is the bond that brings them to you. And wealth makes friends and relatives. The only friend that the poor and downtrodden have is Baba. We came into this world naked and naked we leave this world.

Birth is followed by death. When a baby is born father distributes sweets; there is joy all around. But when the person dies, there are tears and sorrow all around. The frightening thought of death is the cause of unhappiness. When a friend comes to our door we welcome him. If we welcome death in the same way, then the mind and thought process is ready for death. When this state of mind is reached, sorrows and troubles of life are conquered.

Life and death are both auspicious. Death is also a *swaroop* (form) of God. It is the sweet fruit of the tree of life. The human form is a *maath* or *matka* (earthen pot). The Lord of the cosmos gave shape to these pots. Some are small, some are large and some are brittle, while others are sturdy. Some are old and cracked or broken, while some are new and strong. Having given them different shapes, the Lord of this universe sent them to this earth; so that they may perform good deeds and live in the paradise on earth.

Death is a *maha yatra* (a great journey), a *mahaprasthan* (final journey), a *maha nidra* (a great slumber). At night we sleep soundly, oblivious of our surroundings; that sleep is akin to mini death. If death comes to our door, we cannot send it away empty handed. What can we give it? We give it the numerous happy occasions and events that occurred in our lives. We also give it the sorrows or sad events that occurred in our lives. And finally, we give it all the wealth of *punya* (good *karmas*) that we have accumulated so far.

Above thoughts will make us mentally prepared for death, our final journey. Then we lose the fear of death. Even if we have self-control over our ego, control over the 'I' factor, yet in the end we have to accept that we are weak and feeble, in front of death.

Devotees should not just apply the *udi* and go about doing their chores. It behoves every devotee of Baba to think about the inner and deeper meaning of *udi*. Devotees should reflect on the *adesh* (a message and advice), the *updesh* (instruction) that Baba gave when he applied *udi* to the forehead. So devotees can get rid of the Self or 'I' and reveal the inner 'Self'.

After accumulation of good *karmas* of many lives, do we get good fortune of becoming a human being. Baba is seated in the temple of every human being and is the life force. We keep a temple clean, neat, pure and full of joy. So should we keep the human temple or body neat and clean. And fill it with good *karmas* and spiritual way of living.

When human being becomes '*jeev mukta*' or free from the encumbrances of ego and pride, and is free from possessiveness and the fear of death, then that devotee has achieved a spiritual life. The inner light becomes one with the light of the universe and with it dawns *vivek* and *vairagya*.

55

Baba's Bathing Stone

The bathing stone (**photo 2.28**) was kept in the verandah of Dwarka Mai. After the museum was opened it is exhibited there.

The Three Steps next to the Ota

The three steps (**photo 2.29**) of Dwarka Mai lead into the sanctum sanctorum. These are now used to come out of the sanctum sanctorum. Whenever Baba went for *bhiksha* rounds or to Lendi Baugh and returned, he washed his feet and hands (this is *Upa Snan*) on these steps. Many devotees waited for this ritual, so that they could collect water that flowed from his feet as *paad tirth*. This they drank and took home and distributed, for they knew that it would cure many physical and mental afflictions.

The Ota or Platform with the Agarbatti Stand

There is an *agarbatti* (incense stick) stand (**photo 2.30**) attached to the platform. This platform is on the right side of the main entrance of *Dwarka Mai*. It is about 8′ long and 3½′ wide and has a height of 2½′. Devotees would offer incense sticks to Baba. Then light them and fix them on this stand. Now another movable *agarbatti* stand is kept near the stone on which Baba sat. Hence, this stand is not used anymore.

Baba often sat on this platform. There is an original photograph of him sitting on this platform.

The Palkhi Room

This room is to the right side of the main entrance of Dwarka Mai. Due to the efforts of Radha Krishna Mai, Shirdi was turned into a Sansthan. In 1912 a *Palkhi, Rath* and some silver utensils were presented to the Sansthan. Once the *palkhi* was left outside Dwarka Mai and four of its silver ornamentations were stolen. Distraught devotees ran to Baba and complained about the theft. Baba was unconcerned and said, "Why didn't the thieves take away the entire *palkhi*?" So Purandare and Radha Krishna Mai decided to make a room for it.

Purandare went to Radha Krishna Mai's home and she said, "At present the *palkhi* is kept in the Chavadi, but that is not a feasible option." So Purandare said, "We can keep the *palkhi* next to Dwarka Mai. If we build a small tin room that has a door, that can be locked. Then the *palkhi* can be kept safely inside it. This work can be done tomorrow."

Then Purandare suggested that in the evening the *palkhi* could be kept next to Naryan Teli's home. The reason for this was that the place where Baba stood aught to be vacant. After a great deal of deliberation it was decided to build the *palkhi* room adjacent to the sanctum sanctorum. At that very moment, Dixit came to invite them to his home for lunch. They told him their plan and he approved it. Then he went and asked Baba for permission, which Baba gave readily.

The next morning when Baba went to Lendi Baugh, Purandare started the work. Swiftly he and Fakira (his aide) cleaned the area. There was a lot of rubble lying here and there. When they lifted the broken tiles they found a lot of scorpions below the tiles. The scorpions however did not sting them. Fakira then neatly placed the broken tiles to the side. Then he poured water and washed the floor.

Next, the roof had to be made with tin sheets. But the sheets were unsteady, so Purandare decided to place rafters to support them. One end of the rafters was to be embedded in the outer wall of Dwarka Mai. Meticulously he scooped out about 3″ holes in the outer wall. Purandare had completed two holes and was on the third hole when Baba returned from Lendi Baugh.

Instead of washing his feet, as he usually did, Baba came towards Purandhare. Everyone fled from there leaving Purandare to face Baba's wrath. Baba walked swiftly towards him, picked a brick with one hand, and with the other hand held Purandare by his neck. Then Baba said, "Go away. You give me a lot of trouble. I will kill you. Are you going away or not?" Purandare calmly replied, "I will not leave until I have completed making the room for the *palkhi*. I am not destroying your *masjid*. I am just making small holes to support the rafters and I was about to make the last hole." Baba replied, "Are you trying to compete with me? I have been watching you. Today the *bhadva* (a derogatory name) is very stubborn and extremely determined to make holes in my *Masjid*'. A short while later Baba said, "All right, do what you think fit. Later we can build a nice room. Go! Now go away."

Baba then washed his feet and went and sat in his usual place. Purandare continued to work and with each stroke of the hammer, Baba sitting on the other side of the wall let out a volley of abuses. This continued till the work was completed. Then the noon *arati* took place and everyone went home for lunch except Purandare.

Baba turned to Bade Baba and said, "Look at this *bhadva*. Today he is full of determination and has forgotten hunger and thirst. He won't even go home and have lunch. I am hungry and my children are hungry." (Here Baba meant Mrs Purandare, who was waiting for her husband). Then Baba sent Bade Baba to fetch Purandare, who came and stood below. Baba said, "Come up. Have you finished breaking my *masjid*? Just come up" Timidly Purandare went up. Baba got up, held out his hand to strike him. Instead he held Purandare's hand and made him sit close to him and said, "Now go and have lunch. Why do you trouble everyone? Why do you trouble your wife and children? Why do you trouble me? They are hungry and so am I. Now go and have your lunch. The work can be completed in the evening."

As soon as Baba said this, Purandare laid his head on Baba's feet. As he lifted his head Baba asked him to bring some *udi*. Purandare brought the *udi* and placed it in Baba's hand. Baba applied the *udi* on his forehead and placed his hand of benediction on his head. Then Baba said, "Your faith is steadfast. Don't let it waiver even slightly. *Allah* will bless you. All your wishes will be fulfilled. My *Masjid Mai* will bless you." With these blessings Purandare completed the work and the *palkhi* room was made.

Shirdi che Sai Baba *by Dr Keshav B Gavankar*

Baba never sat in the *palkhi*, but his photograph was placed in it. Every Thursday at 9.15 p.m., the *palkhi* is brought in procession from *Samadhi Mandir* to Dwarka Mai and thence to the Chavadi.

The Tortoise

This marble tortoise (**photo 2.31**) is in the centre of the well. The black tiles surrounding it represent the four flights of steps leading to the bottom of the well.

Numerous meanings are attached to the tortoise: 1. The tortoise is an *avatar* of Vishnu (*Kurma avatar*). In the *Kurma Purana* the story of churning of *Kshirsagar* is given. Then Mount Meru was used as the churning rod and *Vasuki,* the serpent, was used as the rope for churning. Mount Meru then started sinking and Lord Vishnu supported the mount on his back, as he lay prostrate.

Baba is Mount Meru. We have to churn our egos, as we are sinking under its weight. Baba however carries us on his back and supports us. Thus we can cross this *Bhava Sagar* with his support, as he carries us on his back.

The five *pranas* are energy giving sources. The *kurma* is *upaprana* of *Vayana* the ruling deity of 'blinking'. Without the action of blinking, seeing is not possible. Baba being *Kurma* gives us energy, while he watches our every action with his thousand eyes.

Through *Kurma* Baba is instructing us to be aware that we are losing time with every blink of the eye. And also to act to know the Self by withdrawing the *indriyas,* just as the *Kurma* withdraws its feet when it faces danger.

One should enter the place of worship slowly, like a tortoise bowing one's head, in complete surrender. Leaving the ego outside, just as the tortoise is in a prostrate position; one should surrender everything to Baba. It is said, "Enter the temple like a tortoise with the head bowed and do not rush in like a horse with the head held high."

2. In *Bhagvad Gita,* chapter 2 verse 58, Lord Krishna says, "One who is able to withdraw his senses from sense objects just as the tortoise draws its limbs within the shell, and is firmly fixed in perfect consciousness." The tortoise can at any moment wind up its senses and exhibit it again at any time for a particular purpose. The senses should be used only for the particular purpose in the service of the Lord, instead of one's own satisfaction. Keeping the senses in the service of the Lord is the analogy of the tortoise who keeps the senses under control.

3. The tortoise was gifted two things, nourishing and nurturing of her young ones by glancing at them from the other shore. And *sadgati* was bestowed by Lord Vishnu showing his *chatur bhuj* to her. Most importantly, the tortoise is looking at Baba. If we follow her example and turn our complete attention towards Baba, he will surely look after us.

In *Shri Sai Satcharita,* chapter 18 Baba says, "The Guru is the mother and father. When gods are angry, only the Guru protects and preserves. But when Guru is angry, there is no one to protect you." In chapter 19 *Ovi* 68 Baba gives the analogy of the tortoise and says, "Just as the mother tortoise feeds her young ones by her loving glances, so was the way of my Guru". Then in *Ovi* 71 he says, "The mother tortoise is on this bank and her little ones are on the other bank. They are nurtured and reared just by her loving glances."

This could be the possible meaning of the tortoise.

The Tulsi Vrindavan

There are 3 major varieties of this plant. They are called: 1. Rama *Tulsi.* 2. Krishna *Tulsi.* 3. Sri *Tulsi. Tulsi* leaves are extensively used in ritualistic worship of Vishnu and Krishna.

Baba planted the *Tulsi* (oximum sanctum or holy basil) *vrindavan* (container) outside the *masjid.* After the outer pavilion was constructed, the devotees brought this *Tulsi vrindavan* inside and tended it. It now stands in the north-east corner and is looked after by the *pujari* of

Dwarka Mai; its nourishment is not up to mark, due to the lack of sunshine. Every year *Tulsi vivaha* (marriage) is celebrated on the 12th day of Diwali.

The Mythology of Tulsi Vivaha

On 'Karthika shukla dvadasi;' which is the 12th day of the bright fortnight of the month of *Karthika* (October and November), which is also known as *utharadvadasi* the *Tulsi vivaha* (**photo 2.32**) takes place.

Jalandhara was a powerful *asura*, who was a threat to *suras* or gods. The secret of his mighty power was his chaste and devout wife Vrinda. Gods requested Vishnu to save them. Vishnu impersonated Jalandhara and went to her. Vrinda having lost her chastity, Jalandhara lost his power and met his end. When Vrinda came to know of this, she cursed Vishnu. Vishnu then repented and sat next to her on the funeral pyre of her husband.

By Parvati's grace the funeral pyre was converted into a beautiful garden. The garden was full of *Tulsi, Amla* (Indian Gooseberry) and *Jaie* (a type of fragrant Jasmine). Out of these the *Tulsi* plant is Vrinda, hence the garden is known as *Tulsi vrindavan*.

Vrinda, who committed *sati*, became Rukhmani in her next reincarnation and married Krishna on *Karthika shulka dvadasi*.

There was a *Tulsi* garden in Dixit Wada and in the area where the *Samadhi Mandir* now stands. The *Tulsi* plant is supposed to have been born at the time of the churning of the milky ocean. *Tulsi* is said to be dear to Lord Vishnu and is identified with his consort Lakshmi. Its presence in the courtyard of the house in a *vrindavan* is believed to ward off the messengers of death. It is considered to be a purifier of sins, hence its twigs are used in the funeral pyre. Some *puranas* say that all gods and places of pilgrimage dwell in it. The *Tulsi* has the boon of converting *Rajas* and *Tamasic* food into *Sattvic* food. This quality can benefit people, who have a *Tulsi vrindavan* in their homes. Further, the effects can be perceived for a distance of one *yojana* or a distance of nine miles around it. Hence the leaves are placed on the *naivedya* offered to God.

In Shirdi, *Tulsi vivaha* is performed in Dwarka Mai on the 12th day of Diwali. Priests from *Samadhi Mandir* come to Dwarka Mai to perform the marriage. Devotees also can participate in the marriage. A new healthy *Tulsi* plant is brought and the old one is replaced. The plant is dressed like a bride in a small green saree. Small green bangles adorn the branches of the plant. Then the marriage takes place between Krishna and *Tulsi* with due rituals.

After the marriage ceremony is completed, devotees assembled there are given *bathasa*, whole coriander and savouries that are made for the festival of Diwali. It is a very joyous occasion.

The Idol of Shyam Karan

Kasam a horse merchant was distraught, because his mare was barren. He promised to Baba that if his mare had a foal he would offer the first born to him. By Baba's grace the mare had a series of foals. So he came and presented the first born to Baba. Baba called him Shyam Karan (**photo 2.33**). He was dark like Shri Krishna and hence the name.

Bala Sahib Sulthe presented this idol. It was installed on the left side of Baba's stone. The details of the horse are given under the heading 'The Samadhi of Shyam Karan'.

The Stone on which Baba Sat

This stone (**photo 2.34**) is placed in the centre of the eastern wall of the *Sabhamandap*. Baba used to sit on this stone facing west. Small marble *padukas* were installed on this stone. Now the marble *padukas* have been replaced with silver *padukas*.

Baba often sat in the *Sabhamandap*. It was the portico in front of the sanctum sanctorum (Dwarka Mai). There Baba sat on this stone. First this stone was adjacent to Dwarka Mai. Later it was moved to the eastern wall.

Once a *pehelvan* (body builder), who was extremely proud of his strength, came to Shirdi. Baba casually asked him to move the stone, from its original place to where it is now. But try as he may, it did not budge an inch. The *pehelvan* stood silently looking at the stone and then at Baba. Then Baba laughed and with his *satka* played with it as if it was a small ball. Then with three small steps he moved it to the eastern wall. Needless to say the *pehelvan* was humbled and returned home.   Sai Baba Hach Chamatkar *by Dr Keshav B Gavankar.*

The Big Portrait of Baba Above the Stone

DDNeroy was a staunch devotee of Baba. He was a photographer and artist. He made numerous photographic prints of Baba. The prints would have one of Baba's eleven promises printed below. He sold these photographs to various companies and temples.

Neroy was devoted to Kamu Baba (a saint at Girgaon, Mumbai). He got this portrait (**photo 2.35**) of Baba sitting on the stone made and mounted in an ornate frame. Then with the help of four men took it to Girgaon. Happily he offered it to his Guru. Kamu Baba appreciated the portrait and very kind gesture, but he refused to accept it. He told Neroy to take it to Shirdi and place it in the *Sabhamandap* of Dwarka Mai. Dejected he sat at his guru's feet and said, "It took me three years to make this portrait and 1½ months to get it framed. Never mind the expense, now you reject it?" Kamu Baba calmly said, "It is not a question of rejecting it, but a keen desire that you take it to Shirdi and place it where thousand upon thousands of devotees will have the benefit of praying to it." Thus, this portrait came to be installed in the *Sabhamandap* of Dwarka Mai.

The dimensions are 6' by 4'. Originally it had a wooden frame, later the silver frame. Recently it has been enclosed in a glass door cupboard like frame to preserve it. Before *Kakad arati* the priest does *alankar* (decorates it) with *ashtagandh* and garlands it.

The Master by Bejon N Desai

The Idol of the Tiger

This idol (**photo 2.36**) is on the right side of the stone. It was installed on 12-11-1969 and presented by Triambakrao Shripathrao Shiladar of Ozar village. Seven days before Baba took *Mahasamadhi* the *leela* of Baba giving *sadgati* to this ailing tiger is given in *Shri Sai Satcharita, chapter 31*. The details are given under the heading, 'The *samadhi* of the tiger'.

The tiger died in Dwarka Mai at Baba's feet, then how could he ever be reborn?

Shyam Sundar Hall

At the end of the *Sabhamandap* and behind the stone on which Baba sat is Shyam Sundar Hall (**photo 2.37**). if has an east facing entrance and it was the school where Shama taught. Shama was an assistant teacher. He often slept in the school at night. Often at night he heard Baba talk in English, Hindi, Arabic and various other languages. Shama would look out of the window on the western wall and see Baba seated alone talking to some invisible entity. He then realised that Baba was a *Sat Purusha*.

This hall was later used as a stable for Baba's horse Shyam Karan. A ster that it was used to sieve *udi* and store it. Later the sieving was done in the room adjacent to the Chavadi. Then this room was used as a *parayan kaksha*. Devotees could read *Shri Sai Satcharita*, do *naam jaap* or meditate. Later on the *parayan kaksha* was shifted to the room in front of the *kapad koti*. Currently, this hall is again being used to store *udi* and *udi* packets.

Why did Baba call the Masjid 'Dwarka Mai'?

"This is our very own Dwarka Mai. This mother gives full protection to her child. He, who once sits in her lap, has overcome all difficulties. So very kind is this *Masjidmayee*", said Baba to Bala Sahib Mirkar, who was going to Chitali and was to encounter a serpent.

Shri Sai Satcharita chapter 22

Baba's words are always true. Then why did he call this *Masjid* Dwarka Mai? One can geographically, historically and mythologically place Dwarka at Shirdi. B V Dev has researched this topic in great detail. He has written an extensive thesis in *Sai Leela* magazine. Only the salient points are given below.

1.   The Churning of the Kshirsagar.

During the churning of Kshirsagar it was agreed by the gods and demons that whoever drank *halahal* (poison) was also to partake of *amrit* (ambrosia). Lord Shiva drank the *halahal* and made it stop in his throat. Thus he earned the name *Thiru Neel Kantashvar* and the place of occurrence got the name "Ghat Siras" (Taluka Pathardi, which is south east of Shirdi). The temple is called Rudreshwar. The Shiva linga in this temple is *swayambhoo* (i.e., manifested on its own accord). Another interesting feature of this Shiva linga is that it is uneven and looks like it is corroded by *halahal*.

After the *halahal* and ambrosia came into being and the gods partook of it. *Chandra* (moon) and *Surya* (sun) came to know that demons Rahu and Kethu stealthily came to the gods' side and partook the ambrosia. They quickly informed Lord Vishnu of this. Vishnu came in the disguise of beautiful Mohini and dazzled Rahu and Kethu. Then He cut the head of Rahu with His golden *chakra*. The place where Rahu's body was thrown is called Rahuri (about 45 miles from Shirdi). There his temple is said to exist. The place that this incident occurred is Newasa, at Mohini Raj. There is Ardhanari Nateshwar temple. Newasa is 110 miles south-east of Shirdi. Kethu's head fell in Rathangad (60 miles north-west of Rahuri) where a temple exists for him. The nectar that flowed from Kethu's mouth became the exalted Pravara River. This river was originally known as Amrit Vahani (carrier of *amrit*).

Out of the 14 *ratnas* (jewels), Lord Shiva took *halahal*, ambrosia and *chandra*. The place of *chandra* is called Chandgaon (about 130 miles from Shirdi) where Chandreshwar temple is situated. Lord Krishna took Lakshmi, *Kausthab, Shankha* and *Dhanur*. Lord Indra took *Airavatam, Kamdhenu, Rambha* and *Dhanvantari* (Ashvini Kumar) at Belapur's Vilveshvar temple (about 25 miles from Shirdi). The place of *Ashvini Kumar* is called Ashvi about 25 miles from Shirdi. Lord Shiva took seven headed horse at Khollar which is 45 miles from Shirdi.

2. The Yadav Dynasty
As late as the 12th and 13th century, the Yadav dynasty (Lord Krishna's dynasty) ruled most of the present Maharashtra. Its capital was Fort Devgad, near Aurangabad, as mentioned in *Jnaneshvari*.

Rukmini, the wife of Lord Krishna, was born in Kundipur, Amravati district near Nagpur. Her father Bhismak was a king and his capital was Fort Devgad.

3. Pandharpur
The southern tip of Dwarka is Pandharpur, which is situated in Sholapur district and is 450 miles from Shirdi. The story of Pundalik is as follows: Once Rukmini left Lord Krishna in a huff and he went after her to pacify her. He roamed the Dindrivan forest, found and pacified her. On the way, he saw Pundalik doing *seva* to his parents. On seeing the Lord, Pundalik threw a brick and asked the Lord to sit awhile, till he had finished doing *seva*. The Lord stood on the brick and waited, with astonishment his arms *akimbo*.

4. Gopal Kala
Lord Krishna practised *Gopal Kala*; as a child he often broke the *matkis* of the *gopis* and ate the curd and butter. Baba mixed all the food in the *kolamba*, partook in it and distributed it to his devotees. *Gopal Kala* is performed by the Sansthan on the conclusion of all the festivals in Shirdi.

5. Our Dwarka Mai

In the *Skand Puran* the definition of Dwarka is, "The place where the doors are open for all people regardless of caste, community and creed for accomplishing *Dharma, Artha, Kama* and *Moksha* is called Dwarka." Baba's *masjid* in Shirdi is open to one and all.

The sanctum sanctorum is closed at about 9.p.m., while the *Sabhamandap* is left open throughout the night. Before the sanctum sanctorum is closed it is swept and cleaned, a *zaari* full of water is placed in front of Baba's photograph, the mosquito net is hung around the photograph and a lit *kandil* (lantern) is hung above the *kathada*.

In 1996 this *kandil* (**photo. 2.38**) started swinging; many devotees felt that it was an omen, others felt that some great change or event was about to take place in Shirdi. Many devotees gathered around to behold the event. The place of the *kandil* was changed, yet the swinging did not stop. This happened for about a week. The only event that occurred was that Sivanesan Swamiji died on 12th February 1996. He loved Dwarka Mai and from the early 1960's looked after it with tender and loving care.

3

The Chavadi

The word Chavadi (**photo 3.1, 3.1A**) means a meeting place for the villagers. Every village in Maharastra has a Chavadi. Men gather there in the evening to chat, to they discuss their crops, their cattle and solve any problem that the village might have. However, there are two Chavadi*s* in Shirdi; one is south facing, where Baba slept on alternate days. Due to a violent storm devotees entreated him to sleep there, as the *masjid* would not withstand any storm's fury. Baba refused, but perceiving the love and concern of his devotees, he finally agreed. Hence, he stuck to his routine; so every alternate day he slept in this Chavadi. The Chavadi procession is described in *Shri Sai Satcharita* chapter 33.

The north facing Chavadi was used as a reading room. It is now closed and not in use.

The Chavadi of any village is a sort of court for the villagers, where the people brought their grievances and justice was delivered by the elders. It is also the place where the *gram panchyat* took decisions for the betterment of the village. This function is described in detail in *Jnaneshvari*, chapter 13.

In Shirdi, as in any small village, the villagers brought their problems to Baba. It was here that Baba took decisions on true and false statements and acts on *paap* (sinful acts) and *punya* (good or righteous deeds). The devotees for their well-being and welfare, made him go to the Chavadi. Baba did this leaving his tranquil *samadhi* state of Dwarka Mai. We devotees can also go every alternate day to the Chavadi in our *sukshma sharir* (invisible body) and take decisions on our lives. For example, we can ponder if we are on the right path. Are we doing *paap* or *punya karmas*? Are we living the life prescribed

1.1 Gurupaduka sthan (Gurusthan)

1.2 The Cellar Near the Neem Tree

1.3 The Gurusthan or Guru Padukasthan

1.4 Baba's Idol

1.5 Baba's Original Photograph

1.6 Shiva Linga

1.7 Baba's Padukas

1.8 Shri Sainath Mahima Stotra

1.9 The Ever Burning Lamps

1.10 A View of the Interior of the Gurusthan

1.11 The Sacred Neem Tree

2.1 Outer View of the Mashid or Dwarka Mai

2.2 Dwarka Mai in the 1920s

2.3 The Sabhamandap of Dwarka Mai, 1911

2.4 The Entrance of Dwarka Mai

2.5 The Bell

2.6 Nimonkars flag & 2.7 Damu Anna's flag at the Dwarka Mai.

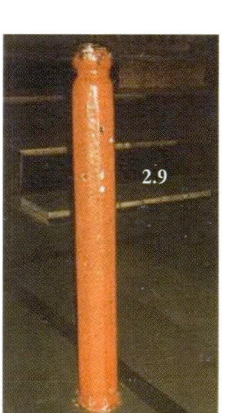

2.8 The Small Red Pillar, 2.9 Three Steps in Front of the Pillar

2.10 Padukas in Front of the Chariot Room

2.11 The Choolh

बाबांचा जुना रथ

2.12 The Old Chariot

2.13 The Chariot (Rath) Room

2.14 The Old Dhuni Mai

2.14A The Dhuni Mai (now)

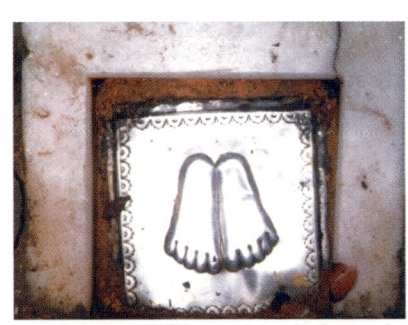

2.15 The Small Silver Padukas in Front of Dhuni Mai.

2.16 Baba near Dhuni Mai

2.17 The Kolamba

2.18 The Maath or Water Pot

2.19 The Magical Chillim (clay pipe)

2.20 The Hooks on the Ceiling

2.21 The Nimbar or Allah Mia
Che Jagha, 2.21A The Ever Burning Lamps

2.22 The Jaath or Quern

2.23 The Sack of Wheat

2.24, 2.24a The Portrait of Baba in Front of
Dhuni Mai (Dwarka Mai pose)

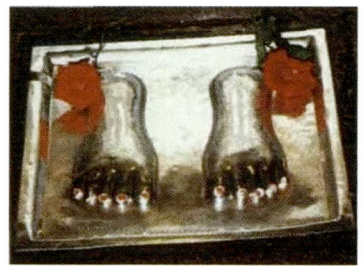

2.25 The Padukas in Front of Baba's Portrait

2.28 Baba's Bathing Stone

2.26 The Kathada (railing) on which Baba
Rested his Hand, 2.27 The Udi Stand

2.29 The Three Steps next to the Ota

2.30 The Ota or Platform with the
Agarbatti Stand

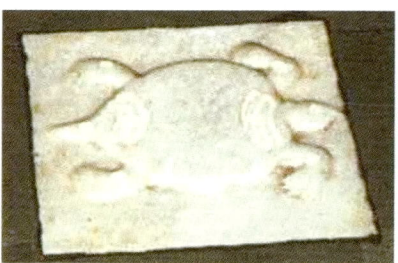

2.31 The Tortoise

2.32 The Mythology of Tulsi Vivaha

2.33 The Idol of Shyam Karan

2.34 The Stone on which Baba Sat

2.35 The Big Portrait of Baba Above the Stone

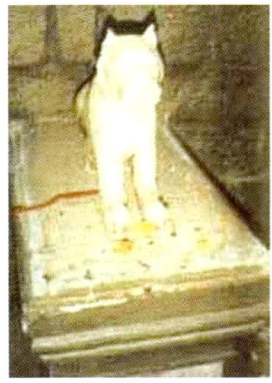

2.36 The Idol of the Tiger

2.37 Shyam Sunder Hall

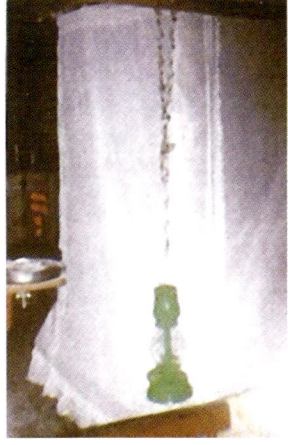

2.38 The Swinging 'Kandil'

3.1 The Old Chavadi

3.1a The Outer View of the Chavadi

3.2 Plaque in Chavadi

3.3 The Big Painting of Baba on the Northern wall

3.4 The Small Photograph of Baba on a Silver Throne

3.5 The Wheelchair and 3.6 The Wooden Cot

4.1 Old Photograph of Lendi Baugh

4.2, 4.2a The Flower Garden

4.4a The Nanda Deep

4.3 The Neem Trees, 4.4 The Nanda Deep,
4.5 The Ashwatha or Peepul Tree

4.6 Baba's Well

4.7 The Dattatreya Mandir

4.8 The Samadhi of Amidas Bhavani Mehta

4.9 The Samadhi of Mukta Ram

4.10 The Samadhi of Shyam Karan

5.1 Sathe Wada

5.2 Dixit Wada (1911)

5.2a Dixit Wada (now)

5.3 Butti Wada (1947)

6.1 The Samadhi of Haji Abdul Baba (outside)

6.1a The Samadhi of Haji Abdul Baba (inside)

6.2 Samadhi of Bhau Maharaj Kumbhar

6.3 Nanavali Samadhi (inside)   6.3a Nanavali Samadhi (outside)

6.4 The Samadhi of V P Iyer

6.5 The Samadhi of Tatya Kote Patil

6.6 Tajim Khan's Darga (outside)   6.6a Tajim Khan's Darga (inside)

7.1 Sakharam Patil Shelke's house

7.2 Narsimha Temple

7.3 Vamanrao Gondkar's house

7.4 Bayyaji Appa Kote Patil's house

7.5 Bayaja Bai Ganpath Kote Patil's house

7.6 Nandram Marvadi Sanklecha's house

8.1 Khandoba Mandir in Shirdi (earlier)

8.1b Khandoba Mandir in Shirdi (inside)

8.1a Khandoba Mandir in Shirdi (recent)

8.2 The Banyan Tree

8.3, 8.3a The Kanifnath Mandir (outside, inside)

8.4, 8.4a Ashta Lakshmi Mandir

8.5, 8.5a Vitthal Mandir

8.6, 8.6a Dakshina Mukhi Shri Hanuman Mandir

8.7 Mahadev Mandir

8.8 Ganapathi Mandir

8.9 Shani Mandir

8.10 The Samadhi of the Tiger

9.1 Interior of Abdul Baba's Cottage

9.2 Chimta (prongs) given by Baba

9.3 Satka and 9.4 Tin Mug

10.1 Akhand Parayan

10.2 Palkhi Procession

10.3 Changing of the Sack of Wheat

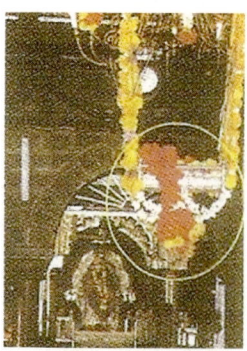

10.4 The Cradle of Ram

10.5 Changing of the Flags

10.6 The Urs and 'Sandal Procession'

10.7 The Rath Procession

10.8 Seemolanghan

11.1 The Butti Wada (old)

11.2 The Beautiful Wooden Doors and the Plaques Behind them

11.3 Samadhi Mandir (1920)

11.3a Samadhi Mandir (1926)

11.4 Baba's Show Room

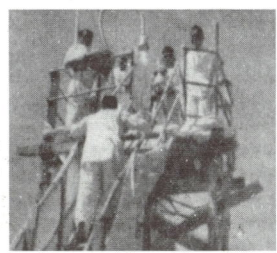
11.5 The Suvarna Kalasha Sthapana

11.6 Samadhi Mandir 1952

11.7 Model for Baba's Statue

11.8 Talim in his Workshop

11.9 Baba's Murty (1954)

11.10 Baba in Dwarka Mai

11.11 Baba with Tukaram's Gatha in Hand

11.12 Baba Sitting with Outstretched Legs

11.13 Original Photograph of Baba Going to Lendi Baugh

12 Baba Going for Bhiksha

13 Invisible Baba

14 Baba Sitting on the Ota in the Sabhamandap

by the *Vedas*? As we have to reap the fruits of our actions. This is the place for introspection; a court where we have to judge ourselves and take decisions on what needs to be corrected.

On entering the south facing Chavadi, one can see a plaque on which is inscribed, "*Shri Sai Nath Babanchi Lakshmi Bai Damodar Babre, Chinchanikar Chavadi, Shake* 1859". Damodar Barbre came from the village Chinchni in Thane district. Hence everyone called him Anna Chinchanikar. He and his wife made Shirdi their home. For many years the couple did selfless service not expecting or asking for any favours from Baba. One day, Shama asked Baba why he had not blessed the couple with a son. Baba smiled and said, "Has it ever happened, that whenever anybody has asked me for anything that I have not granted it?" Baba being *antaryami* saw that a son would only continue their name for one generation. Baba wanted Anna's name to last for a very long time.

A civil suit regarding his fields was then in progress at Dhanu. Anna repeatedly asked Baba about it's outcome. Baba always replied "*Allah bhala karenge.*" A famous lawyer named Achyut Narayan Khare was handling the case. Someone maliciously wrote to him that 'he had lost the case'. Anna informed Dixit. Then both of them went to Dwarka Mai. As they were entering Dwarka Mai Baba shouted, "This old man has no faith in me. Throw away that letter."

Anna finally won the case and a sum of 1,800 rupees along with the court fees was awarded to him. Anna and Dixit then went to Baba with the letter. Baba calmly said, "Have you got faith in me now?" Anna placed the letter at Baba's feet and said, "Baba this is all yours. I do not want it." Baba refused to accept the money saying he was a *fakir*. Anna begged Baba to accept it. This conversation went on for some time. Ultimately, Dixit suggested that the sum could be used to repair the Chavadi and it could be named after Anna and his wife Lakshmi Bai. (**photo 3.2**)

In the 1920s, the Chavadi was a building with three steps leading to it. It had three doors facing south. Then two verandahs were added on either side of the steps. The verandahs are about 13′ long and 8′ wide. In the 1970s, the grills were added. On the Chavadi procession the day's *arati* was performed to Baba and then Baba was given the

69

chillim to smoke. Now a photograph of Baba is placed on a silver *sinhasan* (throne) and *arati,* is performed to it. The paintings of the *leelas* and stories of various Gods and Goddesses were there from Baba's time.

In the 1920's, a glass box was placed in front of the photograph with Baba's *padukas* in it. This box was there till the 1970's. In the 1970's, there were two pairs of *padukas* kept open for *darshan*. Then the *padukas* were kept in the show room of *Samadhi Mandir*. After the museum was opened the *padukas* were brought there. After Baba's *samadhi*, the Chavadi procession was held on every Thursday and holy days.

On 9-12-2008, it was the dawn of the 100th year of congregational *arati* and *palkhi* procession. Shirdi Sai Baba Sansthan had a grand celebration. After Baba's *mangal snan* at 6.45 a.m. there was a grand procession, the silver *padukas* were brought from *Samadhi Mandir* to the Chavadi. There *arati* was performed. This was followed by reading of the 37th chapter of *Shri Sai Satcharita*. This chapter has the title 'The description of the Chavadi Ceremony'. The villagers along with numerous devotees did '*samudayik pathan*' (collective reading) of Das Ganu's *Stavan Manjari*. Then there was *maha prasad* given by the Sansthan. This concluded the first day's celebration.

Throughout the year there are *bhajans* by famous singers. On some days there are *pravachans* (a sort of lecture on spiritual persons and topics) and *satsangs* by various *gurus* and God men.

Big Painting of Baba on the Northern Wall

After Baba's *Mahasamadhi*, in 1953 he gave a dream vision to Ambaram Lalbhai Kahar of Navasari. The dream had a tremendous effect on Ambaram, the artist and he painted this portrait (**photo 3.3**) of Baba. The painting is 6' by 4' of Baba sitting on the stone posture. There is a gigantic *Aum* behind Baba.

Ambaram gifted this painting to the Avatar Meher Baba centre in Navasari. Before this painting was brought to Shirdi, it was placed for public *darshan*. For two days the devotees performed *akhand naam jaap* of Baba and simultaneously they had *bhajans* throughout the day and night. The villagers of Navasari were attracted to the portrait and the enchanting *leelas* of Baba. So they collected subscriptions and got the painting framed. Then after performing *puja* they brought it to Shirdi in procession and gifted it to the Sansthan.

The Shirdi Sai Baba Sansthan proposed to install the painting over Baba's *samadhi*. But as Baba's idol was being sculpted, the painting was placed in the Chavadi. It is placed in the place where Baba used to sit during the *aratis*. The *pujari* of the Chavadi does *alankar* daily with *ashtagandh*.

The Small Photograph of Baba on a Silver Throne

This is an original photograph (**photo 3.4**) of Baba. It is known as the *Raj Upchar* photograph. *Raj upchar* consists of an elaborate ritual that consists of about 30 smaller rituals including a *snan* of various ingredients. They are the *panchamrut snan, sudh dravya snan, chandan snan* and *abhishek*. Since all these rituals cannot be performed to a photograph, only *panch upchar* is performed.

It is taken to the *Samadhi Mandir*, every Thursday in the afternoon. There it is placed on the *samadhi*. After *dhup arati* at 8.45 p.m. it is taken in the *palki* procession.

It is the only photograph that has been clad with a silken *sovale*. Here an explanation is necessary. Some Brahmins, who are considered pure and holy (*sovale*), have by ablution or other purification rituals attained the state of the highest and most sacred. If they come into contact with persons or articles that are *ovale* (impure) their state of *sovale* is tarnished. This word is used for clothes, utensils, food and things in general. These are made fit for use after washing and other purification rituals. But silk and woolen clothes are used by the *sovale* person without any restriction.

Baba's photograph is taken to the *Samadhi Mandir* where the *pujari* does *panch upchar*. That is applied with *gandh* or sandalwood paste. It is offered *pushpa* (flowers), *dhup* (incense), *deep* (lighted lamp) and *naivedya* (food offering).

Then the photograph is clad with the silk *sovale*. This is the dress code or way of tying the *dhoti* with pleats covering the genital organs tightly for males. And for females the pleats of the *sari* do the same. Earlier, for both sexes the tying of the *koupina* or *langoti* was compulsory, over which the *dhoti* or *sari* was tied, with the pleats covering the *koupina*.

What is the meaning of this dress code? It could mean: 1. Baba by wearing the *sovale* is then in the state of *sovale*. This state of *sovale* requires a great deal of discipline and self-control. When in this state one cannot randomly touch anything or even go to the toilet. To maintain this state of purity, one has to lead a very disciplined and self-controlled life. So this way of dressing could mean that one should be disciplined, and follow chastity very strictly in all *ashramas* of life.

"Why should Baba be dressed with the *dhoti* in this particular fashion when he is *Parabramha* himself"?

Baba by example is showing us how to lead a disciplined, pure and chaste life. To state it rather explicitly, He is instructing us to use the genital organ to pass urine. And by tying it so tightly indicating that the organ be used to procreate and produce progeny, during *grihastha ashram* only with our lawfully wedded spouse. In other words, we should not become a slave of lust.

The next question is, "Why did Baba sleep in the Chavadi on alternate nights?"

Sleeping should be understood at a higher parlance, that is, a state of *samadhi* or a rehearsal of death. In death one is alone, as neither spouse nor the children will accompany us. Baba by doing this himself taught us this truth.

Finally, why are women not allowed in the sanctum of the Chavadi?

The Chavadi is the soul or core of the *jeeva*. Human nature is attracted to *kamini, kanchan* and *kashyap*. By following this rule strictly,

Baba is teaching us not to be trapped by sexual lust. To look at a woman as a mother will ensure spiritual advancement.

The Wooden Cot and the Wheelchair

This chair (**photo 3.5**) was placed next to the wooden cot (**photo 3.6**) in the Chavadi. It was in the north-western corner of the Chavadi where ladies are allowed to go. After the museum was built, this chair and cot were moved there. They are displayed on the ground floor, in the central area.

The glass lampshades (glass globes)
Radha Krishna Mai was a young widow who hailed from Pandharpur. She heard about Baba's *leelas* and divinity from Chandorkar. She came to Shirdi and made it her home.

Radha Krishna Mai loved Baba and wanted him to have a royal Sansthan, which would take care of all the silverware and fine clothes. She worked tirelessly for this, and often asked rich devotees to bring beautiful articles for Baba. She wanted Baba to enjoy the pomp and show like Lord Vitthal of Pandharpur. "Kaka Mahajani on the advice of Radha Krishna Mai brought these glass globes for the lamps in the Chavadi. Govardhan Das brought silk curtains and new uniforms for the volunteers who carry the umbrella and *chanwars*," writes Khaparde in his Shirdi diary.

4

Lendi Baugh

The gate to this garden faces east and is in the north-east corner. It is *vaikuntha* (heaven) on earth. In the early days of his sojourn in Shirdi, Baba used to go early in the morning to Lendi Baugh.

The photograph **4.1** is a very old photograph. The text below it reads, "This is the photograph of the Lendi canal on the bank of which Baba sat every morning and afternoon."

Baba loved the Neem and *Ashwatha* (*peepul*) trees immensely. He watered them daily. Just as Lord Krishna stood under the banyan tree, Baba stood under this *peepul* tree and gave instructions to many a devotee. One day Baba stood under this tree and pulled Moreshwar Pradhan towards him. He then took a handful of corn from his pocket and gave it to Pradhan to sow. Baba then sprinkled some water on it. Pradhan and a whole lot of devotees did the same. This *leela* resulted in two incidents. One was that Pradhan bought this *baugh* and presented it to Baba. The other joyous incident was that the devotees started taking Baba in procession to and from Lendi Baugh. The board above the gate reads, *"Moreshwar Pradhan che Lendi Baugh."*

Lendi Baugh is a treasure trove, sanctified by the dust of Baba's feet and the solitary time he spent there each and every day. This garden was full of trees and flowering plants like *parijata, champa, chameli, jui* and *jai*. These were just a few of the plants thriving there. Indeed up to the 1980s this garden had a beautiful entrance which was a canopy of flowering bouganvillaea (**photo 4.2**). On the left of the entrance there was another rose garden where deer and rabbits roamed about.

The trees were *Aamra* (Mangoe), *Ambore* (*tarvad* an indigenous tree), *Arista* (neem), *Ashwatha* (peepul), and *Audumbar* (*umbar*). In Hindu mythology these trees are considered holy, as a deity is supposed to reside in many of these trees. (*The English language does not have the phonetics of Marathi or Sanskrit nor does it have the sound of half a vowel. So it is transliterated.*)

If you take the *aakara* (form) the above mentioned trees are believed to represent Brahma, Vishnu, Shankar and *Aumkar swarupa* Ganapati. If you take the vowels of the Marathi language from these trees it forms *Aum*. The 'aa' from *Ambore*, represents Vishnu, the 'u' from *Audumbar* represents Shankar and the 'm' from *Malka* or *Nemba vraksh* represents Brahmadev. From *Aamra* the *ardha matra* of 'aa' and the *bindu* from *Ambore* represents *Brahma kaal roop*. The *akar, makar, ardha matra* and *bindu* form an *Aum*, and this is Sai Baba, who like the destroyer of difficulties, Ganapati is ever present at Shirdi.

Sai Baba Hach Chamatkar *by Dr Keshav B Gavankar*

Lendi Baugh was about an acre in length and breadth. *Lendi* was a small, very old and famous river. It flowed underground and then emerged in Lendi Baugh. There it divided the garden into two parts. In Lendi Baugh it flowed slowly and more like a stream. The water was scanty for most part of the year. Baba went to Lendi Baugh, daily and every day he threw some silver coins in the *Lendi*.

Baba tested his devotees to see if they hankered after money and gold. Once he asked Purandare to accompany him to Lendi Baugh. Together they went to the *Lendi* stream and stood near the bank. Then Baba showed him three dazzling plates of gold. The plates were in the stream and Baba pointed to them. Purandare was not in the least tempted and did not even glance at them.

Jyotindra was another devotee that Baba took to the *Lendi* stream. He showed him lumps of gold and asked him to take as much of it as he wanted. Jyotindra was not at all concerned. His only concern was to be with Baba and develop spiritually.

Although Baba was surrounded by devotees, he kept a rather strict schedule. He went to Lendi Baugh at about 8.a.m. and again at about 3.p.m.

The musical band would be ready and waiting for him. He always entered *Lendi Baugh* alone, while the band and the devotees would return. Baba entered *Lendi Baugh* through the west. He also sat facing the west with his back to the *Nanda Deep*.

Abdul Baba brought pitchers of water for him which he threw in all directions and chanted something. The Lord of the west is *Varun* alias *Mitra* (or sun). Varun is the deity of rain and rules over water, wells, rivers, etc. He is the judge of the cosmic power and delivers justice by punishing wrong doers and liars. He is happy when he is worshipped and everyone should turn to the west and pray to him. This is done in the evening with water by pouring a thin stream or sprinkling it. Then we should ask to be forgiven for our mistakes and wrong doings.

Rishis took water in the palm of the hand and cursed a person by throwing it at him. During Baba's *arati* the priest blesses the congregation by throwing water in all directions.

Baba could be pacifying Varun by sitting facing the west and throwing water in all directions along with incantations and chants. The lesson here is that we should pray to Varun every day.

The vehicle of Varun is *Makara* (crocodile) which represents the hand of time. Time is ticking away, so use it fruitfully and spare this life for self-realisation. *Kaal* or time is fast approaching us with outstretched hands to grip us mercilessly as time waits for no one.

Significance of Lendi Baugh

Baba like a gardener went to the *Baugh* to nurture the plants. The plants are his devotees and he pulled out the weeds. The weeds are symbolic of the evil tendencies that pull us in different directions.

Another explanation could be *Pitruyana* or the journey of the soul after death. It is believed that the soul travels to *Chandra loka* which is full of happiness, if the person has dug a well or developed a garden. Just as we are unable to do this our forefathers might not have done this. After death of a parent we are supposed to perform certain rituals on a daily and yearly basis. For example, every day we are supposed to feed the crows and perform a yearly *shradha*. Often we are unable to do this.

Thus, it becomes the *sadguru's* responsibility to see that our journey is smooth. He also teaches us what has to be done to have a smooth journey. So he might have dug the well and developed the *Lendi Baugh*.

The Flower Garden

There were many fragrant flowering plants in the 1920s. (**photo 4.2A**) There were many peacocks, deer, rabbits, mongoose and birds. This was there up to the 1980's. Then that part was landscaped and a waterfall was made.

The Neem Trees

Baba had planted two Neem trees (**photo 4.3**); but they died. So one was cut at ground level. The other is a stump about 6' tall.

The botanical name is *Azadi Rachita Indica*. In Sanskrit it is *Nimba,* which means bestower of health. It is also known as *Ravi Samba* or the suns' rays. The Hindu mythology says that *Amrit* (ambrosia) fell on the Neem tree. Another myth is that the sun took refuge in it to escape the demons.

The neem tree symbolises *Devi Roopam* (Goddess). *Purusha* and *Prakriti* are inseparable. In the case of all Gods (*Sagun roopa* was given by us) this being represented by male and female *roopa*. Whereas Baba is *Paripoorna Parabramha*. So there is no separate *roopa* of *Prakriti*. Thus unlike other Gods, he does not have a female counterpart.

By sitting under the neem tree he is conveying to us that "*Maya,* which is his own creation, is totally under his control and he conditions it." This *maya* cannot act upon him, as it would act on us. But having taken a human form to be in this universe, he too needs *maya*. The whole of the universe, the cosmos and *maya* were created by him.

The only difference is that *maya* is under his control unlike us, who are under the control of *maya*.

Idols of the deities at Jagannatha Puri temple are carved from neem trees. The *Indra Nilamani purana* and *Sutka Samhitha* (religious scriptures) state that those trees that bear certain symbols are selected. The colour of Balabhadra's tree is white and bears the symbol of *hal* (plough) and *langala* (spikes). The colour of Subhadra's tree is red and the symbol is *padma* (lotus). The colour of Jagannatha's tree is black and the symbols are *shankha, chakra, gada* and *padma* (conch, wheel, mace and lotus respectively). The colour of Sudarshana's tree is yellow and the symbol is *nabhi chakra* (the symbol of the naval). Thus, the neem tree is bestowed with different coloured tree trunks. The trees chosen are slightly sweet, instead of being totally bitter.

Worshipping idols carved out of the Neem tree bestow *ayu* (longevity), *shri* (prosperity), *yasa* (fame) and *vijaya* (victory).

Why is a neem tree chosen?

The mythology is that on *Amavasya Mithun Sankranti*(an auspicious day by the Hindu calendar) the primeval *purusha* manifests in the predestined neem tree. Then it emanates a sandalwood odour, instead of bitterness. Then this particular tree is used for carving the deity. The tree also has the *Brahma padarath*.

The *Brahma padarth* is the supreme energy that is mysteriously hidden in the body of Jagannatha. The Buddhists believe that it is the tooth of Buddha. The *Vaishnavas* believe that it is the live *Saligram* and the *Sabaras* (tribals) believe that it is the unburnt naval of Lord Krishna.

The myth is that when Lord Krishna was struck by the arrow of Jarasabara in Mahendragiri, it resulted in his death. Then his body was cremated, the body burnt except for the naval portion, which was kept inside the initial deity. Hence, the *Sabara* tribes worship the deity as *Nila Madhava*. The *Navakalavar* (replacing the old deity) ceremony is an elaborate, time intensive and rather secretive ceremony.

Upon Devi's instruction the are felled with a golden axe. Logs are then sanctified with numerous rituals, like *Rudra abhishek*, recitation of Vishnu *sahasranama*, Narsimha mantra and *havan*. The priest is blindfolded and his hands tied with silk ribbons; so he can neither see nor feel the Brahma *padarth*. At midnight, behind closed doors, he transfers it to the new deities.

To the left of the *Nanda Deep* were two Neem trees. These trees were planted by Baba. Unfortunately, these trees dried up. One of them was cut from the base. The other tree was cut. Over it's stump a creeper is being grown.

Nanda Deep

Baba lit this *akhand Nanda deep*. (**photo 4.4**) When exactly it was lit is not known. In those days it was placed in a pit used to Abdul Baba look after it. Abdul Baba states that Baba sat with his back to the *jyoth*. Daily Abdul brought pots of water and placed them near the Nanda Deep. Baba then threw the water in various directions.

In 1942, Galvankar built a platform over which *Nanda Deep* was mounted. Later it was placed over a marble pillar in a glass case. (**photo 4.4a**) Thus it was protected from the elements. During the beautification plan of 1998 it was placed in the present container.

Till a few years ago the *pujari* of the *Gurusthan* used to attend to it, to keep it perpetually burning. Then the *Parayan Kaksh* was moved to the hall adjacent to the *Kapad koti*. So the *pujari* of the *Parayan Kaksh* looks after it now. He also looks after the *Dattatreya Mandir*.

Meaning of Nanda Deep

In *Mahanaryanopanishad* this verse explains it beautifully. "O! fire, the life force of all living beings, you glow so powerfully. By your light let all the obstacles in my *sadhana marga* be warded off. Protect everyone and all those who are under my care."

The Ashwatha or Peepul Tree

This aged Peepul tree was already there when Baba came to Shirdi. This Peepul tree (**photo 4.5**) began to dry up and Baba gave life to it by installing the *Navgraha* in it. Hence, this tree had nine huge branches and nine huge roots. Subsequently, many of the branches have been cut off. Baba watered this tree daily and looked after it. There is also a *Ganesha* formation on this tree.

Devotees perform *pradakshina* here to receive blessings of the numerous deities that reside on these trees. The *Brahma* and *Padma puranas* state, "Once there was a fierce battle between the Gods and the demons; Lord Vishnu sought refuge by hiding in the *Ashwatha* tree." This tree represents the *trimurti*. The roots are Brahma, the trunk is Vishnu and the leaves are Shiva.

Lord Krishna chose this Peepul tree to depart from this earth. The *Ashwatha* is sacred for the Buddhists also as Lord Buddha received *nirvana* under this tree. This tree is also called the Bodhi tree. It is said that Lakshmi sits on it on Saturdays.

In the *Jnaneshvari, chapter 15 Ovi 1-3*, Lord Krishna explains the meaning beautifully. The Lord said, "The tree has roots on the top and branches downwards. The tree is endless and is called *Ashwatha*. The *Vedas* are its leaves and one who knows this tree is also knower of the *Vedas*."

Ovi 2, "Fed by the three *gunas*, it has sense objects as tender leaves. The branches in the shape of different orders of creation are spread above and below. Its roots bind the soul according to the actions of the human beings, spread themselves in all regions above and below."

Ovi 3, "On careful observation this tree of worldly life does not prove to be of that nature as it seems apparently to be; because it has no beginning, no end nor even stability. Fell this *Ashwatha* tree with a formidable axe of detachment."

Baba's Well

This well (**photo 4.6**) is in the middle portion of Lendi Baugh. It is adjacent to the western wall of Lendi Baugh. With the help of his devotees, both rich and poor, Baba dug this well. He used to drink water from this well and he called it *Budki*. The water of this well was famous in the vicinity for driving away fevers and many diseases. Previously the devotees used to take water from this well and it gradually dried up. In 1983 A R Shinde deepened this well and water was found in abundance. There were two wells in Shirdi in those days. One was on the left side of the exiting stairs of the *Samadhi Mandir* (this one does not exist anymore) and the other one is in Lendi Baugh.

Suspending the disciple in inverted position in the well is a traditional Sufi technique which would result in his transformation. This conversion experience is known as *tawbat*.

Here the well could mean a place containing cool waters of peace. Here tying the student in an inverted position (head downwards) over a well means turning down or overturning ego. By overturning ego, one could reach the cool waters of peace. This whole process is conducted by the Guru.

In chapter 32 of *Shri Sai Satcharita,* under the title "Greatness of the Guru", the *leela* of Baba being suspended in the well is given.

The other possible meaning could be that 'we' are deep in the well of materialistic world. But when the *Sadguru* comes to us, he being merciful will tie our hands and legs (the organs of movement). Then he will tie us in the inverted position with the head downwards, thus making the body vomit out the false 'I'. So we become detached from worldly pleasures and their consequential results, although we live surrounded by them. In simpler terms, 'He' teaches us to be in this transient world to exist in a most detached way.

The Dattatreya Mandir

In front of Muktaram's *Samadhi* and to it's left is the Dattatreya temple (**photo 4.7**). It was built by two local devotees who would like to remain anonymous. The *pran pratistha* of the idol of Lord Datta and marble *padukas* was performed by the Sansthan in August 1976. There is an *Audumbar* tree behind the temple. The *pujari* from the Gurusthan looks after the temple. In the morning there is *mangal snan, shringhar* and the clothes are changed. *Bhog* is offered three times a day.

Silver *padukas* were installed here on Datta *Jayanthi* on 12th of December, 2008.

On Datta *Jayanthi pujaris* from the *Samadhi Mandir* do *arati* to Lord Datta. The devotees do *pradakshina* of this temple and get their wishes fulfilled.

During Baba's sojourn in Shirdi there was a small Datta *Mandir* here. Baba would often go and stand before it. When the beautification of Lendi Baugh was done, this temple was removed.

The Samadhi of Amidas Bhavani Mehta

His *samadhi* (**photo 4.8**) is in the central part of Lendi Baugh. Amrutal was his real name. He was a Nagar Brahim from Bhavnagar (Kathiawad, Saurashatra). Amidas was from the community of Narsinh Mehta. He was an intellectual poet and a devotee of Lord Krishna. Every time he worshipped Lord Krishna and looked at the Lord's photograph, he saw a *fakir* in the glass. He was perplexed to see a Muslim *fakir* superimposing Lord Krishna and his curiosity was aroused. So, he set out to find this *fakir* who was none other than Sai Baba of Shirdi.

Amidas was a very learned man. He was trained in Indian classical, instrumental and vocal music. He was affluent and was attached to a small king named Dayashankar Revashankar Pandya. In those days, Katheiawad was divided into small kingdoms, which were ruled by Nawabs.

Being well off he visited Shirdi frequently. He rented a room and stayed with Baba for long period of time. He started writing about Baba in Gujarati. Thus spreading the glory of Baba amongst the Gujarati speaking population.

Amidas was a poet. His poetry was about the life, habits, likes, dislikes and characteristics of Sai Baba, who was *purna parabrahma* to him. Swami Sharananand has mentioned his book titled *Purna Parabrahma Sri Sadguru Sainath Maharajni – Janavajog Vigato Temaj Chamatkarion* in the *Shri Sai Satcharita*.

Baba loved Amidas for his kind and gentle nature. When somebody was sick in Shirdi, Baba sent him to Amidas to be taken care of. Amidas gladly tended to the patient with tender loving care and nursed him back to health. His only wish was to die in Shirdi in the close proximity of his Guru.

Baba on hearing his wish replied, "You may die anywhere, but you will always be with me." He breathed his last in Shirdi, where his *samadhi* is in Lendi Baugh. It is adjacent to the *samadhi* of Mukta Ram. There is a plaque on his *samadhi* which reads, "*Shri Satchitanand Sadguru Baba Anand Maharaj. urf* (alias*) Amidas Bhavani Mehta Budhwar (Wednesday) mithi* (Roughly translated it's the date or *tithi*) *Magh* (February –March) *shudh* 14 *Shake.* 2844. (i.e. 31- 1-1923).

The Samadhi of Mukta Ram

Mukta Ram first visited Shirdi in 1911, when he came with a group of pilgrims. Baba's divinity had an overwhelming effect on him. He made several visits thereafter and finally made Shirdi his home. He hailed from Ravierked, where he lived with his wife, mother and extended family. Unfortunately, his real name is not known. It was Baba who called him Mukta Ram. So the villagers and other devotees also called him by that name.

He was very affluent; he owned a *wada* and had many acres of farm land. Soon he lost interest in the crops, the farm and his family. The whole day he did 'Baba's *naam jaap'* (continuous chanting of Baba's name). His only thought was when he could be close to his *Sadguru*. Finally, he left his family and came to Shirdi.

Mukta Ram was an ascetic by nature and was willing to do severe penance to gain the grace of his *Sadguru*. He was very disciplined and would be with Baba from early morning till noon. He sat in front of Baba, next to the *Dhuni Mai*. Whether it was scorching hot or cold, he sat next to the blazing *Dhuni Mai*. Just as Hanuman sat in front of Shri Rama, or Garuda sat in front of Shri Vishnu, one could see Mukta Ram sitting in front of Baba. Mukta Ram's devotion towards Baba was no less than that of Maruti towards Rama.

He survived on whatever Baba gave him from his *bhiksha*. After the noon *arati*, Baba had his lunch, then rested a while. Mukta Ram would go to his room, which was a cramped tin-shed adjacent to Dixit's *wada*. There he sat and meditated in front of the *Dhuni*. Upon Baba's instruction he had an ever burning *Dhuni Mai* in his room. There he sat till it was time for him to go again to Dwarka Mai. This penance he did gladly although the room was hot as a furnace.

Mukta Ram dressed exactly like Baba. He wore a white *kafni*, tied a white cloth around his head and had *langoti* around his loin. It was Baba who gave him the *kafni* and the white cloth to tie on his head. Mukta Ram's intense love, devotion and concentration on his Guru, soon bore fruit. After some time his way of living became the mirror image of Baba's lifestyle.

About three months before Baba's *nirvan*, Mukta Ram was sick with fever and a persistent cough. He spent most of his time in his room. At the time of Baba's *Mahasamadhi* his condition was rather serious. Eight days after Baba's *Mahasamadhi*, he went to Dwarka Mai and returned to his room very quickly. When he was in Dwarka Mai, he sat on his sack and leaned against the central pillar.

Dr Keshav B Gavankar writes that Mukta Ram did not sit on Baba's sack *gaddi'* (mattress) near the railing (*kathada*); nor did he place his left arm on the railing. He sat on his own sack. Many of the devotees thought that Mukta Ram had gone to the Dwarka Mai to usurp Baba's seat. But as he returned to his room, rather quickly, that doubt was dispelled. Nonetheless some people seized the opportunity to malign him. They spread the news that "Mukta Ram went to Dwarka Mai and sat on Baba's *gaddi*. While getting up his foot touched Baba's *gaadi*, and as retribution he died."

After Mukta Ram returned to his room, many devotees questioned him. "Why did you go to Dwarka Mai? Why did you return soon after?" Mukta Ram answered, "My illness had become worse and I suffered a lot. So I thought I would go to Dwarka Mai and entreat Baba to give me some relief. But I could not sit there for long. Besides I was coughing out blood and sputum incessantly. The very thought of spitting in Dwarka Mai repulsed me. So I quickly returned to my room."

Thereafter, Mukta Ram never left his room. With each passing day his condition worsened. In the month of January 1919, he breathed his last. (**photo 4.9**)

Sai Baba Hach Chamatkar. Author Keshav B Gavankar.

In the Marathi *Shri Sai Satcharita*, 5th edition 1955. Nagesh Atmaram Savant wrote in the article titled *"Doon shabdh"* (two words) He states that a householder named Mukta Ram came to Shirdi when Baba was in his physical form. Two days after Baba's *Mahasamadhi*, Mukta Ram said, "Shri Sai Baba has ordered and instructed me to sit on his *gaddi* in the Dwarka Mai. Henceforth I will be occupying his *gaddi* or seat". Tatya, Ramchandra Dada Patil and other devotees asked him not to speak thus. Not heeding their advice Mukta Ram sat on Baba's *gaddi* and a short while later he started bleeding from his rectum. He continued to bleed even after he went to his room. On the eighth day, he breathed his last begging Baba for forgiveness.

I have given both the views with reference to the source of this information. It is upto the reader to believe either view.

The Samadhi of Shyam Karan

I have often wondered why the *fakir* would keep a horse? The word *Ashwa* has many meanings. *Ashwa* means 'the great eater'. So one can possibly say that the horse represents the destruction or eating away of our *karmas*. *Ashwa* also means infinite knowledge. This knowledge could help in dispelling the love for the transient materialistic things. Thus ending the lure for the temporary and worldly things and helping one on the journey from the unreal to the real.

Lord Indra symbolises ego and he rides a horse (Ref. *Nirukti*). The *Brhadaranyaka Upanisad*, chapter1: verse 5 describes the symbolic meaning of the horse as follows:

"The head of the sacrificial horse is the dawn; its eyes, the sun; the vital force the air, its open mouth the fire called *Vaisvanara* and the body is the year. It's back is heaven, belly the sky, hoof the earth, sides the four quarters, ribs the intermediate quarter, members the seasons and joints the months and the fortnight.

"It's foreparts and feet, the days and nights, bones the stars and the flesh the clouds. It's half digested food the sands and it's blood and vessels the rivers. The liver and the spleen are the mountains; the mane is the herbs, trees and the ascending sun. It's yawning is the lightening. The shaking of it's body is thunder. It's passing urine is the rain and it's neighing is the voice and sound."

The word *shyam* literally means black. A flawless black that is pleasing to the eye. But the word in Hindu mythology could mean pure and holy. It has been prefixed to other words to convey different meanings. For example, Shyam Karan is used to refer to Shri Krishna.; Shyam Kant to Shri Shankar.

Shyam Karan was the name of the horse or *ashwa* of the *ashwamedha*. The *rinanubandh* between Shyam Karan and Baba were deep. At every *arati* he danced with joy and after the *arati* was the first to bow to Baba. Baba then applied *udi* to his forehead and then gave the rest of the *bhaktas udi*. The horse symbolises the whole cosmos bowed before Baba and danced with joy when Baba was worshipped. Little wonder that his *Samadhi* is in Lendi Baugh.

This horse was housed in the room situated on the eastern side of Dwarka Mai, now called Shyam Sunder hall. The trainer Khajgiwale saw that the horse was well looked after and decked with all the trappings that are now exhibited in the museum. Shyam Karan was taught to stand in front of Baba, climb the steps of Dwarka Mai and do *namaskar* to Baba and later to Baba's *Samadhi*.

At about one o'clock, noon *arati* was performed with grandeur. At that time Shyam Karan was bedecked with a *mala* (necklace), anklets and tiny bells and looked quite regal and royal. He stood in the centre of the *Sabhamandap* (where the marble tortoise is) and waited patiently for the *arati* to start. The devotees stood on either side of him. When the *arati* started he danced merrily keeping beat with the tiny bells tied to his feet. After Baba's *lalkari* he climbed the central steps of Dwarka Mai and bowed to Baba. Then Baba applied *udi* to his forehead and blessed him. After this all other devotees received *udi* and *prasad*.

After Baba's *Mahasamadhi*, he attended the *aratis* in the *Samadhi Mandir* and bowed to Baba's *Samadhi*. On every Vijay Dashami, he was bed decked with all his trappings and was taken out in procession. Before the procession the devotees would take a one rupee coin and wave it around his head. This is done to dispel the effects of the evil eye.

On Chavadi procession days he led the procession dancing all the way to the Chavadi. After this which Baba entered the Chavadi he stood facing Baba.

Shyam Karan died in 1945. His *Samadhi* (**photo 4.10**) is in Lendi Baugh. In the 1950's there was a board next to his *Samadhi* which read "Krishnaji (alias Nana) Khajgiwala was the trainer of Shyam Karana, Baba's beloved horse, whose *Samadhi* is here." Now there is no such board.

5

The Three Wadas in Shirdi

Sathe Wada

This *wada* (**photo 5.1**) was behind the Gurusthan, and adjacent to one of the exit gates of the *Samadhi Mandir*. Baba asked Hari Vinayak Sathe, "To pull down the village wall and build." What Baba meant was to build a residential building there and to incorporate the village wall in it. So Sathe bought that land and built the *wada*. This *wada* was very useful as it was the sole resting place for devotees who came from far off places.   *Shri Sai Satcharita, chapter 4*

Then Dixit wada was built followed by Butti wada. Sathe states, "I built the *wada* around 1908 or so at Baba's bidding. When the construction was in progress and the walls had to be raised, some of the branches of the Neem tree had to be cut. No one dared to do so. Then Baba said, 'Cut off as much of the branches, which obstruct the construction. Even if our own foetus lies athwart, the womb must be cut.' Yet no one had the courage to do so. Then Baba himself cut the obstructing branches."

This *wada* was replete with history as it housed many staunch devotees, who were worth their weight in gold. Baba gave Tatya Sahib Nulkar *sadgati* in this *wada*. At that time, his childhood friend Neelkant Sahasrabuddhe was with him. Neelkant stayed in this *wada*, of and on whenever he came to Shirdi. Dada Kelkar and Hari Vinayak Sathe stayed here with their families.

Most importantly, Megha and Dada Sahib Khaparde stayed there for long periods. The story, of Megha is given in *Shri Sai Satcharita,* chapter 28, under the heading 'A Gujarati Brahmin named Megha'. It was in this building that Baba gave him a dream vision. Baba said, "Megha draw a trident." Megha could not believe that Baba appeared in his room as the door was locked and bolted. Then Baba said, "No door is necessary for my entry, as I have neither shape nor size. I am omnipresent and in everything that has a name." Following this Baba presented Megha with a *pindi* (*Shiva linga*) that was offered to Baba by a *ramdasi*.

Khaparde stayed in this *wada* and wrote the memorable '*Shirdi Diary*'. K. J. Bhishma wrote "*Shri Sainath Sagunopasana*" (*arati* book). Baba Sahib Tarakad and his family stayed there, as did Jyotindra whenever he visited Shirdi. The devotees who stayed there were like-minded. They had set a daily routine. They got up early in the morning and attended *Kakad arati*. After the *arati* they returned to the *wada* and waited for Baba to go to Lendi Baugh. As Baba's procession reached the *wada*, they came and had *darshan*. When he returned from Lendi Baugh, they had *darshan* again. They also attended all the *aratis*.

In the evenings they had regular reading sessions, when they read the *Ramayan*, Eknath's *Bhagvat*, *Yoga Vasistha* and also discussed it. At night they had *bhajans* usually sung by Bhishma.

The great devotee Swami Sharananand regularly stayed in this *wada* whenever he visited Shirdi till his demise in 1983 at the age of 94.

These are just a few of the devotees that stayed in this *wada*. This *wada* was bought by R S Navalkar on 30th September 1924. Then V N Gorakshkar with a great deal of persuasion advised the heirs of Navalkar to gift the *wada* to the Sansthan. This *wada* was gifted in 1939 to the Sansthan. In 1941, the Sansthan added four double rooms for the devotees to stay in. The devotees used to stay in this *wada* till 1980. Then it was used as the P R O (Public Relations Office). The Shirdi Sai Baba Sansthan broke this *wada* when the Sansthan beautification plan was undertaken (1998-99). Unfortunately, when this *wada* was levelled to the ground, a lot of history of Shirdi was lost.

Dixit Wada

This *wada* (**photo 5.2, 5.2a**) is the double storey building facing south. It has a huge hall which was used as a *prasadalay* in the 50's. Now its the museum. The rooms adjacent to this hall were used as reading rooms. Now they are used as first aid centres and for 'blood donation drives'. The rooms on the first floor are used by the Sansthan to store old records and papers.

I run out of adjectives to describe the great devotee Kaka Dixit. So I will state the salient features of his *Guru bhakti* and the deep *rinanubandhic* ties between Baba and Kaka Dixit. Kaka Dixit first visited Shirdi on the 2nd of November 1909. He was so overwhelmed by Baba's divinity and compassion that it changed his life forever. He visited Shirdi again in December and at that time he was quite sure that he wanted to be at Baba's feet for the rest of his life.

He thought he would sell about 25 shares of his company and build a tin shed with a corrugated roof. But later on he resolved in his mind to build a *wada* instead, that could be used by the devotees. He got permission from Baba on the 9th of December and the foundation stone was laid. His brother also happened to be there. Both of them worked day and night, resultantly the *wada* was completed in six months.

On Rama Navami of 1911, *Griha-pravesh* (the ceremony of occupying a newly built house) was performed with all the rituals.

Dixit was highly educated and was a famous solicitor in Mumbai. He was very affluent and owned property in Mumbai and Lonavala. Politically, he was in the Indian National Congress and was an elected member of the Bombay Legislative Council. His list of achievements is long. It would suffice to say that he had everything any human being would desire. Dixit had name, fame and wealth; yet he gave it all up to stay in Shirdi. Several people said, "A *fakir* called Sai Baba has cast a spell on him and pulled him to Shirdi. He has gone crazy." Indeed Dixit had gone crazy, but with divine intoxication for his *Sadguru*.

Baba had openly and specifically said, "*Kaka tula kalji kasali? Mala saari kalji ahe* (Kaka why should you have any anxiety and worry? All your anxieties and responsibilities are mine.)" So Kaka stayed in Shirdi and read and studied the scriptures that Baba had advised. Baba sent those devotees who had doubts to Dixit. They would find the answer in the portion being read.

Because of Dixit's absence from his law firm, his income started dwindling; but this fact neither saddened, nor disappointed him. Dixit had given his *tan, man,* and *dhan* (body, mind and wealth) to Baba and had surrendered totally. He had developed total *vairagya*.

In this *Wada* a small room upstairs was used by Dixit for *ekanta dhyana* (solitude and meditation). Baba said "Kaka remain in your *wada* upstairs. Do not go here and there. Do not even come to the Dwarka Mai." So for nine months Kaka strictly obeyed Baba's orders. He did regular study of the 10th *Skanda* of the *Bhagvat*, and the 11th *Shanda* of Eknath's *Bhagvat,* that Baba called the '*Vrindavan Pothi'*. He studied various other books and had discussions on them. Kaka was given only nine months of *sadhana,* while others were prescribed many years of *sadhana*. Baba like a mother after nine months gave birth to a 'new Dixit'. He was endowed with *vivek, vairagya*, calmness, kindness, compassion and unshakable devotion to Baba.

Baba told Dabholkar, "Dixit is a good man; be with him." So Dabholkar stayed in Dixit wada whenever he came to Shirdi. On one occasion he and some other devotees were sitting on the upper floor of this *wada*. A serpent slid through a hole in the window and sat coiled up. Soon it was noticed and the people ran to bring sticks to kill it, but it beat a hasty retreat and slithered away. The next day they asked Baba whether it should have been put to death. Baba replied, "God resides in all creatures, be it a snake or a scorpion. No creature will act without His command. So love and have compassion towards all living beings."

Baba from the very beginning said, "I will take my Kaka in a *vimana*." A *vimana* is a chariot of the Gods, serving as a conveyance through the skies. It is self-directed and self-moving. Tukaram was also carried to heaven in a *vimana*. On 5th of July, 1926, *ekadashi,* Dixit was in a train with Dabholkar when he said, "Anna Sahib, just how merciful Baba is. He has sent us the train, without making us wait even for a minute. This is Sai's grace." Having said this he slipped into the sleep of death. There was no fear, struggle or anxiety; only eternal peace.

The third *wada* is Butti *wada* (**photo 5.3**) whose details are given under the heading '*Shri che Samadhi Mandir* or *Dagdi wada* alias Buttiwada.'

The Takiya or Asool garh

This is a spacious room used by *fakirs*. When they go on pilgrimages, they can break journey and stay in a *takyia*. Before Baba came to live in the *masjid*, he stayed in this *takiya* for some time. Baba often tied *ghungrus* (small bells) on his ankles and danced with abandon.

Shri Sai Satcharita, chapter 5

This *takiya* was located in front of the 'exit gate' on the northern wall of the *Samadhi Mandir*. Later this room was used as an *udi* distributing centre. After *Kakad arati* this room was used to distribute *prasad* and Baba's tirth. Most recently, this room is used as an announcement centre.

6

Samadhis on the Way to Lendi Baugh

There were many *Thagdas* here in the 50s. A *thagda* is a sort of *samadhi*. Possibly these *thagdas* were of the many *Gosavis* that were staying in Shirdi. Then there was a water fountain. Now the land is paved with gate number four in front of it.

The Samadhi of Haji Abdul Baba

Abdul Baba was a resident of Nanded in Khandesh. He first came to Shirdi in 1889. He was under the care of *fakir* Amiruddin, who had a dream vision of Baba. In that vision Baba gave him two mangoes to give to Abdul and send him to Shirdi. The *fakir* did this and Abdul came to Shirdi.

This is the first *samadhi* (**photo 6.1, 6.1a**) on your right, opposite the museum. He was the premier *sevak* of Baba and toiled from early morning keeping Shirdi clean and taking care of Baba's needs.

Under Baba's tutelage and care he progressed spiritually. Baba made him read the Qur'an daily and asked him to meditate on it. Abdul had the habit of writing down everything that Baba said. After Baba's *Mahasamadhi*, he used this manuscript to make prophecies.

He took *samadhi* on 16th August 1954. His *samadhi* is looked after by his descendants. His descendant Ghani Bhai is given the honour of cleaning Baba's *samadhi* and doing *puja* to it. This ritual is done daily at about 10 a.m. *Urs* is also celebrated on Rama Navami day in Shirdi. This celebration is described under the heading, 'The *urs* and sandal procession.'

Samadhi of Bhau Maharaj Kumbhar

This *Samadhi* (**photo 6.2**) is adjacent to Nanavali's *Samadhi*. *Sant* (saint) Bhau Maharaj Kumbhar was highly spiritual and an ascetic from a very young age. His ancestors lived in a small village called Kairey Neemgaon, (Sangamnere District) and were *kumbhars* (potters) by caste and profession, hence the surname. Bhau Maharaj came to Shirdi, from that village as a young man and never went back.

In Shirdi he stayed near the Shani temple. At other times he stayed below the huge banyan tree, on the way to Rahata. Sometimes, he went to Rahata, Sakori, Neemgaon and other neighbouring villages; but always returned to Shirdi.

He took *bhiksha* and survived on the food that he thus received. He was sensitive to other people's needs. Sometimes he begged for alms or asked visiting devotees for money. But as soon as he received it he distributed it to the poor and homeless. On rare occasions he kept a small amount of it and bought some sugar and gave it to children; at other times he bought medicines that a child was prescribed and gave it to the mother. The clothes or blankets that he received, he gave it to the needy. He loved all living things and was known to wrap a blanket around a tree, as he felt the tree also felt the bitter cold of Shirdi.

Bhau Maharaj had cordial relations with everyone. He spoke softly and respectfully. The villagers and visiting devotees liked and respected him. Sometimes mischievous people fought with him and stole the money or the clothes that he had received. This did not bother him and he showed no rancour towards the thieves.

He did not hoard anything; his earthly possessions consisted of a staff, a *khadi dhoti*, a *khadi* turban and vest. On his shoulder he always carried a blanket made of sheep's wool.

His daily routine
Bhau Maharaj kept himself busy in keeping Shirdi clean. Between 8 a.m. to about 2 p.m. he swept each and every street of Shirdi. This he did with his own blanket. Besides, he cleaned every gutter and *moori*

(an outdoor sink where housewives wash their utensils and clothes). Thanks to him there was never a clogged gutter or sink. He swept the streets again before dusk and pulled out any floating debris from the gutters. Whether it rained or was scorching hot, he did not deviate from his daily routine.

At about 5 a.m., he went and had Baba's *darshan*. This he did rather secretly. In fact, he went to him many times in the day and Baba communicated with him verbally or silently. Other devotees did not know when he went for *darshan*. Nor could they decipher the spiritual guidance given by Baba.

Although it was quite evident that Baba did so. Bhau Maharaj treasured these *adhyathmic* (spiritual) sessions with Baba and would not divulge their contents to anyone. Once Butti *Sahib* asked him about it. Bhau Maharaj smiled and replied, "My father gives me 1/4th of his *bhakari* and tells me sweet stories." After Baba took *Mahasamadhi*, Bhau Maharaj took *darshan* of his *samadhi* several times in the day. This he did secretly and no one could figure out when he went for *darshan*. The *rinanubandhic* ties between Baba and Bhau Maharaj were deep and strong.

About a week before he took *samadhi* (died) Bhau Maharaj was sick. He had loss of appetite and did not eat anything. He drank a great deal of water. The symptoms indicated that he had severe diabetes. Raghuvir B Purandare and Sagunmeru Naik looked after him and took great care of him. He breathed his last in *Chaitra Krishna paksh* on wednesday the 12th *Shake* 1860 (i.e. 27th of April 1937). The news of his demise spread like wildfire. Devotees gathered together and built his *samadhi* under the neem tree on the way to Lendi Baugh.

On 7th May 1937 (that was the 12th day of his demise) there was a grand *bhandara* (feast) in honour of the gentle saint. The next day (the 13th day) there was another feast of *shira* (semolina *halva* made with jaggery) and a multitude of devotees were fed to their hearts' content. On this auspicious day a beautiful portrait of Sant Bhau Maharaj Kumbhar was given a place of honour in the *Samadhi Mandir* photograph gallery.

Every year in *Chaitra* the Shirdi Sai Baba Sansthan performs his *punyathithi* and a grand *bhandara* is organised. Any one can partake in it. Even today many mothers bring their infants and lay them on his *samadhi*. They take a little dust from it, and apply it to the forehead of the child with a prayer that the child may grow up to become just like him.

The Samadhi of Nanavali

Shankar Narayan Vaidya, an ardent devotee of Baba, was misunderstood by many of the other devotees. There were two factions; some respected him, while others thought he was a troublemaker. Nanavali was like an *avadhuta* and would do strange acts that annoyed devotees. He would keep scorpions in his mouth or drink water from the gutter. Sometimes he would slap a devotee on his cheek and at other times he would pick up quarrels with the visiting devotees. Baba would then gently rebuke him saying, "If you behave like this the devotees will stop coming to Shirdi." Sometimes he would smear his body with dirt; this amused children. Then he along with a group of children would go to Dwarka Mai and create a raucous scene.

Nanavali addressed Baba as *kaka* (paternal uncle) as Baba loved him a lot. When Nanavali first came to Shirdi, Baba said, "Nanavali, I have put on the lock and the key is with you. Do not betray me and I will not betray you." These words convey deep *rinanubandhic* ties that existed between the two.

He took a keen interest in keeping order in Dwarka Mai and would see to it that every devotee got *darshan*. He was a well built man. He could walk extremely fast or run when he chose to. Once he took Jyotindra to Chavadi, as he wanted to show him a trick. The two of the then went to Chavadi. And Nanavali jumped up, simultaneously reducing his size and sat in the glass globe. He looked like a monkey sitting there. Sometimes he tied a rag on the rear portion of his pant like a tail and put on a mask of Hanuman. He then collected children of the village and went to *Sabhamandap* and created a racket. His love and devotion for Baba was no less than Hanuman's love and devotion for Rama.

Once Nanavali came to Baba and holding his hand made him get up. Then he sat on the *gaddi* for a minute or so. Then with a great deal of respect he made Baba sit on it again. Then he prostrated before him and said, "Oh lord, only you can occupy this seat, as it befits your divinity. My place is at your feet." This *leela* is narrated in *Shri Sai Satcharita,* chapter 10.

Nanavali was shattered with grief by Baba's *Mahasamadhi*. He felt it was futile to live any longer, as life without Baba was worthless. On the 13th day of Baba's *Mahasamadhi*, he cried "*Kaka, Kaka*" and left his mortal body. His *samadhi* (**photo 6.3, 6.3a**) is built over his body. It is next to Abdul Baba's *samadhi*.

The Samadhi of V P Iyer

Just behind Nanavali's *samadhi* is this *samadhi* (**photo 6.4**). He lived with his wife and six children in Lucknow. Iyer was kind hearted, affectionate and devoted to Baba. He loved Baba immensely. Once he heard someone talk ill of Baba and cried inconsolably.

He was a sugar technologist by profession. In those days, the job was on a contract basis. So he had to go and work at various sugar mills till the season was over. In 1943 he went through a rough period, as he did not have any job contract.

This did not bother him and he told his family not to worry, as Baba knew what was good for him.

In 1944, he got a job in the Lakshmi *wadi* sugar mill near Kopergaon. Iyer was extremely happy. He told his family and friends that Baba had called him close to Shirdi. Being an ardent devotee, he visited Shirdi frequently. The contract was to last up till the 7th of May; but he had decided to spend the rest of his life in Shirdi.

On May 27th, on one of his visits to Shirdi he fell ill and was diagnosed with cholera. The doctor was summoned to treat him. Soon his condition worsened and he became semiconscious. He lay with his eyes closed. When he did open them it was to look lovingly at Baba's photograph. Then embracing Baba's photograph he said "Baba! Sai Baba" and breathed his last. The villagers loved him immensely and requested the Sansthan to build his *samadhi* in Shirdi.

The Samadhi of Tatya Kote Patil

This is the last *samadhi* (**photo 6.5**) and is next to the compound wall of Lendi Baugh. Tatya, the beloved son of Baijama, died on 12th March 1945. He was enveloped by Baba's grace right from birth. He and Baba had a very loving relationship. Although outwardly they had a playful relationship, Tatya left his home to sleep in the Dwarka Mai with Baba for fourteen years. Baba on the other hand is said to have 'given up his life for Tatya'. Tatya recovered from his illness and led a peaceful and fruitful life.

Tatya had three wives; the first wife did not have any children. The second had a daughter and the third had a daughter and three sons. Baba had promised Baijama to look after Tatya's welfare and to give him *santhati* (children).

Unfortunately, his date of birth and other details of his life are not known; but a detailed account of his and Baba's *rinanubandhic* ties is given in the book titled *Baba's Rinanubandh*. His descendants are leading a fruitful life at Shirdi.

The Lendi Route

Baba went to Lendi.Baugh twice a day. He went in procession to the accompaniment of musical instruments. After the small *durbar* at about 9 a.m. he went along with his dear and near devotees. Nana Sahib Nimonkar was always on his right, while Gopalrao Butti was on his left. He held Baba by placing his hand under his armpit. Butti had so much reverence for Baba that he always looked at his feet, nor did he speak to Baba directly. The entourage was completed with Bhagoji Shinde at the back holding the embroidered umbrella. *Chopdars* in their bright uniforms accompanied him and uttered *lalkari* (sonorous salutations).

They came out of Dwarka Mai and then proceeded to the corner in front of Gurusthan. There Baba stood facing Gurusthan and made gestures with his right hand. The devotees staying in Sathe wada would eagerly await the arrival of the procession and prostrate at Baba's feet. Many devotees visiting Shirdi also availed of this opportunity to do *namaskar*. This they did when Baba went to and from Lendi Baugh.

The procession then turned left and proceeded towards Pilaji's house. Here Baba rested against the wall of this house for some time. *Padukas* were installed at this sacred site by the family. The original black and white photograph of the Lendi procession shows Baba leaning against this house. They then passed the Vitthal Mandir, which is opposite the Seva Dham building. From there they proceeded to Kanif Nath's Mandir. This temple is blessed, as Baba sometimes entered it. This temple is across the road and adjacent to Seva Dham.

After proceeding they walked along the 'trunk road', now known as Nagar Manmad highway. Baba always entered Lendi Baugh alone. The devotees then returned to their rooms, along with the musicians. After an hour they assembled outside Lendi Baugh and the musicians played their instruments. Then Baba came out and the *chopdars* uttered a sonorous *lalkari* and the entourage proceeded towards Dwarka Mai. They took the same route back to Dwarka Mai.

Bhiksha Route

Baba did not have a fixed *bhiksha* routine. He took *bhiksha* as often as he pleased. This he did till his *Mahasamadhi*. Baba started his *bhiksha* rounds at about 8 a.m. He took *bhiksha* from five selected houses, as he had deep *rinanubandhic* ties with these families. Baba placed a cloth over his head, which when folded and knotted, became a *jholi*. In this he placed dry food. In his right hand he carried a tin *tumrel* (mug) in which he collected liquid food.

From Dwarka Mai Baba walked past Chavadi, and stood in between the houses of Sakharam Shelke and Vamanrao Gondkar. He stood at a fixed place and called out *"Bai bhiksha de"* (Lady give me some alms). There is an original photograph of Baba standing there. It is kept in the museum. Shakaram's house was to his left (now Punnami hotel) and Gondkar's house to his right. From there he proceeded to Bayyaji's house.

On the way, there was a small hillock. Baba stood there for a while and fed the birds, dogs and cats. This sacred site was marked by the installation of *padukas*. The uniqueness of these *padukas* is that they are not raised, but engraved in the stone. In front of the *padukas* there is a bowl where Baba kept water for birds and dogs. These *padukas* are now in Shri Sai Baba Mandir, Kohrale.

Bayyaji's and Tatya's houses were adjacent to each other. After getting *bhiksha* from there he proceeded to Nandram's house. He walked past Tajim Khan's *Darga* (**photo 6.6**). It is said that he often went inside this *Darga* (**photo 6.6a**) and then came to Nandram's house. Unfortunately there is no valid information about this saint. He was the patron saint of the Kote family. Legend has it that once there was a flood in Shirdi following torrential rains. Tajim Khan was also the caretaker of the Kote estate. So he asked the family to leave their home and move to a higher place. A fight ensued between him and the family and he was killed. The family repented for their folly and built the *darga* in his honour. The family looked after the *darga*. Now their descendents do so. There is an annual *urs* held at the *darga*. The villagers pray to this saint and offer coconuts at the *darga* during auspicious ocassions in the family. But the most important fact is that Baba respected this saint and when on his *bhiksha* rounds went inside the *darga*.

After receiving *bhiksha* from Nandram, he came to Dwarka Mai. He then mixed all the food together *gopal kaala* and kept it in the *kolamba*. The lady who swept the floor of Dwarka Mai, took a few *bhakaris* home everyday. After mixing all the food together, Baba gave it as *prasad* to many devotees. It was also distributed at lunch to the devotees.

The significance of Baba taking bhiksha

Baba taught us the four *mahayagnas* by example. *Pitru yagna* is conducted by the right of human beings. *Dev yagna* is his *swaha* right i.e., by saying *swaha* and putting offerings into the *Agni*. By slaughter of an animal *Bhoot yagna* is accomplished. By offering food to *atithis* (guests) and doing *annadaan, manush yagna* is performed.

Baba took *bhiksha* everyday, thus performing *bhoot* and *manush yagna* for our welfare. He often asked the devotees who came to Shirdi to take the *jholi* and go for *bhiksha*.

By taking *bhiksha* from Nandram, a Jain *Marwadi*, he taught equality of vision that caste or creed mattered little. Thus we should treat food as *Brahman* and not hanker after delicious food. Life may shower bitterness or sweetness. We should accept it with good grace as *prasad* given by Baba

Why did Baba do *a-pradakshina* on his *bhiksha* route?

During *shraddh* karma *(apara* karma) the procedure followed is *apasavia* (anti clockwise). He is receiving *bhiksha* and offering it to our ancestors, which we are supposed to do with every meal. This is *aposana* or *Yama* karma. We are also required to perform yearly *shradha*, which we forget to do after some years.

Baba took *bhiksha* from five houses instead of seven houses, as is followed in the *madhukari* of *Datta parampara*. The five houses symbolise the five *pranas*, which are: 1. *prana* are the vital forces that receive the food into the body. 2. *aapana* excretes what is not required. 3. *samana* receives all that is brought by *pranas* and assimilates it. 4. *vyana* is the circulatory system that carries assimilated food to the different parts of the body. 5. *udayana* protects and serves as a bodyguard to the individuality and the ego helping it to lift the thoughts to a new height of better understanding.

7

The Five Blessed Houses that Baba took Bhiksha from

1. Sakharam Patil Shelke's house

This house (**photo 7.1**) was near to the Chavadi with a west facing entrance. Sakharam was a farmer, a wealthy landlord and was devoted to Baba.

Sakara Bai the wife of his grandson, Hari Bhau, states that Baba loved Sakharam immensely. Baba stood at the crossroad between his and Vamanrao Gondkar's house and called out "Sakharam *roti de*". She also stated that Triambak, (Hari Bhau's father), donated some land to Baba's Sansthan. The land for the Shirdi bus stand was donated by him. Triambak's *samadhi* is inside the compound of Narsimha Temple (**photo 7.2**), which is behind Sakharam's house. The other two *samadhis* are of Thana Bai (Triambak's wife) and Ramgir Bua, who is mentioned in chapter 33 of *Shri Sai Satcharita*. There were many *Gosavis* living in Shirdi at that time. Their *samadhis* are in that compound. Unfortunately, their names are not known.

Narsimha temple was constructed by the Shelke family. Narsimha is the Kul devata of the family. A priest performs *puja* daily along with *arati* and offers *bhog*.

Around the year 2000 this house was sold by his descendants. A multi-storey shopping complex now stands in its place.

2. Vamanrao Gondkar's house

This house (**photo 7.3**) is on the right side and opposite to Sakharam's house. Vamanrao was born and bred in Shirdi. His family was affluent; were farmers and landowners. His descendants say that he owned 500 acres of land in and around Shirdi. They also state that they owned Lendi.Baugh and the adjacent lands. They sold Lendi Baugh to Moreshwar Pradhan, who then gave it to the Sansthan. This is one of the blessed houses that Baba took *bhiksha* from.

Mention is made of this house in *Shri Sai Satcharita*, chapter 19, when Baba placed a ladder against this house and climbed on the roof. Then he crossed the roof of Radha Krishna Mai's home and descended on the rear side. At that time, Baba was very sick and so was Radha Krishna Mai. Purandare had pleaded with Baba to cure Mai and this was Baba's unique remedy.

Baba gave two rupees to Venku Shimpe Kambleker, who brought the ladder. Other devotees objected saying that Baba had paid too much. Baba told them that any work that was done should be paid for promptly and adequately. Kambleker had no children but after he received the money he prospered and had two sons.

Vamanrao Gondkar after leading a prosperous life died on 15th April 1964. His descendants are living in Shirdi and carrying on his legacy. The *palhki* and *rath,* when taken in procession through the village on festivals, stop first at this house. The family is given the honour of doing the first *puja* to Baba and the *palkhi* and *rath.*

3. Bayyaji Appa Kote Patil's house

His home (**photo 7.4**) is named 'Sai Kutir' and is at the end of Kote gully. He was born in Shirdi and was close to Baba since infancy, as his father was a staunch devotee. He started serving Baba at the age of eleven. Bayyaji noted that Baba was very fair and just and would enjoin silence on the Hindus when *namaz* was being performed and *vice versa*. Sweets were distributed to all alike.

He worked as a revenue officer and police officer in Biragaon. He was very affluent and owned 84 acres of land. Baba used to give him four rupees daily and say, "Do not eat and excrete it". So he invested it in land. Baba advised him as to what and when to cultivate on it. Once he did not heed Baba's advice and there was no yield. He incurred a loss of 300 rupees.

He was with Baba when his *Mahasamadhi* occurred. Baba distinctly told him, "I am leaving. Carry me to the *wada*. All Brahmins will be near me." Baba was sitting when he breathed his last. Nana Sahib Nimonkar poured some water in his mouth; but the water came out. Bayyaji tried to collect the water by placing his cupped palm below Baba's chin. Baba leaned on him and took *samadhi*.

His descendant Gopinath Kote still lives in that very house. The Shirdi Sai Baba Sansthan has given that family the honour of carrying Baba's *padukas* (holy footwear) and *satka* (baton) for the Chavadi procession.

4. Bayaja Bai Ganpath Kote Patil's house

This house (**photo 7.5**) is situated adjacent to 'Sai Kutir'. Bayaja Bai came to Shirdi after she married an affluent landowner, Ganpath Kote Patil. She was a dutiful, loving wife, who did all the household chores. She loved to cook and feed various guests and relatives that came to her home. 'Food is *Brahman*' she knew and was the first lady to feed Baba. In chapter 8 of *Shri Sai Satcharita* her love, devotion and caring is beautifully described.

Her trouble ended when Baba came to live in Dwarka Mai. Everyday Baba took *bhiksha* from her house. As soon as she heard Baba's voice, she left whatever she was doing; whether it was attending to the cattle or the horses, went inside and prepared fresh *bhakri* and curried vegetables for him. Baba was very pleased with her love and devotion.

Once Baba asked her, "Bai what do you want? *Sampathi* (wealth) or *santhati* (children)?" Unhesitatingly she asked for Tatya's welfare. She was very concerned that though Tatya had three wives, he had no children.

When Baba was in his physical form, *arati* was performed to him. Usually during Madhav Adkar's *arati* '*Arati Sai Baba sowkya dathar jiva*' he was offered the *chillim*. Baba would take a puff or two then pass it around.

The Shirdi Sai Baba Sansthan has bestowed the honour of carrying Baba's photograph during the *palkhi* procession on their descendants. A brief note of the Chavadi procession is given below.

Viju Kote Patil, who is Tatya's grandson and Gopinath Kote who is Bayyaji's grandson go to the *Samadhi Mandir* just before the *palkhi* procession commences. The *pujari* gives Baba's photograph to Viju and the case containing the *padukas* to Gopinath. (Earlier they would ascend the steps of the *samadhi* to pick them up. This was stopped about four years ago.) They then carry them to the waiting *palkhi* and place them inside. Then the *palkhi* proceeds to Dwarka Mai. Viju then takes Baba's photograph and places it on the stone for a short while. After Baba has sat on the stone for sometime, he's taken to the *sanctum sanctorum*. The photograph is then placed in the *mandap* for sometime. Then it is brought to the *palkhi* and placed in it.

Until Viju signals to the *palkhi* bearers to lift the *palkhi*, it is not lifted. Just as Baba would not get up until Tatya came and lifted him and asked him to go for the *palkhi* procession. The *palkhi* then goes to Chavadi and *arati* is performed. At that time Baba is offered a lighted *chillim* by Viju.

5. Nandram Marvadi Sanklecha's house

Nandram was a rich landowner and moneylender by profession. He was a kind-hearted and gentle person. His grandfather came to Shirdi from Rajasthan (Kharade village). Nandram was born in

1866 and grew up in Shirdi. He came close to Baba in 1875. His devotion increased by leaps and bounds. In fact, he spent most of his time with Baba. His house (**photo 7.6**) was one of the five blessed houses that Baba took *bhiksha* from. It is said that Baba visited this house last, although it is very near Dwarka Mai. Baba loved this family and would call out to Nandram's wife, Radhabai, who had a lisp. "*Oh! Bhobadi bai bhiksha de.*" If she was late in offering *bhiksha*, he would shower abuses on her and return to Dwarka Mai. Whenever Baba wanted to eat *puran polis* (wheat *chapattis* filled with sweet stuffing of *chana dal*) he would call out to Radhabai and ask for *polis*. Radhabai would hurry and prepare *puran polis*. But it took a long time to prepare. Baba would lose his patience and go to Dwarka Mai. After making all preparations, she would take the platter to Dwarka Mai. Baba would eat very little and distribute the rest.

Radhabai was devoted to Baba. She knew Baba's abuses were blessings in disguise. Every Diwali she used to get five yards of white *manjarpat* (coarse cotton), stitch a *kafni* for Baba and present it to him. Baba used to wear it immediately with great joy and happiness.

In 1911 when plague was rampant in Shirdi the villagers started fleeing. Nandram met some villagers, who told him that his eyes were red and that this was the first sign of plague. Alarmed and frightened out of his wits he thought he would go to his village Ekruka. He mounted a horse and went to take Baba's permission. As soon as Baba saw him he said, "I won't let you die till I die." Baba gave him *udi* and he recovered.

On another occasion, there was a terrible sickness. Many villagers were seriously ill with it. It was believed that sugar was not to be ingested during the illness. Those who did ingest sugar were gravely sick and some lost their lives. Nandram was also afflicted with the disease. When he noticed the first signs of the disease, he went straight to Dwarka Mai and sought refuge at Baba's feet. Baba took out a packet of sugar from his pocket and gave it to him. Nandram had utmost faith in Baba. So he ate it at once and recovered.

Nandram's grandmother asked Baba to look after her family, as the male children used to die in infancy. Baba gave her three mangoes and she had three sons. After this "*aam leela*" all her sons survived.

The best deed that Nandram did was to donate the land between Butti wada and Dwarka Mai. This deed was done through Damu Anna; hence the *Samadhi Mandir* was extended. Nandram believed in doing good, in giving rather than receiving. He also repaired and laid the floor tiles of the *Maruti* and *Ganapati* temples. He died on 13th October 1946. His philanthropic and social work is carried on by his descendants.

As related by Nandram's grandson, Dilip Sanklecha

8

Temples in Shirdi

Khandoba Mandir in Shirdi

It is said that this temple (**photo 8.1**) is more than 500 years old. The date of construction is not known. This small temple is situated opposite to the bus stand (**photo 8.1a**) and adjacent to Sainath hospital. Mhalsapati was the priest of this temple. Since then the upkeep of this temple has been in the hands of his descendants, the Nagre family.

The temple is 15 ft long and 15 ft in breadth (**photo 8.1b**). In the centre is a stone idol of Khandoba. Mhalsa is on the left and belonged to the *Vaishya* caste. Banai is on the right and belonged to a shepherd's family. They are incarnations of Parvati and Ganga. Khandoba is an incarnation of Shiva and is the presiding deity of Maharashtra.

Two *Shiva lingas* are in front of Khandoba; a tiger in front of Mhalsa, and a dog is in front of Banai. The temple's wooden door is fitted with grills, so that the devotees can have *darshan* of the deities even after the temple door is closed.

Mhalsapati was performing *puja* in this temple, when the marriage party of Chandbhai Patil arrived. There was a Muslim looking *fakir* with them. This *fakir* immediately went into the temple. Mhalsapati sensing that there was somebody behind him, turned and saw the *fakir*. He welcomed him saying *"Aao jee Sai Maharaj"*. Then Mhalsapati did *namaskar*, and seated the *fakir* with respect. After he completed the *puja*, Baba and Mhalsapati smoked and shared a *chillim* between them. Then he took Baba to the village and introduced him to Kashiram Shimpi and Appa Jagle.

Shiladhi *written by Dr Keshav B Gavankar*

Later Baba went to the temple and said it was a fit place for a *fakir's* residence because of the solitude. Mhalsapati objected, saying that, "No Muslim should get into his Hindu temple."

Shri Sai Satcharita *chapter 5*

Baba asked Upasani to sit quietly in this temple for three and a half years for his spiritual advancement as Baba would do the rest. In 1929 Upasani reconstructed this temple with bricks and mortar and installed a *gopuram* (temple spire) in gratitude to Baba for showering his grace.

Two *aratis* are performed there daily at 12 noon and at 6 p.m. On the festival of *Champa Shasti* a grand ceremony is held there annually. This falls in *Margashirsh shuddh shasti* (November-December). Many devotees after fervent prayer walk on burning coals that are kept in the 12′ long pit. This ceremony has been going on since 1850. The *pujari* completes the ceremony by walking on the burning coal.

On *Vijaya Dashami* the ritual of *Seemolanghan* is performed at this temple. It is described under the heading "*Vijaya Dashami* or Baba's *Aradhana vidhi*".

The mythology of Champa Shasti
Two demons Mal and Mani were granted the boon of immortality by Lord Brahma. Then they became evil and killed people. Lord Shiva reincarnated as Khandoba and fought oils the demons. Khandoba's wife Champa (alias Mhalsa) prayed for her husband's victory. On the sixth day the demons were slain. Champa happily gave a huge feast of brinjal *bharit* and *bhakri* made of *bajri*. Since then it is called *Champa Shasti*.

Lord Khandoba repented. So he set up a long *Agni kund,* and walked back and forth on the burning coal barefoot.

The Banyan tree

This is the blessed Banyan tree (**photo 8.2**) that gave shade to Baba and the marriage party of Chandbhai Patil. This tree is to the right upon entering the compound. A small parapet is built around it. A small shrine of Baba's *padukas* is placed there to commemorate the wonderful return of Baba to Shirdi.

In Shirdi *Vat Purnima* is performed around this tree. In the *Skanda purana* this story is given. Savitri's husband Satyavan lost his life, as she was late in coming to meet him. Then she pleaded with Yama to give back her husband's life and succeeded. So girls of marriageable age, as also married women perform this ritual to get a good husband and for their longevity. In this ceremony, women tie a white thread around the tree during ritual circumambulation.

The Kanifnath Mandir

The temple (**photo 8.3**) is adjacent to the Seva Dham building. It is an old temple. Unfortunately, the date of construction is not known; but it was there in the 1800s. Kanifnath (**photo 8.3a**), one of the Navnaths manifested from the ear of an elephant and hence his name. Baba visited this temple on his way to Lendi Baugh. Festivals are conducted in this temple in the month of *Shravan* (August), on *Gokulastami* and other holy days. Daily *pujas* are conducted by the village priest.

Ashta Lakshmi Mandir

This ancient temple of *Ashta Lakshmi* (**photo 8.4, 8.4a**) is on Pimpalwadi road, adjacent to the Pilgrim's Inn Hotel. In chapter 13 of *Shri Sai Satcharita* is given a wonderful *leela* of how Bala Ganpat Shimpi was cured of malaria by feeding a black dog a mixture of curd and rice. Baba said, "Bala go to Mahalakshmi Temple and feed a black dog some rice and curd." And so it came to pass that Shimpi was cured.

In the 50s, I remember it to be an old temple with beautiful wooden beams and pillars. In the centre was the panel of Ashta Lakshmi that was venerated and covered with a paste of *sindur*. Later, many idols were added. Now when you enter the temple on your left are the *nav grahas*. On the right three rooms have been constructed. The first room or temple, houses the Ashta Lakshmi deities.

The panel above has been added on later, while the panel below is the original and ancient.

The next room houses Maha Lakshmi and the third houses the Goddess Durga. In front of her and to the rear is a Shiva Linga with Nandi. Touching the eastern wall there are seven stones that are covered with *sindur*. These stones are symbolic of the seven holy rivers.

The temple was reconstructed in August 2001.

Vitthal Mandir

This temple (**photo 8.5, 8.5A**) is situated on the left side of the street and opposite to Seva Dham. The descendants (seventh generation) of Laxman Mama say that Shirdi was full of small hillocks. This temple was next to Shama's home. When the area was levelled and the road was defined, they shifted the temple to the present location.

Legend has it that Nanu Mama Ratna Parkhi was a staunch devotee of Vitthal. Once he was having a bath in the Chandrabhaga River at Pandharpur, when the idol of Vitthal emerged from the river. He did ritualistic *puja* to it and brought it home. Then he constructed a temple, where daily *puja* was performed. It bothered him that Vitthal was alone without his beloved Rukhmini. On another visit to Pandharpur, he met Das Ganu and told him the story. Das Ganu obliged him by getting a suitable idol of Rukhmini made of the same type of stone.

The priest Lakshmanrao alias Lakshman Mama, (the son of Nanu Mama) was very orthodox in his views. In the beginning he was against Baba, as Baba's way of living, speech and routine were not acceptable to him. Once he was seriously ill and he lost all hope of survival; but Baba saved him. This was his turning point and thereafter he became a staunch devotee. He was the *gram pujari* (priest of all the village temples). His daily routine was to perform Baba's ritualistic *puja* and then perform the *puja* to all the village deities.

The day after Baba's *Mahasamadhi*, Lakshman Mama had a vision in a dream early in the morning. In his dream Baba asked him to come and perform *Kakad arati*. At once he got up, performed his morning ablutions and took all the *Puja* materials to Dwarka Mai. There he uncovered Baba's face, not heeding the protests of the *maulvis* and other Muslims; and performed *Kakad arati* as he had always done.

Shri Sai Satcharita, *chapter 43*

Baba on his way to Lendi Baugh often visited this temple. Because of its solitude, Baba asked Das Ganu to stay in this temple and not to come to Dwarka Mai where there were many distractions.

Dakshina Mukhi Shri Hanuman Mandir

This village *mandir* (**photo 8.6, 8.6A**) has two *Maruti Vigrahas* (idols), denoting one for Shirdi and the other for Biragaon. This temple is unique, as it faces the south and has two idols. The idol of Maruti has one hand raised above his head and the other hand below covering his loin. This is symbolic of human life, the upraised hand represents ego, pride and power, while the other hand represents sexual urges. These are the very things that ruin us. Maruti is very powerful, extremely intelligent and he controls our urges. He is the *gram devta* of Shirdi; so it behoves us to do *namaskar* to him everyday.

This temple welcomed saints like Devi Das and Gangagir of Puntamba to stay there. Baba often went to this temple to have *satsang* (discourse) with them. (Shri Sai Satcharita, *chapter 5*). At other times he went and sat in this temple alone and in solitude.

Baba had a special bond with Maruti. On his way to Chavadi, he stood facing this temple and waved his hands, making some mystical signs. Baba is by example showing us that we too should take some time out to pray to Maruti. Even today, every Thursday and on holy days, when there is a *palkhi* (palanquin) procession the *palkhi* stops at that very spot. The *Chopdars* (mace bearers) proclaim *lalkari* (sonorous salutations). This temple is used by devotees to conduct *akhand naam jaap* and *bhajans*. Daily *aratis* are performed; Hanuman *Jayanthi* (birth of Lord Hanuman) is celebrated on a grand scale as are other festivals. In April 2009, soon after Hanuman *jayanthi* erected the temple was demolished by the Sansthan and a new temple will be constructed. This is rather unfortunate as that was the last heritage temple left with the Sansthan.

In Shri Sai Satcharita, *chapter 7*, under the heading "Renovation of the temples", Baba got this temple renovated by Tatya Patil. Out of the money received as *dakshina*, Baba allotted the money for the repairs of all the temples in Shirdi.

Ganapathi, Shani and Mahadev Temples

These ancient temples (**photo 8.7, 8.8, 8.9**) were near each other and situated in front of the Old Bhakt Nivas. Out of the money that Baba received as *dakshina*, he got Tatya to repair these temples. On December 26, 1998, after due *Utthapan vidhi* the deities of these temples were moved to the *Kalasha Mandir*. This was done under the temple extension plan. New temples were built; these temples are contiguous with each other and located in front of the Queue complex. On 3rd July 1999, the deities were housed back in these temples with elaborate ritual and ceremony. Unfortunately the heritage temples were destroyed.

The Samadhi of the Tiger

This *samadhi* (**photo 8.10**) is in front of the Mahadev temple. In the *Shri Sai Satcharita,* chapter 31, the *leela* of the ailing tiger is narrated. In 1918, a week before Baba's *Mahasamadhi*, a bullock cart with four *Darveshis* and an ailing tiger came to the door of Dwarka Mai. The *Darveshis* pleaded for permission to bring the tiger inside. They exhibited the tiger that was the source of their income. They had heard of Baba's miraculous cures so they had brought it to Shirdi. Shama told Baba about their request and permission was granted.

The tiger was brought inside. It climbed the steps of Dwarka Mai and looked lovingly at Baba for a few seconds. Then it extended its paws and laid its head on them and did *namaskar*. Then it let out a terrible roar, dashed its tail on the ground and breathed its last. Baba took out 50 rupees from his pocket and gave it to them. Thus a debt was paid. Here there was a *rinanubandhic* tie between the tiger, the *Darveshis* and Baba. Thus the cycle was completed. The tiger attained *sadgati* (salvation) at Baba's feet and the *Darveshis* were paid a debt of 50 rupees.

At that time Jyotindra Tarkad, was sitting next to Baba. Later, he asked Baba as to what had happened between the tiger and him. Baba replied, "That tiger was tormented by terrible pain from illness and was pleading to be relieved from it. I felt a lot of compassion for it; so I asked *Allah Mia* to relieve it and grant it salvation. Now that tiger is free from the cycle of birth and death. So I asked them to bury it in front of Mahadev's temple."

Live experiences of the Tarkhad family with Shri Sai Baba of Shirdi.

The houses of Baba's devotees in Shirdi
It is impossible to write about every devotee residing in Shirdi; but it will appear in the next book, Baba willing.

9

Abdul Baba's Cottage

This cottage (**photo 9.1**) is in front of Chavadi. Abdul Baba was conferred the title of *Sultan* and was called '*Chotu Sultan of Nanded*' village. He was married to Umran Bi and had a son. Abdul was serving Amiruddin Baba and following a dream vision, Amiruddin sent him to Shirdi. In Shirdi he worked as a *sevak* doing all sorts of menial jobs. As he did not have any income, he begged for his food. He strictly followed Baba's instructions of, "Eat very little and sleep very little."

He slept wherever he could. Then he built a small mud house, where his cottage now stands. When the Sansthan was formed they leased the land and cottage to him. He kept busy looking after Baba's *Samadhi*.

The devotees, who visit his cottage, have an opportunity to venerate the *chimta* (prongs) (**photo 9.2**). It is said that it was given to him by Baba. Abdul treasured it and venerated it daily with *loban* (incense). After Baba's *Mahasamadhi* Abdul used this for curing the pains and ailments of devotees. One can have *darshan* of the original photographs of Baba that are hung on the left wall.

Baba is also said to have given him a *satka* (**photo 9.3**) and a tin mug (**photo 9.4**). But we devotees are most grateful to Abdul for writing down the sayings, teachings and parables of Baba. He read them daily like a Koran.

His descendant Ghani Bhai is given the honour of doing the *alankar* of Baba's *samadhi* ever day at 10 a.m. The *samadhi* is cleaned and a floral arrangement is done.

10

Festivals Celebrated in Shirdi

All the Hindu festivals are celebrated in Shirdi. There are three major festivals that are celebrated on a grand scale. They are *Rama Navami, Guru Purnima* and *Vijaya Dashami*. These are celebrated with pomp and show. Each is a three-day event. The festivities for each day are described under *Rama Navami*. The temples are decorated beautifully with lights, ornate tents and it looks like heaven. In the evening there are cultural programmes and *bhajans* by famous artists. There is *annadan* on the main *utsav* of these three festivals. The *prasadalaya* serves free meals.

The Shirdi Sai Baba Sansthan, sanctioned by the district court of Ahmednagar had after mutual deliberations entrusted the management of the *Rama Navami utsav* to Das Ganu Maharaj and Tatya Kote. The second major *utsav* was *Guru Purnima,* and it was managed by Gopalrao Mukund Butti. The sons of the late Gopalrao Butti, managed this *utsav* till 1940. From 1941 the Sansthan managed this festival. The descendants of Butti send donations for this festival to date.

Baba's *punyatithi* was entrusted to Baba's devotees outside Shirdi especially from Bombay. The permanent fund of the Sansthan had been started from the savings of the collections and contributions of the first *bhandara*, which was held on the 13th day of Baba's *Mahasamadhi*, in 1918.

The festival of Gokul *Astami* was entrusted to the villagers of Shirdi, headed by Tatya Kote Patil.

Gudi Padava, the Maharashtrian New Year

This festival falls on *Chaitra, shuddh* 9 *prathipada* (Hindu almanac). On this day the *'gudi'* on a post is hoisted on top of the steeple of the *Samadhi Mandir*. The *'gudi'* is a copper *kalash* hoisted on a staff. A new cloth is draped on it and has small branches of Neem tied to it. It is garlanded with a flower and *'bathasa maala'* (*bathasa* is a cookie made with a concentrated sugar solution). This is hoisted before sunrise. This is a *Brahman Dwaja*.

Till the 1950's and 60's, they used to perform *abhishek* to the *samadhi* and then distribute *puran poli* (A sweet dish) as *mahaprasad*. The *samadhi* and Baba's idol was draped with a beautiful shawl of velvet with ornate *zari* work. The idol was garlanded with a *'bathasa maala'*. In Dwarka Mai, an ornate garland of roses made of gold was placed on the portrait. This beautiful garland was donated to the Sansthan by a devotee named Indira Pendarkar. This unique celebration has been discontinued. Now the *samadhi* and idol are bathed as usual and the *gudi* is hoisted before sunrise. The *rath* is taken through the village at about 9 p.m, while years ago the timing was between 4 and 5 p.m.   *Shiladhi* by Dr. Keshav B. Gavankar

Rama Navami, the Festival of Rama's Birth

In *Chaitra Maas* (April-May), *shuklapaksh* (bright half of the month) 9th *mithi*, (date), the birth of Lord Rama is celebrated. It was in 1911 that *Rama Navami* was first celebrated. K G Bhishma conceived of this idea from the *urs*. He consulted Kaka Mahajani, who liked the idea very much. Both of them went to Baba and sought permission, which Baba readily gave. Since then Rama Navami is celebrated on a grand scale. It is a three day festival.
Shri Sai Satcharita, chapter 5

On the 1st day, there is *akhand parayan* (continuous reading) of the *Shri Sai Satcharita*. The devotees can submit their names a day before the festival. In the evening a child is asked to pick up the chits (by lottery). Fifty three names are thus chosen and the chapters are assigned. Five names are chosen as standby. After the *Dhup arati* (evening *arati*) these names are announced and lists posted at various places. This procedure is followed for all the three major festivals.

After *Kakad arati, akhand parayan* (**photo 10.1**) commences. The *Pothi* is brought in procession from *Samadhi Mandir*. The procession consists of a devotee (usually a trustee) who carries the sacred *Pothi*. Alongside him another devotee carries a *veena* (a stringed musical instrument). The *veena* is symbolic of Saraswati's *Brahma-veena*. Another devotee carries the portrait of Baba. The *kirtankar* (who is also the *pujari*) sings all the way from the *Samadhi Mandir* to Dwarka Mai.

The procession commences with *mantra upchar, laghu arati* and *lalkari*. The procession comes out of *Samadhi Mandir* through the south gate. *Paad Puja* (washing their feet) and *arati* of camphor is performed by the Iyer family who reside in Shirdi. The procession then goes to *Gurusthan* where again *mantra upchar, laghu arati* and *lalkari* is performed. The procession then turns right and in front of Dixit *Wada Paad Puja* is performed by the Sansthan. It then proceeds through the *Maha Dwar* past the *Maruti Mandir* to Dwarka Mai. This entourage is followed by numerous devotees.

In Dwarka Mai the area in the verandah next to the railing is decorated with banana trees. A silver shrine is kept to welcome Baba's portrait and the *pothi*. A *laghu* (small) *arati* is performed to Baba and the *pothi*. Then the reading commences. Dwarka Mai is open through the night. Late in the evening there is *Palkhi* procession (**photo 10.2**)

The second Day is the main *utsav* (festival). There is *Kakad arati*. Then after the completion of the *akhand parayan*, the *Pothi* is taken in procession to the *Samadhi Mandir*.

There is *mantra upchar, laghu arati* and *lalkari*. The *pothi* is then taken in procession. It goes out of Dwarka Mai and passes from behind the *Samadhi Mandir* and enters Gurusthan where a *laghu arati* is performed. The entourage then goes towards the main *Dwar* of *Samadhi Mandir*. Just before entering it *Paad Puja* is performed to the bearers of the sacred articles by the Sansthan. They then enter *Samadhi Mandir;* thus the entourage would have completed the *pradakshina* of the previous day.

In *Samadhi Mandir* there is *mangal snan* (holy bath of Baba's idol). The villagers and numerous devotees go to (Kopergaon) and bring water from the Godavari for the holy bath. Water is also brought from the Ganga and other holy rivers by many zealous devotees. The *Kavadis* (or water bearers) are allowed to wash Baba's *padukas* with the holy water.

At about 8.a.m. the changing of the sack of wheat (**photo 10.3**) takes place. A new sack of wheat is brought in procession from *Samadhi Mandir* to Dwarka Mai. The old sack is taken to the *prasadalaya* (canteen) and the new sack is placed in the cupboard.

At 12 noon is the birth of Rama. A cradle is tied in the *Samadhi Mandir,* symbolic of the birth (**photo 10.4**). Radha Krishna Mai supplied a cradle when the first *Rama Navami* was celebrated in Shirdi. The Sansthan now performs this ceremony. Following this there is the noon *arati*.

Between 2 p.m and 4 p.m, changing of the flags takes place (**photo 10.5**). This is described in *Shri Sai Satcharita,* chapter 6.

Every year two new flags were taken out in procession. Since then this ceremony is performed. The descendants of Dammu Anna Rasne supply the embroidered flag, while Nimonkar's descendants supply the green flag. These flags are kept on Baba's *samadhi* and *arati* is performed to them. Then the noon *arati* takes place. They are taken to Tukaram Sutar's house (his surname was Bhalerao and his profession was that of a *sutar* or carpenter). At about 2 p.m. the *geru* (ochre) flag is brought in procession from *Samadhi Mandir* to the open area in front of Pilaji Gurav's house. Then the other two flags are brought from the *Sutar* home where they are fixed to a long staff (pole). Then all the flags are taken in procession through the village. There is lot of dancing and merriment and finally two flags are fixed atop Dwarka Mai, while the ochre flag is fixed inside Dwarka Mai.

The Urs and Sandal Procession

In 1897 Gopalrao Gund wanted to honour Baba with a special festival. Thus the *Urs* (**photo 10.6**) was started. *Urs* literally means a wedding with God or uniting the soul with God at death. It is an annual celebration, and the saints' spiritual power is at its peak at that time.

Between 9 and 10 p.m, the 'sandal procession' takes place. The descendants of Abdul Baba perform this. It is a beautiful ceremony. A platter with sandalwood scrapings along with incense is taken in procession around the village to the accompaniment of musical instruments. The platter, the incense and gifts to be offered are carried under a canopy. This canopy consists of a *gailif'* or *chaddar* that is attached to four wooden posts. The *gailif* is green in colour with golden *Kalmas* (*Kalmas* are verses from the *Quran*) inscribed on it. On top of every post is a *panja* (a silver replica of a hand). This sandal procession is to venerate *Auhlias* (Muslim saints). It is described in chapter 6 of *Shri Sai Satcharita*. At the *Samadhi Mandir,* gifts like a *chaddar* (shawl), fruits and sweets are offered. The procession then goes to Abdul Baba's *darga* and again gifts are offered. The procession ends in Dwarka Mai, where sandalwood mixed with rose water and *ittar* (perfume) is pasted on the *nimbar* with bare hands.

In the evening there is the *rath* procession (**photo 10.7**). The whole night there is *bhajan sandhya* in the *Samadhi Mandir*.

The next morning, i.e., on the third day, there is no *Kakad arati*. After the morning *arati* till 12 noon there is *Kaala kirtan* and then the *gopal kaala* is done. This ceremony is celebrated with joy, merriment and feasting at the end of any festival. A *handi* (earthen pot) filled with the ingredients mentioned below is hung high up and is broken. Then the contents are distributed. The earthen *handi* is filled with a mixture of curds, *lye* (puffed Jvari grain), turmeric powder, cumin seeds, coriander seeds and honey. At the auspicious time it is broken and the contents are distributed as *prasad*. The above ingredients cool the body thus bringing calm and peace.

Some little known facts about Baba and the festival of Rama Navami

Baba celebrated *Rama Navami* right from the early days of his stay in Dwarka Mai. On that day he washed the entire Dwarka Mai himself. At about 12 noon he bought a little oil and lit a few lamps. From the rest of the money he bought some *gulal* (a dry vermilion powder). Having done this he first put some on the Dhuni Mai and then on his own head. Then he put some on each of the steps leading to Dwarka Mai, in every corner finally applied some to the entrance door. Later when the devotees started flocking to Shirdi they had *katha* and *kirtan* in the *Sabhamandap* followed by the birth of Rama, following which Baba distributed *pedas* and *burfi* (sweets).

Shiladhi written by Dr Keshav B Gavankar.

Puja of the Sadguru, or Guru Purnima

Baba, accepted *Dakshina*, and *Namaskar* (prostrating at his feet) from his devotees. Yet he actively discouraged and forbade ritualistic *puja* directed towards him. Instead he asked them to perform *puja* to the pillar in front of the Dhuni Mai. Baba sat for hours in front of this pillar leaning his back against it. When the devotees went to Dwarka Mai even at about 5 a.m. they found Baba sitting there gazing into the Dhuni Mai.

In the year 1908, Tatya Sahib Nulkar, who was a subjudge in Pandarpur, came to stay in Shirdi. Baba asked him to stay in the Chavadi.

One day, in the morning Baba told Shama, "Ask *Mhatara* (old man) to perform *Puja* to the pillar." Shama went and told Nulkar (*Mhatara*) exactly what Baba had said. Both of them discussed the reason for this; but could not come up with an answer. At last they consulted the almanac and found that it was *Vyas purnima* or *Guru purnima*. But Baba had asked him to perform *puja* to the pillar and not to him. Nonetheless they were happy that at least he had allowed *puja* to be performed in the Dwarka Mai. Nulkar was performing *puja* to the pillar when Shama turned up. Baba said, "Why is he performing *puja* all by himself? Why can't you too perform the *puja?*" Shama replied, "I will not perform *Puja* to this pillar. But if you will allow me to perform *puja* to you, I will gladly do so. I will only worship you and not this or any other pillar". After a lot of debate and discussion, Baba finally agreed.

Dada Kalker was aware that it was *Guru purnima*. So he sent for Tatya who had gone to his farm. Both of them went with *puja* materials, and performed *Guru puja*. The rest of the devotees followed suit. They offered fruits, *dakshina* and *vastra* (*dhotis*) to their Guru. The *dhoti* was of no use to Baba; but they got the opportunity to do *Guru puja* that day and they hoped it would continue in the future.

Thus the festival of *Guru purnima* started and now it is a three day function. On the first day there is *akhand parayan*, the second is the main festival and it concludes on the third day with *gopal kaala*. *Guru Purnima* is celebrated in *ashad maas* (i.e. June-July).

Shiladhi written by Dr. Keshav B. Gavankar

Vijay Dashmi or Baba's Aaradhana Vidhi

It was on the 11ᵗʰ day of the lunar cycle *Ekadashi*, that Baba's *niryan* took place. The *Dashmi* had passed into *Ekadashi*, when Baba's *Seemolanghan* occurred. *Seemolanghan* (**photo 10.8**) is crossing the border in procession on *Dassera*. From time immemorial the *punyatithi* of *sadgurus* are performed in memory of the compassionate and worthy deeds done by them. So it behoves a devotee to participate in the *aradhana puja*. This is also an excellent way of performing *seva* to the *sadguru*.

The Shirdi Sai Baba Sansthan performs *aradhana vidhi* in the following ritual. In 1920s four Brahmins were invited; the belief being that the *Sadguru* had not passed away, but he had taken the form of the universe (*vishvaroop dhara*).

Each Brahmin is given a place of honour. First is the *Sadguru* (Baba's *sthan*). second is the *param guru* (Baba's guru's *sthan*). third is *parmesti guru* (*Brahma Dev's sthan*) and fourth is the *parathpar guru* (God's *sthan*). They are seated and *Paad Puja* is performed. The Brahmins are given *aachaman* water, which is sipped, and *puja* is done with the recital of the *Purusha sukta*.

After the *Paad Puja* a *mandala* is drawn, over which plate for the meal is kept. Then a feast of *panch pakvan* is served. After the meal is over they are given *tambul*, *dakshina* and clothes. Then the *tirthrajachya* Puja commences. On the floor sanctified with the slurry of cow dung, beautiful *rangoli* is drawn. On this four *chowrangs* are placed, on top of which a bed of wheat and rice is laid. On top of the grains a *kalasha* filled with water is placed. With the invocation that the water is *Ganga Mai, puja* is performed. This *kalasha* is worshipped amidst chants of the *Purusha sukta* and other mantras; to be used as tirth.

Following this *puja* each Brahmin places the *kalasha* on his head and dances so that a little of the *tirth* or Ganga falls on his body. After this the *kalasha* is placed on the bed of grain. *Arati* is performed to the *kalasha*. Then the Brahmins are circumambulated. *Tirth* from the *kalasha* is given first to the Brahmins, then to the rest of the devotees. Thus the *aradhana vidhi* is concluded. About 200 to 300 people are given a feast. Now on the third day the villagers are given free meals at the *Prasadalaya*, in fact any and everybody is welcome.

On the first day there is *akhand parayan*. On the second day there is *Bhiksha jholi* and the names of the *bhikshus* is obtained by lottery. They assemble in *Samadhi Mandir* at 8. a.m. where they are garlanded and ochre coloured *jholis,* that have a small quantity of wheat, is given to them. They are brought in procession to Dwarka Mai. After this they are taken to the five houses that Baba took *bhiksha* from. On this way many devotees give them *bhiksha* and in return receive a little of the contents from their *jholi*.

Shiladhi written by Dr Keshav B Gavankar

At about 5 p.m. the ceremony of *Seemolanghan* takes place. The word *Seemolanghan* consists of two words *seema* (border) and *ullanghan* (crossing it). Centuries ago kings practised this. If they crossed their border first and attacked the neighbouring kingdoms, it would result in fewer fatalities and loss of land. For the nine days of *Navrathri*, the kings fasted and performed *Devi puja*, (*Devi* symbolizses *shakti* or power) and on *Dassera* (the 10th day) they crossed their border and attacked.

Lord Rama crossed the border (*seemolanghan*) on *Dassera* and set out to kill Ravan. It was on this day that Devi Durga killed the *rakshasa* Mahisasur.

The priest from *Samadhi Mandir* along with a multitude of devotees perform *Seemolanghan*. They carry an ochre coloured *nishan* on a pole. This *nishan* is garlanded and *arati* is performed to it at Dwarka Mai. Then in procession they cross the boarder of Shirdi and enter Khandoba Mandir. There *arati* and *puja* is performed to it. After the *puja* is done Shami leaves (*sona*) is exchanged by one and all. The procession then returns with the *nishan* to Dwarka Mai and the *nishan* is hoisted on the grill of *Sabhamandap*

Why are Shami leaves (sona) given after the seemolanghan?

Shami pujan

After *seemolanghan*, Shami tree is worshipped and its leaves are exchanged. The legend of the Shami worship and distributing its leaves is as follows. King Raghu was kind and compassionate. Nobody left empty-handed when they sought his help. Guru Varthanthu asked his disciple Kaulsh for 14 million gold sovereigns to perform some religious ceremony. Kaulsh sought the help of King Raghu. Unfortunately, at that time the king had just distributed all his wealth amongst the needy. Neither did he possess the money, nor could he send Kaulsh away empty-handed.

The king sought Kubera's help, who took him across the border (*seemolanghan*). Kubera accompanied the king; but once they had crossed the border, Kubera got nervous and he showered the gold coins on the Shami tree. King Raghu gave Kaulsh the 14 million gold sovereigns. But the tree was still loaded with gold coins. The king asked Kaulsh to take away the rest of the coins, but he would not accept even a single coin over the amount specified by his Guru. Neither would King Raghu take the gold coins as he did not believe in hoarding money. So the king distributed the remaining gold coins amongst his subjects. This tradition continues even today. After *seemolanghan* the Shami tree is worshipped and its leaves are distributed as *sona* or gold. The lesson is that whatever wealth we have, ought to be considered as *prasad;* so it should not be hoarded.

The second myth is that when the Pandavas were banished from their kingdom and sent to forest, they hid all their weapons in the Shami tree. Upon returning they performed Puja to the tree and requested the tree to return their weapons. Thus the *Puja* of the Shami tree is done after *seemolanghan.* In Shirdi the *sona* (Shami leaves) are offered to Baba seeking his blessings. The artisans offer the *sona* to their tools seeking their blessings.

Kojagiri Purnima

On the night of this festival *abhishek* is done to Baba's *Samadhi.* At midnight the *Chandra puja (puja* to the moon) is performed. The priest goes to the *gopuram, Samadhi Mandir* and performs *Puja.* He takes sweetened milk or *kheer* to be offered as *prasad,* which is later on distributed.

Daring all festivals, the *palkhi* and *rath* are taken in procession through the village. The *rath* is stopped for a while in front of Dixit *wada.* Here *bhajans* and *bharood* are performed. Much of these activities are curtailed now due to over crowding.

Shiladhi written by Dr Keshav B Gavankar

Baba's Daily Routine

Although thousands of devotees flocked to Shirdi, begging Baba for health, wealth and progeny. He maintained a fairly rigid routine. He got up very early in the morning. At about 5 a.m. he was seen sitting infront of Dhuni Mai. After his morning toiletries, he would again sit in front of Dhuni Mai. Purandare says, "Baba sat in front of Dhuni Mai, leaning against the pillar, doing something." The devotees were not allowed to go near, even at a distance of 50'. He used to utter words like *"yade haq"* (remember Allah), *"Allah Malik"* (Allah is the master) and *"Allah vali hai"* (Allah is the redeemer).

Abdul Baba and Madhu Fasle would quietly go about doing their work. They swept and cleaned the *masjid*, replenished the lamps with oil and offered wood to *Dhuni Mai*. The first devotee to enter Dwarka Mai was Bhagoji Shende. He came daily at a fixed time and massaged Baba's right hand and lovingly bandaged it. Baba saved the ironsmith's baby when she fell into the furnace at Nigoj. This *leela* is described in *Shri Sai Satcharita, chapter* 7. Thus, Baba's hand was burnt badly. The only treatment for it was, to bandage it tightly. Early in the morning Bhajoji Shinde came to Dwarka Mai and did this.

Many of his devotees entreated him to take some medicines and get the hand examined by a doctor. But all these requests fell on deaf ears. Once when such a request was made, Baba said, "Get some good cow dung cakes, about a thousand or two thousand, then ignite them. When they are burning brightly put this body over it. [Baba pointed to his body while he said this] Then stand beside it and watch the fun. And see this body burn."

This is called *'Vyaktirek Jnana'*. *Vyakti* means a human being or a person. *Rek* means 'emptying or purging of' i.e., emptying yourself of *arishadvargas*. Possible meaning is that the "I" is so caught up in this materialistic world, that the real I is forgotten. Self-realised people can stand aside and watch their self burning and witness an out of the body experience.
Shirdiche Sai Baba *By Dr K. B Gavankar*

Then Bhagoji gave Baba a total body massage. After the vigorous massage, he lit the *chillim* and offered it to Baba. Baba took a puff or two and gave it to Bhagoji and between them they took five or six puffs and then Bhagoji left.

Then a few selected devotees came and did *seva* of massaging Baba's feet. After this Baba got up and washed his mouth, face and ears. He used plenty of water. This was a sight worth seeing. He washed himself in a very gentle manner. Baba had a bath occasionally, about once a week in the visible body. He often stated that he had bathed in the 'Ganga and Jamuna'. This he did in the invisible body, for these rivers needed to be sanctified by him. Many a devotee eagerly waited for him to bathe in Shirdi, so that they could collect the bath water. This they carried home and used it to cure many diseases.

At about 8 a.m. Baba went for *bhiksha* to the five blessed houses. There he stood at a fixed place and asked for *bhiksha*. Of the food offered Baba ate very little. He kept the food in the *kolamba*, for anyone to eat. Baba then sat in his usual place near the railing and there was *"chotta hajri"* (a small attendance) when his dear and near devotees came to do *namaskar*. Then he had open *durbar* (sitting) when any and everybody could meet him. This *durbar* lasted till 9.30 a.m. Devotees thronged to pay their respects, to thank him and some to ask for favours. At times during this *durbar* Baba purchased fruits with his money and distributed it to devotees. Sometimes he peeled a banana and fed a devotee; at other times he cut the fruit into small pieces and gave them to devotees. He also told stories or parables, which had profound meaning. This was understood by the devotee for whom it was meant, while others derived valuable lessons from them.

After the *durbar* he went to Lendi Baugh, accompanied by Nana Sahib Nimonkar and Gopalrao Butti, while Bhagoji Shinde held the umbrella. Baba entered Lendi Baugh alone. There he sat with his back to the ever burning *jyot* (lamp). Abdul Baba brought two pots of water and placed them near Baba, who threw the water in different directions. Abdul did not know whether Baba uttered any *mantras* or prayers while doing this. After about an hour Baba returned to Masjid accompanied by his entourage.

The second *durbar* would start at 10.30 a.m. when Baba stayed in the *masjid* till 2 p.m. Baba allowed the devotees to worship him through individual *pujas* and a general *arati*. After *arati* Baba had lunch with a few devotees. The devotees offered their *platters* full of savouries and sweets. Baba mixed all the food together and this *kaala* was partaken of.

After lunch Baba went to Lendi Baugh again for about an hour.

127

11

Shri Che Samadhi Mandir or Dagdi Wada
alias Butti Wada

The *Samadhi Mandir* and Gopalrao Butti are inseparable from each other. It was his home, the *wada* that he built for himself and his family. In chapter 5 of *Shri Sai Satcharita*, a detailed account is given about his dream vision and how the *wada* came to fruition. It is befitting to write a few words about this great devotee.

Gopalrao Mukundrao Butti

It is extremely difficult to write about this great devotee, as none of the adjectives convey an iota of the humility, love and devotion he had for Baba. It would suffice to say, "After spending *lakhs* of rupees in 1917 to build this beautiful mansion he gave it to the Sansthan, so that you and I can have *darshan* of Baba's Samadhi in comfort". The Butti Wada (**photo 11.1**) in Shirdi is identical to his *wada* in Nagpur.

There is no plaque, sign board or name plate proclaiming his name. However the Sansthan put up a plaque of his name at the entrance of the *Samadhi Mandir*. As the wooden doors (**photo 11.2**) are kept open for devotees to enter this plaque is hidden. This speaks volumes about the character and humility of this great devotee. A few devotees sometimes argued with Baba, but Butti never spoke in front of him. If he wanted to ask Baba something, he asked Shama to do so. Butti belonged to the 'old school'. He had so much of respect for Baba that he never looked at Baba directly.

Baba's word was law for him. Once an astrologer came to Shirdi and handed a book on astrology to him. He hoped that Baba would return it with his blessings, so that he could benefit from it. However, Baba gave the book to Butti. Because Baba had given the book to him, he studied it and became quite a proficient astrologer.

A detailed biography of this wonderful devotee is given in the book titled *Baba's Rinanubandh*.

The Samadhi Mandir

B ecause it was a *Wada* turned into a *mandir* (**photos 11.3, 11.3a**), there are different components to it e.g., the installation of *Suvarna kalasha*; sculpting of Baba's *murty* and its installation etc. So I have written it date wise.

In the 50s entrance to *Samadhi Mandir* was through a marble arch, leading to three marble steps. On ascending the steps you would see two huge wooden doors on your right and two buildings on the left. The wooden doors open to a marble *nandi* seated on a marble pedestal about 3′ high and looking at Baba's *Samadhi*. This *Nandi* faces west.

The buildings were separated by a cemented walkway. The building to the right was two storeys high, while the building to the left was three storeys high. The rooms were used as offices. The small verandah of the two storey building was used by the villagers, who brought musical instruments like the *sanai, chowgada, tutaari,* (wind instruments) and *nagaara* (huge drum) and played them during the *aratis*. This had a wonderful rustic effect. However, this practice is discontinued. Now the Sansthan provides the music.

The *dahi handi* of *Gopal kaala* used to be strung between these two buildings. Previously you could not enter Dwarka Mai from the doors near the stage as the home and shop of Jaganath Lute was there. In fact Lute could see Baba's *murty* from his front door. Later the Sansthan bought his property and amply compensated him.

The Beautiful Wooden Doors and the Plaques Behind them

The inscription behind the door to your left reads:

श्री साईबाबांच्या आज्ञेने कै. श्रीमंत गोपालराव मुकुंदराव बुट्टी रा. नागपूर यांनी हा वाडा स्वखर्चाने सन १९१७ ते १९१८ मध्ये बांधला. विजयादशमी शके १८४० मंगळवार या दिवशी व्यापीने एकादशीच्या ९ दिनांक १५ ऑक्टोबर इ.स. दि ई मोहरम हिजरी सन १८२५ दुपारी ३ वाजल्याच्या सुमारास श्री साईबाबांनी द्वारकामाई येथे देह ठेविला. येथुन ते समारंभपुर्वक आणुन त्यांच्या ईच्छेनुसार या वाडयात ठेवण्यात आला.

Shri Sai Babachya adnana kailash vasi Shrimanth Goplalrao Mukundrao Butti rahnar Nagpur swa kharchani sun 1917 te 1918 madhye bandhalae. Vijaya Dasami Shake 1840 Mangalwar ya divishi aparan vyapini Ekadishi cha 9 Dinak 15 October Isvi sun. Tariq 9 Mohrrum Hegri sun 1825 dupai teen vajnacha somaras Shri Sai Baba ne Dwarka Mai yethun deh tevela. Thethun tho samararambha purvak anun thyancha itche anusar yah Wadyath thevnyat aala.

Roughly translated. "According to the command of Shri Sai Baba late *Shrimanth* Gopalrao Mukundrao Butti, living in Nagpur, built this *wada* with his own money between 1917 –1918. On *Vijay Dashami Shake* 1840, a Tuesday, which was *Ekadashi*, 15th of October by the Hindu calendar. And it was *Mohurrum*, 9th of *Hegri Sun* 1825 (Muslim Calendar). In the afternoon at about three o'clock Shri Sai Baba left His mortal body in Dwarka Mai. From there with full ritual and according to His wish, His body was placed in this *wada*."

The inscription behind the door on your right reads:

सभा मंडपाकरिता लागलेली जागा ही खालील तीन जणांनी दिली आहे.

१) कै. श्रीमंत दामोधर सावळेराम रासने (अहमदनगर)

२) कै. श्रीमंत आण्णासाहेब चिंचणीकर (ट्रस्ट चिंचणी)

३) कै. श्रीमंत रावसाहेब यशवंतराव गाळवणकर (बांद्रा) मुंबई सभामंडपाचे बांधकाम विजयादशमी (दसरा) शके १८७१ (इ.स. सन १९४९) या दिवशी सुरू होऊन श्रीरामनवमी शके १८७३ (इ.स . १९५१) या दिवशी पूर्ण झाले. सभामंडपाच्या बांधकामास रुपये ६५,०००/- खर्च आला. या सभामंडपाची योजना व बांधकाम संस्था व व्यवस्थापक संस्थान समितीतर्फे पुणे येथील दा.पू. नगरकर आणि कंपनी यांनी केली

130

Yeha Sabhamandap karetha lagnelele jagha he khale theghene dile ahayeh.
"Aum Sai"

1. *Kailashvasi Shriyuth* Damodar Savalram Rasne, Ahmednagar

2. *Kailashvasi Shriyuth* Anna Saheb Chinchinikar, Trust Chinchni.

3. *Kailashvasi Shriyuth* Rao Sahib Yaswanthrao Galvankar. Bandra, Mumbai.

Yaha Sabhamandap bandh kaam. Vijaya Dasami Shake 1871 (Isvi sun 1949) ya deveshi shuru ho-un Shri Rama Navami Shake 1873 (Isvi sun 1951) yeha deveshi purna zale. Sabhamandap cha baandhya kemath Rs. 65,000 kharcha aala. Sabhamandap che yogana va bandh kaam sanstha yogana sansthapak samathi tharf Pune yethil Da. Pu. Nagarkar ani Company yene kela.
"+"

"The land for the *Sabhamandap* was donated by these three devotees:

Late Shri Damodar Savalram Rasne, Ahmednagar.

Late Shri Anna Sahib Chinchinikar Trust, Chinchni.

Late Shri Rao Sahib Yaswanthrao Galvankar, Bandra, Mumbai.

"The construction of the *Sabhamandap* started on *Vijaya Dashmi, Shake* 1871 (A.D. 1949), and was completed on *Rama Navami, Shake* 1873 (A.D.1951). The cost of the *Sabhamandap* was 65,000 rupees. The *Sabhamandap yojana* and construction *Sanstha Samithi* hired D P Nagarkar and Co. Pune for this work".

श्री साईबाबांच्या ३८ व्या पुण्यातिथीच्या उत्सव प्रसंगी इ.स. १९५२ संस्थान व्यवस्थापक समिती तर्फे श्रीसंत पारनेरकर महाराज यांच्या हस्ते या मंदीरावर स्वर्णकळस लावण्यात आला व ३६ व्या पुण्यतिथी उत्सव प्रसंगी समावेश इ.स. १९५४ श्री साईबाबांच्या संगमरवरी मार्बलच्या पुर्णाकृती मुर्तींची विधीपुर्वक स्थापना संस्थान व्यवस्थापक समितीतर्फे करण्यात आली.

Shri Sai Baba cha 38th vaya punya thithi cha utsav prasanghi Is 1952 Sansthan vasasthapak Shamithi tarffae Shri Santh Parnekar Maharaj yancha hasthe ya Mandir avere suvarna Kalasha basvayan aath aala va 36th vya punatyhya ththi utsav prasangi samaier [1954] Shri Sai Babacha sangamraure purna kruthu Murty chi vidhi purvak sthapan sanasth vasathapakak samethi tharfath aale.

The plaque reads, "On the 34th *punyathithi utsav* of Shri Sai Baba in the year 1952, the Managing *Samithi* Trust, asked *Shri Santh Parnekar Maharaj* to install the *suvarna* (golden) *kalasha* atop this *mandir*. On the 36th *punyathithi utsav* of 1954, the '*purna*' (from head to toe) marble idol of Shri Sai Baba was installed with all the rituals and *vidhis* by the *Sthapana Sanstha Vasthapak Samaath*."

Beyond these doors you enter a hall which has many rooms on the first floor. Along the railings of this floor hang the photographs of Baba's near and dear devotees, many of whom gave up name, fame and wealth to be near him. These rooms are used as offices. On your left is the show room.

Baba's Show Room

It now houses the portrait of Baba that is brought in procession (**photo 11.4**) for festivals. In front of it is a plastic case with Baba's *padukas* and on the lid Baba's *satka* wrapped in plastic is fixed. These *padukas* used to be kept in a glass box in the Chavadi, till 1980s.

The *satka* was kept open on top of the box till 1990s and many devotees could anoint it with sandalwood oil or either. Now it is encased in a plastic wrapping. The Sansthan takes every precaution to make sure that these sacred articles are safely preserved. Behind the *padukas* and *satka* is a portrait of Baba sitting in front of Dhuni Mai. This portrait is brought in procession to Dwarka Mai on holy days and *utsavs*. They are worshipped during *parayan* of *Shri Sai Satcharita*.

There are collapsible grill doors on either side, thus dividing this huge hall into two. The central areas of both halls are kept vacant. Everyday central area beyond the grill doors used by the priests and musicians during *aratis*. On festivals this is used for *Gopal kaala*, and to hang the cradle for *Rama Navami* etc. On the ladies side there is a wooden door placed on the floor, which leads to basement. This cellar houses Baba's numerous golden *mukuts*, and valuables.

Previously the exit was just beyond and to the right of the *nandi* through another marble archway. Now it is near the temple *Pramukh's* office. Next to it are two rooms.

The Pothi

If you enter the old *prasad* gate, there is a room that houses Baba's articles. These are articles that are used for the *aratis*. The *pothi* is kept in this room, as one chapter is read daily by the *pujari* at 4 p.m. The date that this was started is not known. Dabholkar got permission to write the book in 1910. Actual writing of the book started in 1922. Then it was serialised in the *Sai Leela Magazine* in 1923 and the book was published in 1929.

In the 50s the *pothi* was not bound and the sheaves of pages were kept between two covers. The *pujari* Vitthalrao Marathe would read that day's chapter then tie it in the *gheru* cloth and keep it away. Through the years where those sheaves of pages have gone is not known. Now a regular bound edition is being read.

The Suvarna (golden) Kalasha

Baba's 34th *punyathithi* was on *mithi, Ashwin sudh 9 Shake 1874 dinank* 29th September 1952 when the golden *kalasha* was installed. It was celebrated from 28th to the 30th Sept. The whole of the temple complex was illuminated with numerous coloured light bulbs and it looked like heaven on earth.

The *sthapana* (**photo 11.5**) was on the 29th and this day ought to be written in gold. In 1918 when Baba took *Mahasamadhi, Dashmi* was over and *Ekadashi* had dawned about two hours earlier. This same constellation occurred again after 34 years.

To perform the *vidhi* of *Kalasha sthapana* many *pundits* and scholars from Pune, Aalandi and Nasik were invited. At 6.30 a.m. the *yagna* started; this was followed by various rituals and *pujas*. At about 8 a.m. the three and half feet long golden *Kalasha* was taken in procession through the village. A multitude of devotees got a chance to do *namaskar*, touch it and pray it. The *suvasini* (married) ladies performed *pancharati* at various places during the procession. The devotees chanted Baba's name and loudly proclaimed *"Sainath Maharaj ki Jai."*

Simultaneously Vedic chants and religious rituals were being performed. At 10.45 a.m. the *kalasha* was taken to the top of the *Samadhi Mandir*. There was a crane on which a special *Vyas peeth* or platform was constructed. On this platform Dr Ramchandra Prahlad Parnekar and the members of the Sansthan were hoisted to the top of the *Gopuram*. Exactly at 11 a.m. Dr. Parnekar fixed the golden *kalasha* on the *Gopuram*.

The devotees who were standing below joyously proclaimed salutations and victory to Sainath Maharaj. The Sansthan had got a special device that gave a 25 gun salute. A huge ochre coloured silk flag was brought by N A Savant, which was fixed next to the *Kalasha*. Thus ceremony of *sthapana* of the golden *kalasha* was concluded. Sai Leela *Ank 4 year 29 issue October, November and December 1952.*

In 1952 there was only a photograph of Baba on top of the *Samadhi* (**photo 11.6**). The Sansthan realised that devotees were flocking to Shirdi and soon the crowds would increase manifold. So they decided to have a *murty* of Baba. The next task at hand was to select a renowned sculptor, who could carve a beautiful lifelike *murty*.

The Sansthan selected and met five famous sculptors from Maharashtra. Talim was one of them. Each of the sculptors was given a small black and white photograph of Baba.

Talim met the Sansthan and raised the question of compensation for the four rejected sculptors, "No matter who is chosen, do not disappoint the others, as they have invested a great deal of time, energy and hope. At least give each sculptor 5,000 rupees."

The Sansthan heard his plea and said, "We are not an affluent Sansthan and the sum is huge; but somehow we will get the amount and present it to the sculptors."

The sculptors felt very fortunate and honoured but the task was formidable. When a *murty* is made, the person is asked to sit before the sculptor. In this case none of the sculptors had seen Baba. The next hurdle was that only one small photograph was given to each of them. If the person is not available for the 'sittings' numerous photographs taken from many different angles are given.

The procedure to make the model was a long and complicated one (**photo 11.7**). The model is kept in a 'wet state' for two months, so that the fine facial features can be made. Following this the model is draped with a transparent film. Talim took all the necessary steps. Every morning at *Brahma muhurth*, he went and did *namaskar* to Baba in the model. He prayed earnestly saying, "Baba give me *darshan* once. Let me look at you intently and to my heart's content. Baba give me the strength and courage to make this *murty* resemble you." In fact, this prayer was on his mind and lips every moment of the day. Days rolled by; but Talim did not have Baba's *darshan*, nor had he sculpted Baba's face. The deadline for the completion of the model was about 10 days away. He received a call from the Sansthan asking him if the model was completed, as they would be coming to see the model.

Talim continued praying day and night as he eagerly awaited Baba's *darshan*. Talim was a very devout and disciplined man. Every morning he got up before dawn, had his bath and performed *puja* to his *ista Dev Vitthal*. Then he went downstairs to his studio, performed *puja* to the deities there and only then did he start his work.

One day, he went to his studio at the crack of dawn. His studio consisted of two rooms; the model was in the rear room; so was the switchboard for the lights of both the rooms. He made his way in the darkness to the room in the back. The room was engulfed in darkness. He stepped into the room and lo! Baba's model lit up like a myriad suns. So brilliant was the light that he closed his eyes. Then he heard "*Bagh. Mala bagh*" (Look! Look at me) and there stood Baba in front of him. Their eyes met and he became oblivious of everything except Baba's eyes. In a trance, Talim worked day and night and completed the model.

The Sansthan committee informed him that they had seen other models and were coming to see his model. Talim took them to the rear room. They stood before the model and Talim unveiled it. As he did this, the committee silently looked at the model; soon their eyes filled with tears of wonder, they came to Talim and held his hand and said, "You, and only you can carve Baba's *murty*."

As narrated by Harish B Talim in Sai Anubhav

On the 7th of October 1954, the life-like marble idol of Baba was installed next to the western wall on the platform, behind Baba's Samadhi.

Shilpa Maharishi Balaji Vasantrao Talim alias Bhau Sahib

Balaji was born in 1888, in Hyderabad. His father died early leaving behind his wife Saraswati and three small children. They then came to Bombay where Balaji got his education.

After Balaji completed his schooling he joined the J J School of Arts. He won the 'Dolly Kurshetjee' scholarship, that enabled him to complete his education. Balaji was a brilliant sculptor and painter; portraits being his specialty. In 1918 'Talim Art Studio' was established. He won many prestigious awards, gold medals and accolades. The committee for 'Beautification of Mumbai' chose him to sculpt the statues that dot Mumbai and Pune. The British appreciated his work and gave him numerous assignments. This is a short sketch of the life of this great sculptor.

The Sculpting of Baba's Murty

The Shirdi Sai Baba Sansthan gave Talim humongous assignment of sculpting Baba's *murty*. A huge block of Italian A grade marble from the Karkara mines was sent to his studio. The contract was to carve a five and half feet statue of Baba in the 'sitting on the stone' posture. That meant the idol was much larger than a 'life size' idol. When carving a marble idol the size of the block is much larger than the size of the statue. It is slowly and painstakingly chiselled away.

Since the block of marble was to sculpt Baba's *murty*, Talim was not anxious about the quality of the marble. He was confident that only the best marble would be used. The sculpting of a marble idol is full of uncertainties and risks. If there is a defect inside the block, it is not evident from outside, nor is there any instrument to verify any defects. The defects range from a hairline crack to a huge crack. Sometimes there are air pockets or hollows inside the marble. These holes or hollows cannot be filled with any material. At other times there are coloured stains, which show up after the idol is polished and washed with water. An idol that has any sort of defect, or a crack however small and minute is not worshipped. The sculptor has to stop working on it and sculpt another idol.

At an auspicious time, the carving was started. The block is carved from the top and then proceeds below. Talim kept the model in front of him while carving and the work progressed smoothly. His daily schedule was that as soon as the studio opened his assistant sculptors came and started work. They smoothed the rough edges and chiselled away any spikes or irregularities. Talim came to the studio at 11 a.m. and continued his work (**photo 11.8**).

He had carved the statue upto Baba's right knee. One day when he came to the studio he found all the assistant sculptors sitting idle with forlorn faces. He wanted to know what had happened. They said, "When we started to chisel, we heard strange noises. We got frightened and stopped the work." Talim took his chisel and tapped the area above Baba's right knee. He also heard the dreaded sound. His head spun, this was the sound of disaster and calamity. He thought, 'This is not possible, as Baba gave me *darshan* and his blessings.' He gathered himself together and told the assistant sculptors to wait for two days. For the next two days he tapped his chisel at different times, but the sound persisted. This was the sound of an air pocket or hollow in the marble.

At last, Talim bought a beautiful garland and garlanded the unfinished *murty*. Then he broke a coconut and prostrated before the *murty*. His assistant sculptors did the same. They prayed earnestly to Baba, to bless them. Talim then tapped his chisel below the right knee. With a thud a huge piece of marble, about 2′ fell to the ground.

Talim could not believe his eyes; for that was the very piece that had to be chipped away and removed. Baba in his mercy had left about 2″ of marble. So it could be chiselled smooth. The chunk of marble that fell was below Baba's right knee and left leg down to his foot.

Thus the beautiful idol of Baba was sculpted and sent to Shirdi. The work was commissioned in 1952 and *pran prathistha* was performed in 1954. At the age of 82, on December 25th of 1970, Talim breathed his last.   *As narrated by Harish Balaji in* Sai Anubhav

The Pran Prathista of Baba's Idol

October 2nd 1954, the idol arrived in Shirdi, in a special container. The van carrying the idol halted at Khandoba temple. From there it was taken in procession through the village and placed next to Baba's Samadhi.

Vishnu yagna

The *Samithi* decided to perform a *Vishnu yagna*, a *Pavman panch sukta yagna* and a *til yagna*. The repetition of 48 *Pavman Panch Sukta* is equivalent to two *Laghu Vishnu yagnas*. It was a 3 day function. To perform the *Yagna* two prominent *Veda Shastra* scholars were invited; Pundit Madhavrao Joshi and Balchandra Shripad Kanitkar from Mumbai. To assist them were Tatya Joshi, Vinayak Athavle Narayanrao Joglekar and Gaganrao Kelkar. Along with them another six pundits from Mumbai came to perform the *yagna*.

On Tuesday the area of the *yagna* was segregated with a rope. This was the area where Baba sat. According to the *shastras* a *havan kund* was made. The members of the *samithi* offered *paan vida, supari* and a coconut to Baba's photograph in Dwarka Mai, to the photograph in Gurusthan, to the *padukas* in *Samadhi Mandir* and all the village deities. They prayed for blessings and success of the function.

A gold *pratima* (image) of *Shri Vishnu* was bought. It's weight was that of three *annas*. The *pratima* of *Garuda* was made of silver. On one *vedi* (low stool) the *sthapana* of the *pratima* of *Maha Vishnu* and

Garuda was done. On another *vedi* the *sthapana* of *Nav Graha* was done. The Vishnu *puja* was performed with *Tulsi* leaves. *Tulsi* garlands and beautiful flowers were offered during the *sahasranaam puja* (the chanting of the thousand names of Vishnu). After the *puja* the *Tulsi* and flowers that were offered took the shape of Vishnu himself. Every devotee who saw this miracle was filled with joy and wonder. At about 8 p.m. the havan was completed with *purna ahuti* by the committee and numerous devotees. Then there was *balidan*. These were the *pujas* performed on Wednesday *Ashvini shuddh* 9ᵗʰ.

The Unveiling of the Murty
On Thursday *shuddh* 10 *Vijaya Dashami* after *Kakad arati* there was *mangal snan* of Baba's *Samadhi*. The ceremonies started with *pran prathista punyahavachan vidhi*. This ceremony was started by Ganapati *puja* for the removal of difficulties and obstacles. This was followed with the *punyahavachan puja*. Broken down, the word is: *punya* means good deeds, *aha* means that day or during the day and *vachan* means chanting of mantras. The removal of all *ashuddhi's* of the place, articles, people and *murty*.

In this ceremony, *kalasha sthapana* is done. This *kalasha* is then filled with holy ingredients and then *Varun sthapana* is performed. The *sthapana* of the Vedas are on the four sides of the *kalasha*. The *puja* is done to Varun and his blessings are sought in the form of *punya, kalyan, vriddhi, swasthi* and *shri*. This *puja* was performed by Dev and his wife Nalinibai. Then the idol was unveiled. The devotees had brought water from the Ganga, with which *mangal snan* of the *murty* was performed. This was followed by *Laghu Rudra-abhishek*. The unveiling of the idol was performed by Swami Sharnanand. He was a staunch devotee of Baba and had stayed with Baba for many years. It was a joyous occasion and the entire *puja* and ritual was filmed by the Nandadeep Film Productions.

At about 11 a.m., distinguished guests were presented with shawls from Baba's Samadhi. Then there was a *kirtan* programme that was performed by Anantrao Athawale. a student of Das Ganu Maharaj. The content of his *kirtan* was about Eknath Maharaj's Guru, Shri Janaradhan Swami, who was fortunate to have the *darshan* of Lord

Datta. The *kirtan* was very successful and enjoyed by everyone. Anantrao apologised that his own Guru Das Ganu was unable to attend the ceremonies for some unavoidable reason. The *kirtan* was over at about 1.30 p.m.

Thereafter *Aradhana vidhi* was started in the *Bhojangrah*. It was decided in 1953 to have 16 Brahmins for the *vidhi*. Nine Brahmins were from Shirdi and seven Brahmins came from Mumbai. The Brahmins then recited *mantras* in front of Baba's *Samadhi*. Then there was *Dhoop arati*.

The next day was *Ekadashi*, when clothes were distributed to each and every employee of the Sansthan. During the day and night there was *kirtan* performed by many renowned *kirtankars*. The day was charged with spiritual energy.

The next day was Saturday the 9th; the final day of the festivities. As with the conclusion of any major festival, at Shirdi also there was *Gopal kaala*. The *Kaala kirtan* was performed by the renowned *kirtankar* Sadashiv Bua Puranik Alandikar. Thus the *pran prathistha* of Baba's *murty* was performed with love, devotion and a great deal of joy.

Shri Sai Leela Magazine *Varsh 31 Ank 10 1954. Written by Shri Padanth Baba chaya Balache Bal*

On the 50th anniversary of the idol in 2004, a three-day *yagna* was performed in Lendi Baugh.

The Samadhi

The *Samadhi* is 6′ long, and 2′ wide. Surrounding it is an altar 9′ by 9′ with a height of 3′. Three steps lead to this altar; on the third step these words are inscribed

श्री साईबाबा हे मिती अश्विन शुध्द १० रोजी मंगळवार दि. १५ ऑक्टोबर १९१८ रोजी समाधिस्त झाले.
1918 roji samadhisth zale''

(Roughly translated) In the month of *Ashsvin sudh* 10th day on Tuesday the 15th of October 1918 Shri Sai Baba took *Samadhi*. This is the inscribed in Marathi on the central portion of the step. On either side there are Urdu inscriptions. On the left is the Islamic Tariq. The inscription reads *"Tariq vafat Sai Baba 9 Mohorrum 1339 Sun higari nani"*. On the right side is inscribed *"Likhe ek jaane majmun khali aur Sikander mohib dar duniya dono haath khale"*

The rough translation is "It is written in a well-known article that both the learned philosopher and Sikander (Alexander) entered this world empty-handed and left this world with both their hands empty"

Many questions arise from this inscription. When was this added on? As the photographs in the old *Shri Sai Satcharita* do not show this, only the central inscription is there. Why should this be written on the step of Baba's *Samadhi*? If it is meant to be a sort of epitaph, then judging from the crowds Baba is fulfilling everyones' desires and no one returns empty-handed. Is it a note of caution for us to remember the ultimate truth that finally after asking him for a thousand things and receiving them, we will leave this world empty-handed?

Everyday *mangal snan* is performed to Baba's *murty* and s*amadhi*, and then *alankar* is done with *ashtagandh*. Then *samadhi* is covered with a beautiful shawl. Care is taken to cover *samadhi* and *murty* with a warm shawl during the winter months, while a cotton shawl is used in summer. Meticulous care is taken to give Baba a warm shawl starting from Diwali *Padava* i.e. *Karthik* (October-November) through the winter. The use of the warm shawl is discontinued on *Holi* in *Phalgun* (March).

On Monday, 8th March, 1936, during *Kakad arati* it was noted by Shama and numerous devotees that the warm shawl covering *samadhi* had moved aside of its own accord. Thus leaving only the cotton shawl to cover it. The significance of this was that Baba was feeling hot and had pushed the woolen shawl away. This is the reason meticulous care is given to change the fabric of the shawl on those particular dates.   Sai Leela Magazine *Ank 1,2,3. Year 13, Shake 1858 (1936)*

This routine is also followed in Dwarka Mai. The other caring practice is to place a kerosene lantern through the night next to Baba's *murty*. A copper *zaari* (container with a spout used for water) filled with water is placed next to the lantern. Radha Krishna Mai lovingly did this during Baba's sojourn in Shirdi.

After *Sej arati* a mosquito net covers the *murty* and the *Samadhi*. It is removed just before *Kakad arati* the next morning. Baba's *murty* is offered butter sweetened with sugar at *Kakad arati*. The significance of butter is that it is present in milk in the invisible form. After certain irrevocable process it becomes visible. Once the butter is formed it floats and does not dissolve either in milk or water. Baba wants us to offer ourselves as butter sweetened with sugar of 'total surrender' to him.

Every living being on earth is as pure as milk at birth. But as one grows the family and society influence and adulterate that human being with illusions of *maya* to 'set as curd'. At this juncture only the grace of the *Sadguru* can churn this curd from which butter of 'self realization' can be extracted. Once the butter surfaces it will float on this *Bhavsagar* without being dissolved.

Breakfast is given before the *laghu arati; "Shirdi majhe Pandharpur"*. Lunch is given before the noon *arati*.

Dinner is given before *Dhup arati*. It is usually *"Jhunka Bhakar"* with raw onions. On *Ekadashi* he is offered *'upavas'* food. *Ekadashi* is a day of fasting (*upavas*)

Upavas means "to stay near the almighty" i.e. to concentrate on him. A person can concentrate when his *indriyas* are not working outwardly. The first step is to have *sattvic ahaar*. We have to give *sattvic ahaar* to our mind by doing *puja, naam smaran,* etc.

Baba's food is cooked in the *Naivedya Koti* which was a room in the rear of the *Samadhi Mandir*. The *Naivedya Koti* has now been moved upstairs.

Baba's Murty (idol)

Baba's *murty* is hewn from a single block of marble, which cost 22,000 rupees. The *murty* faces east and the face is tilted towards *Ishanya disha* (north-east). This is the abode of Lord Vishnu. Every devotee who goes to *Samadhi Mandir* feels that Baba is looking only at him or her, no matter where they stand. In fact Baba is not just looking at them; but he is searching for them with his benevolent gaze.

On the 7th of October 1954, (**photo 11.9**) the idol was installed next to the western wall, on the platform behind Baba's *Samadhi*.

The brick

This brick was Baba's constant companion, his *Sangani*. Mhalsapati, Kashiram Shimpi and Madhu Fasle performed *mangal snan* and worshipped it everyday. One day, accidentally the brick broke. The breaking of the brick is symbolic of death. A detailed account of the brick is given in the book titled *Baba's Rinanubandh*.

Baba was distraught and said, "It's not the brick; but my fortune that is broken. She was my constant companion! Now that she has gone, so I too will leave." Thereafter Baba's health started deteriorating and on the 5th day he took *Mahasamadhi*. Mention of this incident is made in *Shri Sai Satcharita*, chapter 44.

Why did Baba take Mahasamadhi in Dakshinayan?

Death and rebirth have fascinated mankind through the ages. It has resulted in strong beliefs. It is believed that if one dies on a *shubh* day, a *shubh muhurth*, a *shubh kaal* one is not reborn.

When a person dies there is a *marg* or pathway that he traverses. The *Shukla marg* is bright, illuminated and the person reaches Brahman and is not reborn. While the Krishna *marg* is dark and rebirth occurs. However, the accumulation of good karmas also determines rebirth. All these pathways are for ordinary people like us.

In the *Jnaneshvari*, chapter 9 Ovi 23, it is clearly stated that *Yogis*, Saints and *Jnanis* do not follow this *marg*. An apt example is of Jnaneshvar, who chose to leave this earth in *Karthik, Krishna paksh*. His Guru Nivratinath, took *samadhi* in *Jesth, Krishna paksh*. Both of them took *samadhi* in *Dakshinayan* and both were *yogis, jnanis* and *siddhas* of the highest order.

In *Manu Smriti* chapter 10 it is written that, "He who has resorted to taking *bhiksha*, lives under a tree, who neither builds a hut or house is truly a *mukt yogi*. He wears tattered clothes, does not depend on anyone, nor seeks help from others and is carefree. He looks at every living being with equality of vision, is forgiving, loving and in a state of *Sat-chit-anand*. These are the signs of a Self realised yogi". Baba had all the above features and more. So if he took *Niryan* in *Dakshinayan* did it lessen his divinity and spirituality? It did not matter one iota. He was *purna parabrahma,* he manifested on this earth when he chose to and left when he wanted to.

The wooden cot

Devotees were devastated by shock and sorrow after Baba's *Mahasamadhi.* Later the question arose as to what was most befitting way to bid farewell to the body. Unfortunately there was a difference of opinion between them.

Baba was laid on this cot for two days till their differences were sorted out. In chapter 42 of *Shri Sai Satcharita* under the title *"Niryan* of Shri Sainath" the description of Lakshman Mama's dream vision is given. It was on this cot that Baba lay when he performed ritualistic *Kakad arati.* Then he placed *dakshina* and *tambul* in Baba's closed fist without heeding the objections of Muslims and the *Maulvis.*

Shri Sai Satcharita *chapter 42*

It was finally decided that Baba's *Samadhi* would be in the sanctum sanctorum of *Butti wada.* The devotees then took out a huge procession, in which Baba's body was carried on this cot around the village.

This cot was kept in Dwarka Mai in early 50s. Later it was kept in Chavadi. After the museum was built, it was placed there.

When it was in Chavadi, it was placed against the western wall, next to the wheelchair. On Thursday and on other holy days this cot was decorated and Baba's Raj *upchar* photograph was placed on it. Thus the female devotees had a chance of venerating and worshipping it. Then the photograph was taken to *Samadhi Mandir.* The cot was brought out; so that Baba's *palkhi* could be placed on it.

Baba's museum

The museum is aptly situated at the rear of Dixit wada. This hall was used as a *prasadalay,* then as a tea canteen. The museum was opened on *Vijaya Dashami,* Friday 23rd of October 2001. This museum is charged with a great deal of spiritual energy. It is one of the most powerful places in Shirdi, nay, in the world. All the articles that were touched, handled and used by Baba are kept here.

Due to editorial constraints each and every article will not be described in detail, unless there is a story or meaning to it. I have given the photographs of all the articles and they are self-explanatory. The Sansthan has provided information next to the exhibits.

Upon entering the Museum to the left is the original photograph of Baba. The photograph in a ornate silver frame is placed on a silver *sinhasan.* It is the photograph of Baba sitting on the stone pose. The silver *sinhasan* is embossed with peacocks and apsaras on either side. There is a silver *chattri* above the photograph. A *chowri* (fly whisk) with a silver handle is placed in front of it.

This photograph and the silver *sinhasan* were kept on the *Samadhi* till 1954. On the wall to your left is the photograph of *Samadhi.* On either side there is a bunch of peacock feathers. This exhibit is a replica of *Samadhi,* complete with marble trellises.

The meaning of peacock feathers needs to be given here; this motif was seen in the small Gurusthan temple and on Baba's silver *mukut.* The materialistic world looks so beautiful and colourful just like the peacock feathers with a thousand eyes of *maya* drawing us. Once we are under the spell of these eyes we are churned by the vicious cycle of *maya.* Only by the *Sadguru's* grace, when we have surrendered to him in totality,can we reach him in totality. This is under the surveillance of the thousand eyes of the *Sadguru.* Thus the peacock feathers represent thousand eyes of the *Sadguru.*

A staircase on your left leads to first floor. As you enter you see a beautifully embroidered red *Taj.* It was probably taken for the Chavadi procession. Next to it is a life size painting of Baba standing. In front of it are three bails of cotton fabric. Ramchandra Atmaram Tarkhad was the secretary of Khatau Group of Mills. He often brought bails of

Manjarpat for Baba, hoping that Baba would get a new *kafni* stitched. Baba however was quite content with his torn *kafni*.

The word *kafni* comes from *kafan* or the shroud that the dead body is wrapped with. He who dons a *kafni* is a dead man walking i.e. though he is breathing and alive, he is dead to all the attractions and distractions in this world. The *kafni* is symbolic of *maya*. Maya functions through two powers known as *Avarna* (covering) and *viksepa* (projecting). *Kashya* or white represents the state of having burnt all desires. White is a symbol of purity and flawlessness. One learns that though we are covered and mired in *maya*, yet we should be dead to it.

Another explanation is that as the *kafni* is shapeless, it can be worn by both sexes. Even though the physical features are different, in both the sexes same *kafni* can be worn by males and females. So it represents the *atman* which is genderless, formless and not affected by anything. By wearing *kafni* Baba is telling us that like the *atman* is not affected by anything, so we to can live in this world of *maya* and be detached.

Next is a painting of Baba. It's unusual as it is a silhouette. The original painting is in Mhalsapati's home. Next to it is a handheld fan. The next exhibit *kafni* is possibly made of silk. Next to it is a pair of *padukas* placed on a pedestal.

The Significance of Padukas

Baba walked barefoot and sanctified the soil of Shirdi. However, he did give *padukas* to some of his devotees. This he did after wearing them for a short while or by touching them. Then he asked the devotee to worship them.

One wears footwear to protect oneself from the dirt. The *paad raksha* acts as non-conductor against *kamani*, *kanchan* and *kashyapa*. These are the root causes of pride, jealousy and even litigations against our dear and near.

All *vasanas* are generated from the earth. So by wearing foot-wear we are protected from them just as we are protected from dirt. Baba being *Parabramha* did not need these artificial protections. He taught his devotees to overcome *vasanas*. To lead a life of *Sammyama* (control of the wandering mind), while living in this world of attractions. This can be achieved by *antakarana chathustitaya* which acts like protective *padukas*.

To your left the wall has photographs of Baba and below are articles used by him. The first photograph is a black and white photograph of Baba sitting on the stone posture. Next is a painting of Baba going to Chavadi in procession. This painting is noteworthy as it has numerous devotees that were near and dear to Baba. The central figure as always is Baba. To his right is Nana Sahib Nimonkar and on his left is Gopalrao M Butti. Moreshwar Pradhan has a garland in his hand and his son Bapu has the silver platter with *puja* materials. The other little boy with the silver mace is Chotta Sainath who is Shamrao Jaikar's son. In the second row Das Ganu is barebreasted. Next to him is Kaka Sahib Dixit. Bhagoji Shinde is as always holding the umbrella. Balaram Mankar is next to him. Behind Bhagoji is Lakshmi Bai Shinde. In the rear or last row you can recognize Bala Shimpi with a *pheta*.

In front of it is pedestal, on which are four *chillims* and a broken clay flint stone. On the same pedestal there are two tumrels. Next to it is the famous portrait painted by Shamrao Jaikar. This masterpiece is popularly known as the Dwarka Mai pose.

In front of it is a gramophone with a record on it and six records are placed next to it. For those of you who are old enough to remember the logo on the record made by a company called His Master's Voice is an apt message that we can use in our daily lives. It was a picture of a dog sitting before a phonograph and listening intently to it.

Kaluram was the blessed son of Shantaram B Nachane. He liked the logo very much and once he told his father that it was special, because it had a deep meaning. His father questioned him further about it. Kaluram replied, "Just look at the dog, so steady from head to tail, listening so intently. You should be equally firm and steady. You too should sit like that and listen (meditate) and then you will hear Baba speak to you."

The next photograph on the wall is Baba sitting in front of Dhuni Mai. It is titled "Baba in a pensive mood". The original photograph is in Dammu Anna's home in Ahmednagar. This photograph is described in Dwarka Mai section with the possible meaning of the pose.

In front of this photograph is the cloth '*songate*' or game of dice. In the nights that Baba slept in Chavadi, he played *songate* with Tatya, and the other devotees. Radha Krishna Mai along with Baba's other requirements for the night (e.g. tumbler of water) would send this 'dice board' and they played far into the night. Often they were heard shouting and fighting.

The next three photographs are rare photographs of Baba.

This unusual photograph of Baba sitting in Dwarka Mai was taken with Baba's consent. Vasudev Sadashiv Joshi of Sholapur had visited Shirdi. Upon his return he met the owner of V. S Photographers, an ardent devotee of Baba (**photo 11.10**).

Joshi requested him to go to Shirdi and take a photograph of Baba for him. He paid for and made all arrangements for his stay at Shirdi. The photographer went to Shirdi and had Baba's *darshan*. After some time Baba said, "*Aare*, didn't Joshi Bua of Satnarayan Company send you to take a photograph? Then why are you just sitting there? Take a photograph in any pose that you want." Then without hesitation and a great deal of joy, Baba allowed the photograph to be taken. Then he stood up and allowed another photograph to be taken. At Sholapur they registered the photographs under the name of "*Bhiksha Sanstha*". Unfortunately the photograph of Baba taken in a standing pose is not to be found. This original photograph is in Dabholkar's home.

Next to it is another rare photograph of Baba with a book in his hand. On *GuruPurnima* numerous devotees came for Baba's *darshan*. Often they brought a book and placed it in Baba's hand, hoping that he might return it with his blessings. So that they could study it and benefit from it. Baba however took a book from one devotee and gave it to another. This photograph is from the first edition of *Shri Sai Satcharita* and the original photograph is in Dabholkar's home. The title is '*Baba with Tukaram's Gatha in Hand*' (**photo 11.11**).

Below is the photograph of Baba sitting with outstretched legs. Mhalsapati is on his left and Shama on his right. The name of the Muslim lad, who rests his head in Baba's lap, is not known (**photo 11.12**).

On a pedestal is another pair of *padukas*. Next to it is a beautiful red velvet coat.

There is a big hall below. As you enter the hall on your left is a small quern or hand mill. This was used by Baba when he wanted to do *annadaan*. Next to it on a pedestal is a stone oil container with an ornate silver spout and stopper. Next to it, Baba's *tumrels* are placed on a small pedestal. One of them is large and the other two are smaller in size. There are 4 *chillims* placed next to it. In a stand adjacent to it 6 *chillims* are mounted.

The next showcase has a *nishan* of Hanuman on either side of the wall. There is a photograph of Khajgiwala (Shyam Karan's trainer) and Shyam Karan. This showcase has all the beautiful trappings that adorned the horse. There is also a statue of the horse.

The next showcase has idols of Hanuman, Rama, Lakshman, Sita and Krishna. On the wall there are photographs of Shirdi of the bygone days. The next photograph is of the *Samadhi Mandir* before 1952. Next to it is the *Samadhi* as it was in 1920s.

The next showcase has a *chowri* mounted on the wall. Next to it is a beautiful red shawl. In front is a circular coil of cloth that was used as a stand for the *maath*. Next there is a marble idol of Dattatreya mounted on a slab of marble inlay. The next exhibit is an ornate red umbrella and its wooden handle.

As you make a left turn there is a crimson shawl with a green border. It has *zari* work done all over. It was probably placed on Baba during the *Chavadi* procession.

There is an isle in the centre of the hall, where the exhibits are openly displayed. The bathing stone is the first exhibit. This stone was presented to Baba by Rambaji of Nasik. He had heard of Baba's *leelas* and wonderful cures of many diseases by him. He came to Shirdi in a mentally disordered condition. He used to drink Baba's bath water and used some of it on his body. By doing so he got rid of his mental disorder. Gratefully he gave the stone to Baba to sit on and have his bath. This practice of using Baba's *abhishek tirth* to cure mental and physical ailments is in practice even today. Devotees carry the *tirth* to their homes, not only in India, but to far off countries also.

This bathing stone was kept in the verandah of Dwarka Mai and is now kept in the museum.

There is a set procedure for taking a bath. One is supposed to take a bath in the river that is flowing in the village. If a river is not flowing nearby, the bath is taken in a *talab* (lake). If that too is not feasible, then water is drawn from the village well and a bath is taken.

One should not take a bath nude or in the standing position. They should sit on a stone and should face east. This could be the reason for building *ghats* near the river. Of course it also ensures safety, as no one would slip, if they sit on a stone or a *ghat*.

A bath cleanses the body; but a bath in any river especially the Ganga by following the proper procedure prescribed by the scriptures also purifies the mind. Everyday one has to invoke the Ganga in the water used for bathing.

Dr Keshav Gavankar and Baba had deep *rinanubandhic* ties. Baba often instructed him in dreams and visions. Once Baba said, "There are four types of bathing. They are 1. *Agni snan*, 2. *Bhasma snan*, 3. *Vayu snan*. and 4. *Bhagirithi snan*. I wander about here and there. So I take a *Vayu snan*. You take a *Bhagirithi snan*."

Agni snan is when fire is lit on four sides of the person who is seated under the blazing afternoon sun. Following this the person is cleansed and purified. Sharada Ma had this type of bath.

Bhasma snan is what is performed in Maha Kaal temple in Ujjain. There the *mangal snan* of *Shiv Linga* is performed with *Bhasma* from the crematorium. Some *sadhus* and followers of the *Aghori* sect also cover their bodies with *Bhasma*. The *sevakaris* who clean the Dhuni Mai from the inside are blessed with *Bhasma snan,* as the dust and *udi* falls on them.

Some *satpurushas* and *sadhus* don't take a bath; yet they are clean, odourless and fresh looking. They have *Vayu snan*. Those devotees who do *pranayam* on a daily basis avail of *Vayu snan*.

150

The *Bhagirithi snan* is bathing in water as described above.

Baba rarely had a bath with water and he walked about in the alleys of Shirdi barefoot yet his feet were clean, soft and tender like a 12-day old baby's. The soles of his feet had a pinkish hue and produced smell of pure sandalwood oil and the fragrance of musk. In those days Shirdi was not a very clean village. It was through the dedication of Radha Krishna Mai that the streets that Baba walked on were kept clean. She was up at the crack of dawn and would sweep the streets that Baba used. Another unique feature of her *seva* was that she swept the streets backwards; so as not to step on the area that she had swept. Bala Newaskar did this job after her and so did Abdul Baba.

Significance of the bathing stone

Spiritually, one will not slip if he makes his *indriyas* as hard and rigid as the stone. He then sits on them to have a bath in the ever flowing Ganga. There is nothing as pure and energetic as this water. So anybody would be cleansed and purified.

For Baba, who is *parabrahma*, bathing does not become necessary. But he wants to teach and show us the path to reach him. We may earnestly choose any *marga* or a blend of them and the cleansing process starts. When devotee is unaffected and untouched by the incidents in this mundane life, one can reach him. That is the cleansing process and is symbolic of having a bath.

The *rath* was presented by Bala Saheb Rege and Daji Saheb Awasthi and other devotees from Indore. But Baba never sat in it. Reluctantly he granted permission. So his photograph was taken in procession on *Guru Purnima* of 1918. The *rath* was kept in *Sabhamandap* of *Samadhi Mandir* and later shifted to the Museum.

The honour of pulling the rath is given to Ramnath Varpe, Rahul Vedie, Lahanu Aiher and Dattu Shaelke, all of whom belonged to Navi caste. Now another *rath* is taken in procession on all major festivals.

Baba had asthma and coughed often. This wheelchair was presented to him by a concerned devotee. The devotee hoped that Baba would use it to move about in his old age. When he was sick or had taken on someones' illness and was feeble and weak, his devotees helped him to go on his daily rounds. Baba did not stop going for *bhiksha* till about two days before his *Mahasamadhi*.

Next to the wheelchair is the *palki*. It was presented by Saddubhayya, Chottubhayya, Rajubhayya and Naryanbhayya of Harda. Baba never sat in this *palki*. Reluctantly he granted permission for the *palkhi* procession. The devotees placed his photograph in it and had a joyous procession.

To your right is the wooden cot on which Baba's dead body was laid till the devotees decided how to bid farewell to his body.

On the wall is the original photograph of Baba going to Lendi Baugh (**photo 11.13**). Baba is leaning against Pilaji Balaji Gurav's home. The descendants have placed *padukas* at that sacred site. Gopalrao M Butti is on the left of Baba, while Nana Sahib Nimonkar is on his right. The little boy standing next to him is his grandson, Goplalrao Nimonkar. This photograph is given on the cover of this book.

Next to this photograph is an *Ovi* written in Marathi from *Shri Sai Satcharita*.

In the centre is a sketch of Baba's *Mahasamadhi*. Below the sketch this is written, "For the last two-three days Baba remained seated and did not move out of Dwarka Mai. On Tuesday 15th October 1918, Baba rested his body on Bayaji Patil's lap and breathed his last. Later that night Baba appeared in Laxman *mama* Joshi's dream urging him to perform *Kakad arati* (morning prayer) which *mama* did. The last rite of bathing was performed on this cot."

Above the sketch the captions are in Marathi and English. Below it is written, "Four months before his *Nirvan* Shri Sai Baba sent Rs. 250/- to Shamsuddin Baba and requested him to perform *Mauli* (prayer to Allah) and *Nyas* (mass feeding). He persuaded Shri Vaze to repeat the reading of Rama Vijaya continuously for 14 days".

There is a sketch of Baba with some devotees. This is written in Marathi and English, "Baba sent an emissary to Bannemiya an eminent

Sufi saint of Aurangabad to convey the message: "*Nav din: Nav tariq : Allah miyan apna Dhuniyia le jayage*". "*Allah miyan* will take away his servant on the 9th day and date". Hearing this Bannemiyan shed tears and raised his hand.

The next showcase has two huge copper *handis*. On the wall is a sketch of Baba with his hand inside the *handi*. Baba is churning the scalding contents as he prepares the food for *annadaan*. Baba used two sets of *handis*, the smaller *handi* could feed about 50 people. These are the larger *handis* and could feed 150 people to satiation.

As you exit from the museum there is a gallery of photographs. The exhibit is titled 'Contemporary Saints During Baba's Time'. The photographs are of Bale Kundri Maharaj, Manik Prabhu, Swami Samarth, Gangagiri Maharaj, Vasudev Anand and Tajuddin Baba. There is also a black and white photograph of Baba going in procession to Lendi Baugh dated (1914).

The other photographs are of the old *Dixit wada, Samadhi Mandir* or *Butti wada* without the *gopurum* and *kalasha*. There is the birds' eye view of Dwarka Mai. Next to it is the old *Samadhi Mandir* with Baba's photograph on it. Next is the photograph of the installation of the *suvarna kalasha* by Dr Parnekar. The last photograph is of Balaji Vasantrao Talim and his son Harish Talim carving the idol of Baba.

12

Baba Going for Bhiksha

This original photograph (**photo 12**) shows Baba going for *bhiksha*. The villagers would often bring their wares and set up temporary shops. Baba is in the vacant space near the Chavadi between Vamanrao Gondkar's and Sakharam Sheilke's homes. He has the *tumrel* in his hand and a cloth over his head.

13

Invisible Baba

This photograph (**photo 13**) was taken by a devotee named Gopal Dinkar Joshi in the year 1912. Every morning after breakfast, Baba went to Lendi Baugh. The devotees who stayed in Sathe wada would eagerly wait for Baba and the procession to approach the corner in front of the *wada*, so that they could have his *darshan*. Baba responded to their wishes by standing there for a while.

Joshi wanted to take a photograph of Baba. He kept his camera mounted and ready for Baba to return from Lendi Baugh. Before doing this he asked Baba for permission to take his photograph. Baba said, "I don't want a photograph of mine; but you can certainly take a photograph of the devotees accompanying me."

Upon Baba's return from Lendi Baugh, he stood a while near Sathe wada. Joshi seized the opportunity and took a photograph of Baba. Shama saw this and told Baba that Joshi had taken his photograph. Again Baba repeated the same saying "I don't need any photograph of mine. What am I to do?"

Joshi got the photograph printed and to his utter surprise Baba is not visible and only his feet can be seen. The umbrella, Bhagoji Shinde and other devotees are clearly seen; but in place of Baba there is a luminous light and only his feet can be seen.

Sai Leela Magazine *year 4. Ank 4-5. Jesth and Ashad Shake 1848 (1826)*

14

Baba Sitting on the Ota in the Sabhamandap

This rare photograph (**photo 14**) shows Baba sitting on the *ota* with Abdul Baba, who is seated on the first step of the central stairs of Dwarka Mai. Tatya Kote Patil is sitting on the third step with a book in his hand, as identified by his descendants. Nanavali is next to him seated on the third step of the southern staircase.

Conclusion

I have tried to give a glimpse of Shirdi in the 20s, 70s and 80s so that devotee can experience it at the present times. To me Shirdi is like my mother's womb; warm, safe and protective. I feel nothing can go wrong here and even it everything goes wrong, I know that my mother will protect me.

People talk about those who are dear and near to them. Mothers talk about their children and vice versa. The urge to share my feelings about a place that I am enamoured of, is intense. I have been visiting Shirdi from a very young age and I have seen it change. But no matter how it changes, there is one constant factor, the earth on which Baba trod remains and will remain. Baba loved his devotees when he was here and they experienced it. After his *Mahasamadhi* his devotees still experience it and it will last forever.

This book came about by this irresistible urge to share Shirdi, so that readers can profit from it. The articles used and handled by Baba are still with us. So the readers can see them and gain insight in their significance.

Baba's Gurukul – Shirdi is based on all prerequisites mentioned in the introduction. These evoke compassion, discipline, cleanliness and truthfulness; all these acts leading to self-realisation. This educational system will naturally produce ideal individuals. Such exemplary graduates will graduate which is beyond doubt due to the *Kul -adhipathi* (Baba) of this *Gurukul,* who is beyond words and speech and cannot be grasped through logic.

Glossary

Aagami or *Kriyaman* – all the Karma performed in this life plus the *Sanchita* that is not exhausted

Aakara – form

Aamra – mangoe

Abhangs – devotional songs

Abhishek – ritualistic holy bath

Adesh – a message and advice

Adhyathmic – spiritual

Adi Maya – primordial illusions

Agarbatti – perfumed incense sticks

Agyan – ignorance

Aham – the false ego

Airavatam – the celestial white elephant, carrier of Indra

Akhand – continuous

Akhand parayan – continuous reading

Akshata – consecrated rice

Allah Malik – God is powerful

Allah vali hai – Allah is the redeemer

Amavas or *Amavasya* – dark night prior to new moon

Amla – Indian Gooseberry

Amrit – ambrosia

Angara – burning coal

Angrakha – a coat with ties instead of buttons

Anima – the ability to reduce the body to the size of an atom

Ankush – goad

Annadaan – feeding the poor

Antahkarna chatusya – a group of four, i.e., the ego complex; *manas, budhi, aham,* and *chitta*

Antahkarna chatusya with *adimanas* – a state where the self is merged with the *Parabrahma*

Antaryami – omnipresent

Annas – old Indian coin, 16 annas to a rupee

Anna-shuddhi – clarified butter added to food for purification

Apasavia – anti clockwise

Aposana – *offerings made to ancestors*

Arati – circular waving of lamps along with singing praises to deity or guru

Archana – ritual of performing worship

Ashwin – 7th month of Hindu calendar

Ashtagandh – a mixture of sandal wood powder and saffron powder

Ashta dik bandhan - The eight direction bondage

Ashuddhis – impurities

Arshidvargas – lust, anger, covetousness, delusion, pride and envy

Ashta Lakshmi – the eight different forms of the goddess Lakshmi

Atithis – guests

Atma – soul

Avarna – covering

Avatar – incarnation

Ayu – longevity

Babul tree - a small tree full of thorns

Balidan – sacrifice

Barood – ballad of deities

Bathasa –a cookie made with a concentrated sugar solution

Bhadva - a derogatory name or a derogatory term

Bhajan – devotional song

Bhakri – thick bread of jowar (sorghum), bajri (millet)

Bhakta – devotee

Bhakti – devotion

Bhandara – feast

Bharit – brinjal

Bhasma – sacred ash

Bhau – loving brother

Brahma gyan – divine knowledge

Brahma padarth – a constituent of Lord Brahma

Brukuti – the centre between the eyebrows

Bua – saintly person

Chaddar – shawl

Chakra – wheel

Chamatkar – miracle

Chandan – sandalwood

Chappi – a wet cloth that is wound around the end of the *chillim*

Charan – feet

Chattri – umbrella

Chillim – smoke pipe

Chimta – prongs

Chiplis – small hand held wooden sticks beaten to keep rhythm

Chitta – subtle state of mind used to reflect on the soul

Chopdars – mace bearers

Chotta hajri – a small attendance

Chowgada – wind instrument

Chowri – fly whisk

Darga – a tomb of a Muslim Saint

Deep – lighted lamp

Deh ahankar – pride of the body

Deh siddhis – powers attained by a spiritual person. They are *Anima, Mahima, Laghima, Garima*

Devi Roopam – Goddess

Dharamshala-Piligrim's Inn

Dharana – fixing the mind on him

Dhup – incense

Dhyana – meditating on him

Divas – earthen lamps

Ekanta – solitude

Fatiah – prayers

Gada – mace

Gaddi – mattress

Garima – the ability to make the body heavy

Ghungrus – small bells

Gomukhi – a glove shaped like a cows mouth, in which the hand holding the rosary is placed when doing *naam jaap*

Gopuram – temple spire

Gow – cow

Gow daan – donation of cattle

Gow Shalla – a barn alike shelter for cattle run by volunteers.

Gram pujari – priest of all the village temples

Griha-pravesh – the ceremony of occupying a newly built house

Gudi – represents a flag hoisted to symbolize good over evil

Gulal – a dry vermilion powder

Gunatita – beyond all attributes

Hal – plough

Halahal – poison

Handis – large utensils to cook in

Indriyas – the senses

Ittar – perfume

Jaap mala – rosary

Jeev mukta – free from the encumbrances of ego and pride

Jholi – a bag for collecting alms

Jnana – knowledge

Jyot – fire

Jyoth – lit end

Kaal – time

Kaala – *naivedya* mixed together

Kaka – paternal uncle

Kakad arati – morning prayer

Kalmas – verses from the *Quran*

Kalyan – welfare

Kanchan – attraction to wealth/gold

Kandil – lantern

Kamini – attraction towards women

Kashyap – land/property

Kathada – railing

Kavadis – water bearers

Khadi dhoti – *Khadi* is pure cotton which is coarse, and *dhoti* is Indian dress worn by men

Kolamba – an earthen container used by Baba to mix the food received by *bhiksha*

Koupina – loincloth

Kripa – grace

Kshetra-sacred soil

Kul Devata – family deity

Kulkarni – The Revenue Officer

Kumbhars – potters

Laghima – weightlessness and levitation

Lalkari – sonorous salutations

Langala – spikes

Langoti – loincloth

Lavni – a style of singing verses

Maath – water pot

Madhukari – the tradition of seeking alms

Mahamaari – the great killer

Mahaprasthan – final journey

Maha nidra – a great slumber

Maha yatra – a great journey

Mahima – the ability to expand the body to any size

Man – mind

Manas – mind

Mangal snan – holy bath

Manjarpat – coarse cotton

Matka – earthen pot

Matkis – small earthen pots

Mauli – prayer to Allah

Maya – Nescience, the veil of Brahma, the Creator

Meetha chawal – sweet rice

Mhatara – old man

Mitra – sun

Moksha – salvation, release from cycle of existence

Moori – an outdoor sink where housewives wash their utensils and clothes

Mothi krupalu – full of compassion

Mukuts – crowns

Mumukshu – seekers

Murty – idol

Mutton pulav – spicy rice with bits of mutton in it

Naam saptha – continuously reciting the lord's name for a week

Naam smaran – remembering/ repeating the name of God

Nabhi chakra – the symbol of the navel

Nagaara – huge drum

Nama – names of objects in creation

Namaskar – prostrating at someone's feet

Namaz – prayers offered by Muslims

Navakalavar – replacing the old deity

Nila Madhav – Lord Krishna with a blue hue

Nimithi – instrumental

Nirlaptha – not affected by anything

Nirlingi – genderless

Nirvikari – formless

Nishkama – selfless

Nista – unwavering faith

Nyas – mass feeding

Ovale – impure

Paad tirth – the water that flowed from his feet

Paap – sinful acts

Paat – low stool

Padma – lotus

Padukas – holy footwear

Palkhi – *palanquin*

Pancha kosas – 5 seats i.e. *Annamaya, Manomaya, Pranamaya, Vignamaya* and *Anandmaya kosa*

Pancha pranas – *prana, apana, udana, vyana,* and *samana*

Pancha bhootha – Earth (*prithvi*), air (*vayu*), fire (*agni*), water (*apas*), and ether (*akash*)

Panch indriyas – consists of five Karma *indriyas*, i.e., touch, taste, smell, sight, and hearing

Panch jnanindryas – skin, tongue, ears, eyes, nose

Panja – a silver replica of a hand

paramaathma – the supreme

Pavaman panch suta yagna – sacrificial fire to render everything touched (e.g. the idol) in the highest state of purity

Pehelvan – body builder

Phool patra – a flat bottomed copper tumbler that is kept over the mouth of a *kalasha*

Pindi – *Shiva linga*

Pipilika – ants

Pitruyana – the journey of the soul after *Chandra loka*

Pradakshina – circumambulation around a temple, a holy tree, a river, or a holy object

Prasad – consecrated food

Pratima – idol

Pravachans – a sort of lecture on spiritual persons and topics

Prithvi – earth

Pukka – ready

Punya – good or righteous deeds

Punyatithi – birthday

Puran polis – a sweet dish

Purna ahuti – complete sacrifice

Pushpa – flowers

Rajas – passion

Rakh – ash

Raksha – protect

Rath – chariot

Ratnas – jewels

Rudra abhishek – ritualistic holy bath

Sabaras – tribals

Saburi – joyous, courageous, forbearance or patience

Sadgati – salvation

Saguna roopa – the living form

Saguna bhakti – devotion and worship of the manifest

Sahaj Samadhi – inborn natural state of deep meditation

Sahasranaam – the chanting of the thousand names of God

Sakshatkar – divine vision and manifestation

Samadhi – super conscious experience

Samnyama – control of the wandering mind

Samodayak pathan – collective reading

Samathi – administrative body

Sampathi – wealth

Sanai – wind instrument

Sanchita – accumulated

Sandhya – ritualistic repetition of mantras three times a day usually done by taking a dip in a holy river like the Ganges

Santhati – children

Satka – small wooden baton

Satsang – discourses usually with holy ascetics

Sattva – purity

Seema – border

Shradha – the annual feast given to the departed ancestors

Shri – prosperity

Shubh muhurth – auspicious time

Shwaan – dog

Shyam – black

Sindur – ochre coloured paste

Sinhasan – throne

Songate – game of dice

Sovale – holy

Sthandila – consecrated platform

Sthapana – installation

Stheer – steady, unwavering

Sukshma – invisible body

Surya – sun

Sutar – carpenter

Suvarna – golden

Suvasini – married

Swaroop – form

Swasthi – health

Swayambho – manifested on its own accord

Talab – lake

Tamas – inertia

Tamasha – street plays held in villages

Tamoguna – inertia, sloth and infidelity

Tapas – austerity

Tatva jnana – principles to live by like truth and honesty

Trigunas – The three attributes, *Rajas* (passion), *Tamas* (inertia), *Sattva* (purity)

Tulsi – Holy basil

Tumrel – mug

Ullanghan – crossing

Uparna – a cloth shawl

Upa Snan – washed his feet and hands

Upavas – fasting

Updesh – instruction

Utsav – festival

Vaikuntha – heaven

Vairagya – renunciation

Varan – soup like lentil or *dal*

Vasana – desire

Vastra – clothes

Vayana – the ruling deity of 'blinking'

Vayu – or the wind and air

Veena – a stringed musical instrument

Vess – entrance

Vibhuti – all pervading or omnipresent

Vidhi – ritual

Vijaya – victory

Vijaya dashami – the tenth and last day of Dussera

Viksepa – projecting

Vimana – chariot of the Gods

Virya – strength

Vishvaroop dhara – form of the universe

Vivaha – marriage

Vriddhi – increase

Vrishaba – bull

Yade haq – remember Allah

Yama – The Lord of Death

Yasa – fame

Yatra – fair

Yojana – nine miles

Zaari – a copper vessel in which water is kept for Baba

***

Our Books on SHIRDI SAI BABA

Shirdi Sai Baba is a household name in India as well as in many parts of the World today. These books offer fascinating glimpses into the life and miracles of Shirdi Sai Baba and other Perfect Masters. These books will provide you with an experience that is bound to transform one's sense of perspective and bring about perceptible and meaningful spiritual growth.

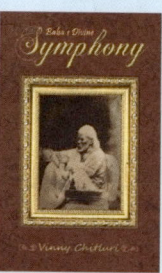
Baba's Divine Symphony
Vinny Chitluri
ISBN 978 81 207 8485 7
₹ 250

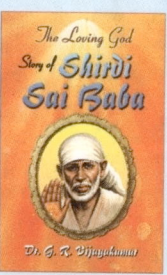
The Loving God:
Story of Shirdi Sai Baba
Dr. G. R. Vijayakumar
ISBN 978 81 207 8079 8
₹ 200

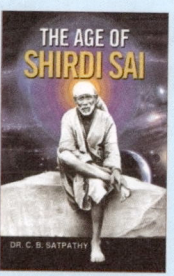
The Age of Shirdi Sai
Dr. C. B. Satpathy
ISBN 978 81 207 8700 1
₹ 225

Sai Baba an Incarnation
Bela Sharma
ISBN 978 81 207 8833 6
₹ 200

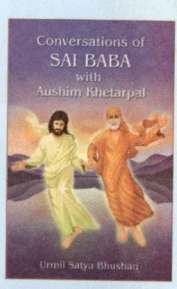
Conversations of Sai Baba with Aushim Khetarpal
Urmil Satya Bhushan
ISBN 978 81 207 8798 8
₹ 200

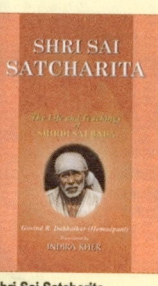
Shri Sai Satcharita
The Life and Teachings of Shirdi Sai Baba
Translated by Indira Kher
ISBN 978 81 207 2211 8
₹ 500(HB)
ISBN 978 81 207 2153 1
₹ 300(PB)

Sree Sai Charitra Darshan
Mohan Jagannath Yadav
ISBN 978 81 207 8346 1
₹ 200

Jagat Guru: Shri Shirdi Sai Baba
Prasada Jagannadha Rao
ISBN 978 81 207 8175 7
₹ 100

Life History of Shirdi Sai Baba
Ammula Sambasiva Rao
ISBN 978 81 207 7722 4
₹ 150

Shirdi Sai Baba: The Perfect Master
Suresh Chandra Panda & Smita Panda
ISBN 978 81 207 8113 9
₹ 200

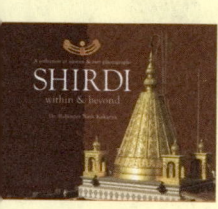
SHIRDI within & beyond
A collection of unseen & rare photographs
Dr. Rabinder Nath Kakarya
ISBN 978 81 207 7806 1
₹ 750

Shri Sai Baba Teachings & Philosophy
Lt Col M B Nimbalkar
ISBN 978 81 207 2364 1
₹ 100

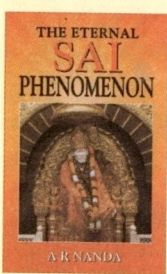
The Eternal Sai Phenomenon
A R Nanda
ISBN 978 81 207 6086 8
₹ 200

God Who Walked on Earth:
The Life & Times of Shirdi Sai Baba
Rangaswami Parthasarathy
ISBN 978 81 207 1809 8
₹ 150

STERLING

Baba's Rinanubandh
Leelas during His Sojourn in Shirdi
Compiled by Vinny Chitluri
ISBN 978 81 207 3403 6
₹ 200

Baba's Gurukul
SHIRDI
Vinny Chitluri
ISBN 978 81 207 4770 8
₹ 200

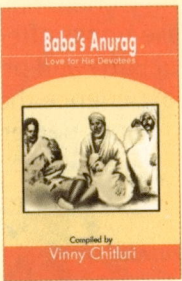

Baba's Anurag
Love for His Devotees
Compiled by Vinny Chitluri
ISBN 978 81 207 5447 8
₹ 125

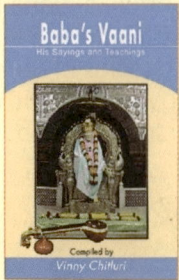

Baba's Vaani: His Sayings and
Teachings
Compiled by Vinny Chitluri
ISBN 978 81 207 3859 1
₹ 200

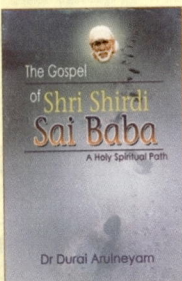

The Gospel of Shri Shirdi Sai
Baba: A Holy Spiritual Path
Dr Durai Arulneyam
ISBN 978 81 207 3997 0
₹ 150

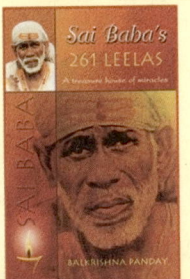

Sai Baba's 261 Leelas
Balkrishna Panday
ISBN 978 81 207 2727 4
₹ 125

Spotlight on the Sai Story
Chakor Ajgaonker
ISBN 978 81 207 4399 1
₹ 125

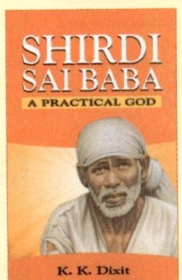

Shirdi Sai Baba
A Practical God
K. K. Dixit
ISBN 978 81 207 5918 3
₹ 75

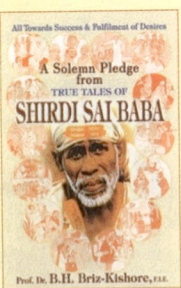

A Solemn Pledge from
True Tales of
Shirdi Sai Baba
Dr B H Briz-Kishore
ISBN 978 81 207 2240 8
₹ 95

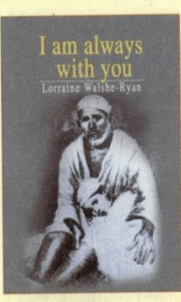

I am always with you
Lorraine Walshe-Ryan
ISBN 978 81 207 3192 9
₹ 150

BABA- May I Answer
C.B. Satpathy
ISBN 978 81 207 4594 0
₹ 150

Unravelling the Enigma: Shirdi S
Baba in the light of Sufism
Marianne Warren
ISBN 978 81 207 2147 0
₹ 400

STERLING

Sab Ka Malik Ek

Shirdi Sai Baba
The Divine Healer
Raj Chopra
ISBN 978 81 207 4766 1
₹ 100

Shirdi Sai Baba and
other Perfect Masters
C B Satpathy
ISBN 978 81 207 2384 9
₹ 150

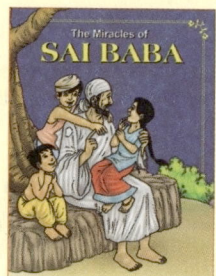

The Miracles of Sai Baba
ISBN 978 81 207 5433 1 (HB)
₹ 250

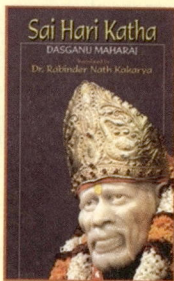

Sai Hari Katha
Dasganu Maharaj Translated by
Dr. Rabinder Nath Kakarya
ISBN 978 81 207 3324 4
₹ 100

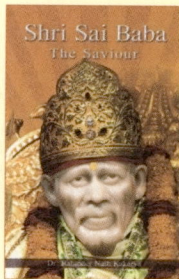

Shri Sai Baba- The Saviour
Dr. Rabinder Nath Kakarya
ISBN 978 81 207 4701 2
₹ 100

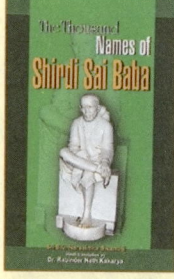

The Thousand Names of
Shirdi Sai Baba
Sri B.V. Narasimha Swami Ji
Hindi translation by
Dr. Rabinder Nath Kakarya
ISBN 978 81 207 3738 9
₹ 75

Sri Sai Baba
Sai Sharan Anand
Translated by V.B Kher
ISBN 978 81 207 1950 7
₹ 200

Sai Baba: His Divine
Glimpses
V B Kher
ISBN 978 81 207 2291 0
₹ 95

Ek An English Musical on the Life
of Shirdi Sai Baba
Usha Akella
ISBN 978 81 207 6842 0
₹ 75

A Diamond Necklace To:
Shirdi Sai Baba
Giridhar Ari
ISBN 978 81 207 5868 1
₹ 200

Shirdi Sai Baba
Vikas Kapoor
ISBN 987 81 207 5970 1
₹ 30

Shri Shirdi Sai Baba: His
Life and Miracles
ISBN 978 81 207 2877 6
₹ 30

STERLING

SHIRDI SAI BABA

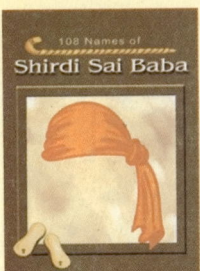

**108 Names of
Shirdi Sai Baba**
ISBN 978 81 207 3074 8
₹ 50

Shirdi Sai Baba Aratis
ISBN 978 81 207 8456 7
(English)   ₹ 10

**Shirdi Sai Speaks...
Sab Ka Malik Ek**
Quotes for the Day
ISBN 978 81 207 3101 1
₹ 200

Shirdi Sai Baba Box

Shri Sai Baba
978 81 207 6920 5
Box size: 23.5 x 16.5 cm
₹ 900

Shri Sai Satcharitra

Sai Baba Mandiramdhil Arataya &
Mantrochar - Mp3

Vibhuti

Sai Baba Photo Frame

Dateless
Calendar

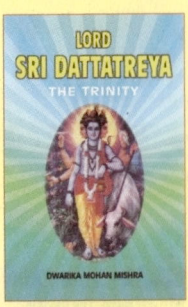

**Lord Sri Dattatreya
The Trinity**
Dwarika Mohan Mishra
ISBN 978 81 207 5417 1
₹ 200

Divine Gurus

Guru Charitra
Shree Swami Samarth
ISBN 978 81 207 3348 0
₹ 200

**Sri Swami Samarth
Maharaj of Akkalkot**
N.S. Karandikar
ISBN 978 81 207 3445 6
₹ 200

Hazrat Babajan:
A Pathan Sufi of Poona
Kevin R. D. Shepherd
ISBN 978 81 207 8698 1
₹ 200

**Sri Narasimha Swami
Apostle of Shirdi Sai Baba**
Dr. G.R. Vijayakumar
ISBN 9/8 81 207 4432 5
₹ 90

श्री शिरडी साई बाबा

साई सुमिरन
अंजु टंडन
978 81 207 8706 3
₹ 90

श्री साई चरित्र दर्शन
मोहन जगन्नाथ यादव
978 81 207 8350 8
₹ 200

श्री साई सच्चरित्र
श्री शिरडी साई बाबा की अद्भुत
जीवनी तथा उनके अमूल्य उपदेश
गोविंद रघुनाथ दाभोलकर (हेमाडपंत)
978 81 207 2501 0 ₹ 250 (PB)
978 81 207 2500 3 ₹ 300 (HB)

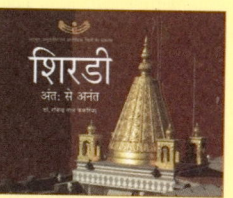

शिरडी अंत: से अनंत
डॉ. रबिन्द्रनाथ ककरिया
978 81 207 8191 7
₹ 750

**बाबा की वाणी-उनके वचन
तथा आदेश**
बेला शर्मा
978 81 207 4745 6
₹ 100

बाबा का अनुराग
विनी चितलुरी
978 81 207 6699 0
₹ 100

बाबा का ऋणानुबंध
विनी चितलुरी
978 81 207 5998 5
₹ 150

बाबा का गुरुकुल-शिरडी
विनी चितलुरी
978 81 207 6698 3
₹ 125

साई की आत्मकथा
विकास कपूर
978 81 207 7719 4
₹ 200

साई संवाद
उर्मिल सत्य भूषण
978 81 207 7777 4
₹ 150

बाबा-आध्यात्मिक विचार
चन्द्रभानु सतपथी
978 81 207 4627 5
₹ 150

साई की महिमा
औशिम खेत्रपाल
978 81 207 8350 8
₹ 200

स्टर्लिंग

श्री शिरडी साई बाबा

श्री शिरडी साई बाबा एवं
अन्य सद्गुरु
चन्द्रभानु सतपथी
978 81 207 4401 1
₹ 90

पृथ्वी पर अवतरित
भगवान शिरडी के साई बाबा
रंगास्वामी पार्थसारथी
978 81 207 2101 2
₹ 150

साई - सबका मालिक
कल्पना भाकुनी
978 81 207 3320 6
₹ 125

साई बाबा एक अवतार
बेला शर्मा
978 81 207 6706 5
₹ 100

साई सत् चरित का प्रकाश
बेला शर्मा
978 81 207 7804 7
₹ 200

श्री साई बाबा के परम भक्त
डॉ. रबिन्द्रनाथ ककरिया
978 81 207 2779 3
₹ 75

श्री साई बाबा के
उपदेश व तत्त्वज्ञान
लेफ्टिनेन्ट कर्नल
एम. बी. निंबालकर   ₹ 100
978 81 207 5971 8

साई भक्तानुभव
डॉ. रबिन्द्रनाथ ककरिया
978 81 207 3052 6
₹ 125

श्री साई बाबा के अनन्य भक्त
डॉ. रबिन्द्र नाथ ककरिया
978 81 207 2705 2
₹ 100

साई का संदेश
डॉ. रबिन्द्र नाथ ककरिया
978 81 207 2879 0
₹ 125

शिरडी संपूर्ण दर्शन
डॉ. रबिन्द्रनाथ ककरिया
978 81 207 2312 2
₹ 50

मुक्तिदाता - श्री साई बाबा
डॉ. रबिन्द्रनाथ ककरिया
978 81 207 2778 6
₹ 65

स्टर्लिंग

सबका मालिक एक

साई शरण में
चन्दुभानु सतपथी
978 81 207 2802 8
₹ 150

साई दत्तावधूता
राजेन्द्र भण्डारी
978 81 207 4400 4
₹ 75

साई हरि कथा
दासगणु महाराज
978 81 207 3323 7
₹ 65

शिरडी साई बाबा - की सत्य कथाओं से प्राप्त - एक पावन प्रतिज्ञा
प्रो. डॉ. बी.एच. ब्रिज-किशोर
978 81 207 2346 7   ₹ 80

शिरडी साई बाबा की दिव्य लीलाएँ
डॉ. रबिन्द्र नाथ ककरिया
978 81 207 6376 0   ₹ 150

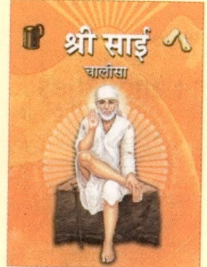

श्री साई चालीसा
978 81 207 4773 9
₹ 50

शिरडी साई बाबा
विकास कपूर
978 81 207 5969 5
₹ 30

शिरडी साई बाबा आरती
978 81 207 8195 5
₹ 10

श्री नरसिम्हा स्वामी
शिरडी साई बाबा के दिव्य प्रचारक
डॉ. रबिन्द्र नाथ ककरिया
978 81 207 4437 0   ₹ 75

शिरडी साई के दिव्य वचन-सब का मालिक एक
प्रतिदिन का विचार
978 81 207 3533 0
₹ 180

स्टर्लिंग

श्री शिरडी साई बाबा

Oriya Language

ଶ୍ରୀ ସାଇ ସଚରିତ୍ର (Oriya)
ଶ୍ରୀ ଗୋବିନ୍ଦରାଓ ରଘୁନାଥ ଦାଭୋଲକର
(ହେମାଡପନ୍ତ)
978 81 207 8332 4 ₹ 300

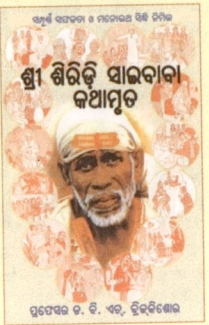

ଶ୍ରୀ ଶିରିଡ଼ି ସାଇବାବା କଥାମୃତ
ପ୍ରଫେସର ଡ. ବି. ଏଚ. ବ୍ରିଜକିଶୋର (Oriya)
978 81 207 7774 3
₹ 80

ଶୀରଡି ସାଇ ବାବାଙ୍କ
ଜୀବନ ଚରିତ (Oriya)
ଅମୃଲ ଶ୍ୟାମଶୀବ ରାଓ
ଅନୁବାଦକ – କିଶୋର ଚନ୍ଦ୍ର ପଟ୍ଟନାୟକ
978 81 207 7417 9 ₹ 125

Other Indian Languages

శిరిడీసాయిబాబా (Telugu)
ప్రో. డా. బి.హెచ్. బ్రిజ-కిశోర్
978 81 207 2294 1
₹ 80

ಶ್ರೀ ಶಿರಿಡಿ ಸಾಯಿಬಾಬಾ ಅವರ
(Kannada)
ಪ್ರೊ. ಡಾ. ಬಿ.ಹೆಚ್. ಬ್ರಿಜ-ಕಿಶೋರ್
978 81 207 2873 8
₹ 80

ஷிர்டி சாயிபாபாவின் (Tamil)
உள்ளார்ந்த கதைகளிலிருந்து
பெருமிதமான வாக்குமூலி
ப்ரோ. டா. பி.ஹெச். ப்ரிஜ-கிஷோர்
978 81 207 2876 9
₹ 80

Shirdi Sai Baba Aratis
(Kannada) ₹ 10

Shirdi Sai Baba Aratis
(Tamil) ₹ 10

Shirdi Sai Baba Aratis
(Telugu) ₹ 10

शिरडी साईं बाबा (भोजपुरी)
विकास कपूर
978 81 207 7558 9
₹ 30

शिडी साईबाबांची दिव्य वचने (Mara)
सबका मालिक एक
दैनंदिन विचार
978 81 207 7518 3 ₹ 180

STERLING PUBLISHERS PVT. LTD.
Regd. Office: A-59, Okhla Industrial Area, Phase-II, New Delhi-110020, CIN: U22110PB1964PTC002569
For Online order & detailed Catalogue visit our website:
www.sterlingpublishers.com, E-mail : mail@sterlingpublishers.com, Tel. 91-11-26386165, 26387070